G000300721

The
Break Up

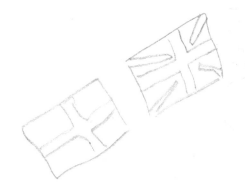

BOOKS BY TILLY TENNANT

TILLY TENNANT

The Break Up

Bookouture

Published by Bookouture in 2020

An imprint of Storyfire Ltd.
Carmelite House
50 Victoria Embankment
London EC4Y 0DZ

www.bookouture.com

Copyright © Tilly Tennant, 2020

Tilly Tennant has asserted her right to be identified
as the author of this work.

All rights reserved. No part of this publication may be reproduced,
stored in any retrieval system, or transmitted, in any form or by
any means, electronic, mechanical, photocopying, recording or
otherwise, without the prior written permission of the publishers.

ISBN: 978-1-83888-241-9
eBook ISBN: 978-1-83888-240-2

This book is a work of fiction. Names, characters, businesses,
organizations, places and events other than those clearly in the
public domain, are either the product of the author's imagination
or are used fictitiously. Any resemblance to actual persons, living or
dead, events or locales is entirely coincidental.

For Georgia, Isabelle and Adam

Chapter One

From the moment they'd met her, Lucien's parents had decided that Lara wasn't good enough for him. According to them, he was better educated, had a better job, was better looking and generally from *better stock* – whatever that meant. They'd never say that to her face, of course (it would be far too vulgar), but they made sure that their opinions found their way to Lara's ears somehow, usually via Lucien himself. For her entire twenty-eight years on the planet, Lara had always assumed that in any relationship, the only opinion she'd have to worry about was that of the man she was dating. But in Lucien's case, if his parents didn't approve, then neither did he. In time, she'd look back on this chapter of her life and wonder why he'd bothered to stay with her for the year they'd been together.

It wasn't until this precise moment, sitting across from him in the wanky jazz bar he loved so much, that Lara had seen fit to question why she put up with it. God, she hated jazz, almost as much as she hated Lucien's stuck-up parents and his pretentious friends. But she was doing her best not to think about these things as she tried hard to concentrate on what he was explaining in an unreasonably loud voice while simultaneously resisting the urge to punch him in the face. The trumpet wasn't helping. Still, she tried to listen to Lucien because it was important, though her brain wouldn't compute the facts. It sounded like he was dumping her. But surely he wouldn't do that, out of the blue like this…?

'And don't get me wrong, I've had a great time with you,' he continued. 'But it's never really been going anywhere, has it?'

Lara shook her head in an attempt to clear it. As far as she'd been concerned it *had* been going somewhere, even if she couldn't be certain exactly where. You didn't put up with Lucien's mother silently criticising your hair with a distasteful twist of her Botoxed lips unless you felt some serious commitment to the relationship.

If he says: 'It's not you, it's me…'

'The thing you've got to take from this is that no blame lies with you,' he said. 'It's not you, it's—'

Lara stood up, ignoring the look of surprise on Lucien's face. She reached for the pint of ridiculously named ale currently sitting on the table in front of him and tipped it over his head. There was something massively satisfying about his gormless look of shock, and even more satisfying about the way the ale dripped onto his £200 jacket. She turned, outwardly calm, although her emotions were anything but, and headed for the door. Inside she was fuming, raging, hurt and humiliated, but she'd never give Lucien the satisfaction of seeing any of that. She left the bar, noise from a keyboard that was almost as dreadful as the strangled trumpet ringing in her ears.

Outside, the night was heavy and the air smelt of thunder. It had been like that all day, sultry and stormy, but so far the weather had held. Lara took a deep breath and pulled her shoulders back as she stepped out onto the pavement. She didn't rush away and she didn't cry because the last thing she wanted was for someone to see her and for it to get back to Lucien. Instead, she started to walk, with as much dignity and outward calm as she could muster. At least he wouldn't be chasing after her right now; he'd be far too busy trying to salvage his perfect hair in the toilets and washing the beer from the designer jacket that she'd once joked he loved so much he ought to date it instead of her. Lara was probably the last thing on his mind right now and she was damned if she was going to cry over such a selfish bastard.

Instead, with shaking hands, she pulled her mobile phone from her handbag and dialled Siobhan's number. Her friend answered on the second ring.

'Wow, that was fast,' Lara said. 'Did you know I was going to call or something?'

'Of course not,' Siobhan said. 'How are you?'

'I've been better.'

'Oh…' Siobhan replied hesitantly. Lara frowned at the unexpectedly reticent tone from her friend. 'What's wrong?'

If Lara hadn't known better, she might have said her friend sounded faintly uneasy. But there was no reason on earth why that should be, was there?

'Is everything OK?' Siobhan continued into the gap. 'Weren't you meant to be seeing Lucien tonight?'

'I did, and he took the opportunity to dump me.'

'Oh, Lara…'

'I feel like such an idiot. Mainly because I've spent so long trying to please his bloody parents, trying to be the sort of girlfriend I thought he wanted me to be. And for what? I should never have compromised myself like that – I don't even know why I did. I should have been myself and done what I wanted.'

Lara grimaced as she stumbled into a stale old puddle on the street, soaking her tights. 'Perhaps he would have liked me better in the end if I'd just been myself; perhaps that was where I went wrong. I shouldn't have been trying to please everyone else; I should have been pleasing myself.'

'It's not your fault – you can't beat yourself up over it.'

'I'm not – though I'd like to beat him up over it.'

'So what did he say exactly?'

'Some bullshit about incompatibility, different backgrounds, different prospects, fun while it lasted… the usual lame stuff.'

'Right.'

Lara paused. 'I have to say, you don't sound very shocked by any of this.'

'Well, you've pointed out your differences so many times, it seemed…' Siobhan's sentence trailed off.

'Inevitable?' Lara finished bitterly.

'Did he tell you anything else?'

'I don't know what else there is to tell. He wanted to end it – there's not a lot I can do about it even if I did get more of a reason than that. Though I'm not buying any of it – I absolutely think there's something he's not telling me.'

'Like what?'

'I don't know – like his precious mother put him up to it.'

'Oh,' Siobhan said. 'I expect that's it. You've always said she hated you.'

'Well, she did, but I can't help feeling that it's funny she didn't do anything about it before now. We've been together for a year after all, and she's had plenty of time to stick the knife well and truly in before now. Apart from the constant snide criticisms, of course, but you can't count those because she does that to everyone.'

'Maybe she thought it would fizzle out by itself.'

'I suppose that could be it.'

Lara was silent for a moment, her steps brisk as the traffic whizzed by her and a couple of drunks rolled out the doors of a nearby pub, shouting at each other as if they were conversing five miles apart, not five inches.

'Either that or he's seeing someone else and he hasn't the guts to tell me,' she added. 'That would be about right.'

Lara paused again as the idea solidified. 'I'll bet that's it. Bastard.'

There was a strange and charged silence on the line, and then Siobhan spoke and it was not what Lara had expected at all.

'I can't do this,' she said miserably.

Lara frowned, her pace slowing as she puzzled at her friend's change of tone. 'What's the matter? Has something happened your end? God, I'm so sorry, and here's me blathering on about that twat—'

'It's not that,' Siobhan said. 'It's... I wanted to tell you so many times before, and I said to Lucien that we ought to, but he wanted to do it when the time was right and now I know I should have done it—'

'What are you talking about?' Lara asked, feeling like iced water had suddenly been poured over her. 'I don't—'

'Me and Lucien,' Siobhan said. 'I know it's just a horrible thing to do but we couldn't help it... I mean, you must understand, if it could have been any other way... And we fought it but... well... you can't help who you fall in love with, can you?'

'*You*?' Lara spluttered. '*And Lucien*?'

'I know,' Siobhan said. 'I'm so sorry, Lara. I do hope it doesn't come between us—'

'*Doesn't come between us*? It's hardly going to bring us closer, is it?'

'Oh, see, I told Lucien to handle it carefully; I knew you'd take it badly.'

'*Take it badly*?' Lara squeaked again in a voice now almost as grating as the trumpet she'd just left playing in the club. '*Take it badly*? What did you expect?'

'I don't know. I feel just terrible.'

'That's a shame, because I feel just dandy about it all.'

'Oh, Lara, if it could have been any other way...'

'There are plenty of other ways it could have been,' Lara said coldly. 'All it would have taken was some self-restraint. Lucien... perhaps I can believe that self-restraint is hard to come by in that quarter, but you... I thought you were capable of better things than this. I thought our friendship meant something to you.'

'It does!'

'If I wasn't so absolutely broken right now I'd go back and kick him in the balls, and then I'd come to your house and smash all your windows. However...' Lara drew a breath. 'I don't have the strength. I hope you're very happy together and if you're not then you've both got what you deserved.'

'But, Lara—'

Lara ended the call and put her phone away. *Don't cry; don't cry...*

It was easier to tell herself not to cry than to do it. It had also been easier not to cry over Lucien than it was over Siobhan. She could feel indignant about Lucien, or she could tell herself that in the end he would see that the loss was all his, but Siobhan... The slice of his blade had come keen, but Siobhan's follow-up had felt almost mortal. How could Siobhan, her best friend in the world, do this to her? She'd known how hard Lara had worked at this relationship, been privy to every twist and turn, witness to every up and down, been there making sympathetic noises as Lara complained and cried and tried (always failing, it seemed) to get it right. She'd been Lara's confidante for many others too – fifteen years' worth in fact. They'd shared hopes and dreams, laughter and tears and a lot of pain in that time.

But apparently fifteen years of friendship meant a lot more to Lara than it did to Siobhan. And all this time Lara had never even considered that Siobhan might be attracted to Lucien. More than attracted, as it turned out – interested enough to destroy everything they had as friends so she could be with him.

When Lara thought about all the things she'd done for Siobhan over the years, how she and her family had saved her, how they'd become more than friends and closer to sisters (or so Lara had thought), the knife twisted in just that little bit deeper. It just went to show that it didn't matter how well you thought you knew your best friend, you never quite knew the whole of them.

Lara thought all this as her determined march home turned into a dejected limp. She didn't know how she could possibly feel any more miserable and wretched than she already did, but then it seemed the weather wanted to get in on the act and challenge that. As if her night wasn't bad enough, a perfectly timed rumble of thunder rolled across the heavens, swiftly followed by fat drops of rain, falling faster and faster by the second.

At least nobody would notice if she cried now, she thought dully.

She stuck out an arm for a passing taxi, but it didn't stop. She hadn't really expected it to – unoccupied taxis on a Friday night in Chester were as rare as Lucien's bad-hair days. The only thing to do was walk. If she caught pneumonia and died, that would round off the evening nicely.

Twenty minutes later she was home, dripping wet, letting herself into her Victorian town house. Tossing her keys onto the kitchen worktop, she kicked her sodden shoes off at the back door, where they slammed against the wall before landing in a heap on the mat. They were quickly joined by her wet clothes. It could all stay there forever as far as she was concerned because she wasn't in the mood to pick any of it up. Dressed in only her damp underwear, she marched through to the bedroom to find something dry to put on.

On the way, she caught sight of herself in the antique mirror hanging in the hallway. Lucien had been with her when she'd bought it from a flea market and he'd absolutely hated every minute of the hours Lara had begged him to walk round it with her. Had she been unreasonable? Perhaps she had that day, although at the time it hadn't seemed like it. Had she been a bad girlfriend? Was that why he'd turned to Siobhan? They'd always seemed to get on well whenever they'd come into contact with each other but Lara had always assumed that they'd made an effort to get along for her sake. Had she really been that blind?

She stopped and stared at her bedraggled reflection. Perhaps, in the end, it hadn't even been that complicated. Her hair was a sort of ash blonde, whereas Siobhan's was far more golden. Longer too, with a natural wave that made it look impossibly glamorous, even when she didn't try. And her eyes were the colour of the Aegean Sea. Lara's were a sort of brownish green, and in some lights they looked like no colour anyone could name. Less Aegean Sea and more sewage outlet.

She let out a sigh as her gaze travelled to the rest of her. Slim enough, she supposed, but nothing about her athletic and rather nondescript figure screamed goddess. Not like Siobhan, who would wiggle her way into the local gym and have every guy in there slobbering over their weights.

Of course Lucien would have his head turned by someone like her, but what really hurt was that Siobhan had let it happen. She and Lara had been friends since high school, and you didn't treat that sort of friendship lightly no matter what man tried to come between you. They'd both been there for the other's darkest hours – there had been more than enough bad boyfriends between them but they'd always got each other through every single one of the break-ups. Lara never imagined that a boyfriend would be the thing to finally break them apart.

She sighed. The fact was, even though she wanted to blame Siobhan – might even want to hate her – she couldn't. Lara and Lucien – it was never going to work in the long run, and even though Lara had let the relationship continue, had even enjoyed it, she had to admit that she could see the inevitable truth now. But though she might have expected it to fizzle out, she'd never expected it to end like this. Maybe they'd have got bored, his parents would finally have persuaded him to give her the elbow, found him a respectable replacement from the glut of well-connected friends' daughters at the golf club… but Lucien and Siobhan?

Lara gave her reflection a sad shake of her head. She'd lost twice over tonight, because there was no way she could be friends with Siobhan again. She couldn't decide if that might hurt more than what Lucien had done, but she thought that maybe it did. His departure had cost her a year of her life, but Siobhan's meant almost all of Lara's adult life was now tainted with memories that she could never look on fondly again.

With a final sigh, she went to the bedroom to get her towelling bathrobe.

Feeling at least a little warmer and dryer, if not more optimistic, Lara went to the kitchen and switched the kettle on. She needed a good strong coffee to clear the last of the alcohol from her system; maybe then she might be able to focus a little more clearly on the situation. She wasn't about to fall apart over that prat, no matter how she might want to sit and cry. What she *was* going to do was exactly the opposite of what he and his stuck-up parents would expect.

She'd talked about starting her own business ever since she'd met him and he'd always just laughed, or told her 'Good for you' in a patronising tone. He'd been derogatory about her job at the call centre and his parents had almost spluttered out their Earl Grey when they'd found out what she did for a living, but still he had hardly been encouraging in any bid she might have made to change.

Lara suspected now that although he'd looked down on her job, he hadn't been keen for her to better herself because then he would have had no reason to look down on her and he rather liked to – it was just another reason to feel superior. She wondered if that might even be why he'd gone out with her for so long. Maybe it was a power thing, a way to keep her in line. So, was that what was happening with Siobhan too? Her job as a secretary in a builders' merchant's was hardly more glamorous than Lara's and she couldn't imagine his parents looking any more kindly on it than they had on hers.

Whatever – none of it mattered now. Now he was out of the picture and Lara needed something to think about other than him and her best friend. What else was she supposed to do with her time? What better way to get over a rough break-up than to get her life back on track as soon as she could? Not only back on track but bigger, more spectacular and more successful than it had ever been. Why not show the world that there was more to Lara Nightingale than her boyfriend? If she got it right, Lucien dumping her for Siobhan might just turn out to be the biggest favour he could ever have done for her. As for Siobhan… well, Lara tried not to think about that. Boyfriends might not matter but best friends did, and they weren't so easy to come by – at least in Lara's experience.

As she stood and stared out at the darkness beyond her kitchen window waiting for the kettle to boil and planning her future, she heard a faint sound. Distant, sort of plaintive... coming from outside maybe? A cat?

She switched off the bubbling kettle to quieten it while she listened again. There it was once more, clearer now – definitely a cat.

Cupping her hands around her eyes, she peered out of the window to see if she could see anything but the garden was too dark. So she rushed to open the back door and it almost tumbled in. It must have been sitting on the step, and Lara couldn't decide which of the two of them looked more surprised to be face to face – her or the cat.

One thing was certain: it was as bedraggled as she'd been when she'd returned from her walk in the rain. It was bold too, because if it had been startled by suddenly finding itself in her kitchen, it didn't show any sign of wanting to run away. In fact, it simply looked up at her expectantly with huge green eyes. It looked very hungry to Lara.

'I wonder where you've been,' she said thoughtfully as she ran a hand down the cat's bony spine. Its coat was sodden but that didn't bother her. The cat began to purr and rub up against her leg, prompting her to tickle behind its ears. 'I bet you wouldn't say no to a nice bowl of tuna, would you?'

It took a moment to find the tin in the cupboard. As soon as the smell was released into the air, the cat started to weave in and out, round and round Lara's ankles as she tipped it into a saucer.

'There you go.'

The cat fell upon the meal, purring all the while.

'You'd be a handsome devil with a bit of weight on you and a good groom,' Lara continued as the cat ate. It was a grey tabby with hair a little longer and shaggier than the usual street cat but not quite as long as some of the posher breeds she'd come across.

Now that she looked closer she could see that it was more of a kitten really, barely into adulthood. She had to wonder if someone had lost it.

As a girl, her family had owned a Russian Blue, a beautiful but temperamental little blighter, and Lara thought that perhaps there was a bit of Russian Blue in this one. It was far friendlier than her childhood pet, though, which she'd later learned was quite uncharacteristic of a usually affectionate breed. Trust her family to get the one diva amongst them.

It didn't take long for the cat to clear the plate and look up at her again.

'No more tuna, I'm afraid,' Lara said, stroking it again. 'I can do milk…'

Going to the fridge now, the cat following, she took the milk out and poured some into another shallow dish. This went almost as quickly as the tuna, and so Lara filled the bowl again, smiling as it went in for seconds.

'Maybe all I need to make a new friend is a never-ending supply of milk.'

The cat looked up and then walked over, weaving around her legs again. She bent to fuss it. 'Will you be my new friend?' she asked. The cat's purr seemed to get louder, echoing around the tiny kitchen.

She was hurting, of course, about the whole Lucien and Siobhan thing, more than she'd admit even to herself. But here was this lost little soul with far bigger problems than hers.

She scrubbed behind its ear, sending it into raptures of pleasure. Her own childhood cat, Bluey (imaginative name, she recalled dryly), had always loved that; in fact, it was the only sort of affection he would tolerate for more than a minute before getting bored and stalking off.

'Well,' she said, glancing up at the window as a flash of lightning lit up the sky, 'you can't go back out in this – you'll drown. You're more than welcome to stay and snuggle down with me until the rain stops. I suppose we'll have to ask around in the morning too, see if you belong to anyone.'

The cat looked up now, almost as if it was taking in every word. And as she stood up and made her way into the living room, it followed, leaping onto her lap as she got comfortable on the sofa and curling up there to sleep.

Reaching over carefully so as not to disturb her new guest, Lara pulled a notebook from a little side table next to the sofa. She opened it up to a page covered in doodles and notes and looked them over. They were plans for nothing in particular, schemes she'd thought would probably never become real, dreamt up on countless idle Sundays. At the top of the page she'd drawn a heart surrounded by flowers and birds and she'd written the name of the business she'd always longed to start up: *Songbird Wedding Services*. What was that old saying: *When life gives you lemons, make lemonade?*

In her lap, the little cat stretched long before curling to settle again. Lara smiled fondly and ran a hand down fur that she quickly decided she might have a go at cleaning up later – if the cat would let her, of course. She hoped so. She was beginning to hope that it wouldn't want to leave after the rain had stopped and that she wouldn't find a rightful owner. Love at first sight might not be something she'd ever experienced with a man, but Lara was beginning to think that cats might be a very different matter.

Chapter Two

'If she doesn't like any of these venues then there's no hope!'

Betsy frowned at her computer screen, and Lara looked up from some notes she was making at the opposite desk. A year had gone by since the night Lucien had dropped his bombshell, a year during which she'd been single, heartbroken and minus one best friend. But it hadn't all been bad. It was also a year since a certain handsome blue tabby had come into her life and a year since she'd quit her call-centre job, cleared out her savings (such as they were) and sold practically anything of value she could find – old heirlooms, pieces of jewellery, collectible pottery that her mother had given to her – to raise funds to start the business she'd dreamt of – Songbird Wedding Services.

Even on days when the memories of what Lucien and Siobhan had done to her hurt, she counted her blessings, and every day she gave everything she had to this new life. And as time went by, the hurt became a little less raw, a little more manageable, though she had to admit that she was still some way off being completely healed.

'Maybe we'll have to look further afield,' she said vaguely.

'Further afield? We live in Chester! Everywhere you look is history and gorgeousness! It's a fussy cow who can't find a building here to like!'

'Maybe she wants something much more non-traditional,' Lara continued serenely. She was getting used to Betsy's impatient outbursts – and they never lasted very long anyway.

For the most part, her assistant was a sweet and cheerful girl, fresh out of a travel and tourism course at college. Apart from role playing in class, she hadn't had very much experience of the world of customer service yet. She'd learn soon enough that there was often no rhyme or reason why a client wanted this or that thing; you only had to know that they did, and it was your job to try and make their dreams come true.

Despite her impatience, she was proving to be a very promising trainee and Lara was becoming increasingly comfortable trusting her with more and more responsibility. She was quick to learn and engaging with clients, and patience would come with practice, as would the standard-issue coat hanger you had to shove in your mouth to keep your smile in place.

'Did you ask her about that?'

'Of course I did – full profile and everything!' Betsy looked as if she might explode with frustration, but then appeared to get a grip on herself, as Lara had predicted she would. 'Apparently she doesn't take any notice of her own taste because everything she said she liked is right here in the list of venues I made for her and she's stuck her nose up at every one.'

Lara gave a vague shrug. 'It's a bride's prerogative. You can't apply logic in this situation – it'll feel right for her when it feels right. Throw some curveballs in there.'

'Like what?'

'I don't know… Try her with a river barge or the amphitheatre or something; see how she reacts to something like that. You might get some surprising responses. And if she doesn't like any of them then getting suggestions that really turn her off might help her focus on what she does want a little better. She's probably just overwhelmed with choice – it often happens. What's her fiancé got to say about it, or is he just keeping out of things?'

'He pretty much sits in silence – probably too scared to voice an opinion on anything.'

Lara looked up with a small smile. 'She can't be *that* bad.'

'She's nice enough, just…'

'Hard to please?' Lara arched an eyebrow.

'Yes.'

'Well, I suppose it's her day and she's entitled to be as choosy as she likes.'

'I bet you wouldn't make all this fuss,' Betsy said, starting to rifle through a pile of magazine clippings spread over her desk. 'Being in the business and everything, you know what it's like from the other side – how hard it is to give couples their dream wedding.'

'Well,' Lara replied, a sudden feeling of irritation sweeping over her, 'I'm not likely to find out any time soon.'

Betsy, seeming to sense that she'd said the wrong thing, bent her head over the clippings and pursed her mouth shut. Of course, Betsy couldn't know what she'd said wrong, and perhaps Lara should have tried harder to keep her personal life away from the office, but it was proving difficult. It was only that morning that the grapevine's sprawling tendrils of news had dropped the bombshell that Lucien and Siobhan were engaged. A Facebook post by a friend of a friend to be exact.

Lara didn't even know why she ought to care. She had no love left for Lucien and even less for her ex-best friend. Perhaps it was the niggling sense of humiliation that she'd never really been able to shake, the idea that mutual friends and acquaintances gossiped and pitied her behind her back.

If anyone asked her about it she'd tell them that she wished Lucien and Siobhan all the best and she'd mean it – truly she would. They probably wouldn't believe her though, and she wouldn't blame them.

Not that she'd be able to tell Siobhan or Lucien that she wished them well. Since the big reveal they'd – perhaps predictably and sensibly – steered clear of any contact with Lara. Lucien wouldn't have cared less about how Lara was taking it, but Siobhan, Lara guessed, would have been too deeply ashamed to see her. Perhaps it was just as well, because Lara couldn't honestly say how she would have reacted had they been faced with each other – certainly not in the early days when it was still raw.

It was likely that Siobhan had done her best to keep Lucien from thinking about any of it too much and had probably asked him to steer clear – if not to spare Lara's feelings, then to make certain he didn't suddenly come to the conclusion that he'd chosen wrongly after all.

Lara liked to think that she'd be calmer now, but she couldn't be certain. Lucien and Siobhan had set a wedding date six months away, and Lara's mother, in a tactless moment, had mused on the possibility of Siobhan being pregnant. Why else would they marry so hastily? she questioned. If Lara knew anything about that particular couple, though, it was more likely that Siobhan didn't want to give Lucien too much time to change his mind.

'Lara…?'

Lara looked up to see Betsy throw her a puzzled look. How long had she been talking to her, completely ignored, while Lara had been lost in thought?

'Sorry… what was that?'

'I was saying I don't know how you've done this job for so long without throttling someone.'

'I only set up a year ago,' Lara said, and even that simple statement reminded her of Lucien.

'I know, but that would be enough time for me to have throttled at least five brides.'

Despite everything, Lara couldn't help a fleeting grin. 'The grooms can be just as bad, you know.'

'Really?' Betsy looked sceptical but then seemed to decide a fussy groom was perhaps a more convincing prospect than she'd first thought. 'I didn't think blokes cared all that much about things like that.'

'Believe me, they do. And wait until the parents get involved too, and you're going through every tiny expense with them and finding ways you can shave a penny off the welcome champagne for the wedding breakfast.'

'Are you actually trying to put me off this job?' Betsy asked, wrinkling her pert, freckled nose.

When Lara had first met Betsy, she was convinced that she'd once owned a doll that looked just like her. Charlotte, her doll, had had glossy chestnut hair in a high ballet bun, huge brown eyes and perfectly distributed freckles across her rosy cheeks. Betsy was like that, only living and breathing, sometimes complaining and definitely eating a lot more; though looking at her tiny frame, it was hard to know where she put it.

Lara's smile broadened.

'Honestly, I'm already lost when you're not here, so no, definitely not. I love having you on board – saves me talking to Fluffy all the time.'

Betsy grinned. 'I bet you get more sense from your cat than me.'

'I get less tolerance though. When Fluffy thinks I've said something stupid he lets me know alright. He hasn't learned what a white lie is yet and I think it might be too late to train him.'

'Can you train cats?'

Lara laughed. 'God no!'

'It's funny; I didn't like cats much before I came to work for you – they made me nervous. I think I'd be alright if I had one of my own now.'

'I'm sure you would.' Lara frowned as a faint gurgling sound reached her ears. 'Was that your stomach?'

It was Betsy's turn to grin. 'Sorry… didn't get much time for breakfast this morning.'

'I can't have you fainting all over the place. It's a bit early but why don't you grab your lunch? I'll have a look at the Millington account while you're gone and see what I can come up with. We can go over it all when you get back.'

Betsy wasted no time getting up from her desk. 'I thought you'd never ask! I'm going to the deli in the next street – do you want me to get anything for you?'

'Don't worry about me – I'll probably grab something a bit later.'

With a brief nod, Betsy let the door of the summer house swing closed behind her as she stepped out onto the decking. Lara watched for a moment as she made her way through the garden and out of the side gate. Not only did she look like a ballerina, but she walked like one too, all pert and perky, though when Lara had once asked Betsy whether she danced, Betsy had said that she'd never had a single dance lesson in her entire life. Lara had told her how nice it must be to have been born with natural grace and beauty, and Betsy had blushed and almost dropped the custard tart she'd been eating all over her laptop.

Running her business from her own garden was one of the things Lara loved most about working for herself. She'd wanted a pretty and romantic place to work, somewhere to inspire her as she put together the perfect wedding packages for her clients, and somewhere like the crumbling, dowdy office block she'd worked in before she'd set up on her own just wasn't going to cut it. It was fine for the customer-service department of a well-known vacuum-cleaner manufacturer, if a little uninspiring and often very depressing. But wedding planning needed something else entirely.

She'd searched high and low for the perfect premises, and then, one day, she'd realised that they were right in front of her face. Or rather, outside her kitchen window. While her house was small – bijou, the estate agent had called it – the garden was actually a disproportionately decent size, big enough to allow a summer house to be tucked away in a corner. Against the advice of just about everyone she knew, Lara began the hunt for the perfect building at the right price and eventually she found it: an ex-display one languishing at the back of a garden-centre lot.

It needed a few new shingles on the roof, a lick of paint and a good clean, but it was a steal, and they had even put her in touch with someone who could install it for her and hook her up to every amenity she would need to work from there. She'd painted it a beautiful sea blue and kitted it out with furniture and heaters. It was breezy in the summer and cosy in the winter and had everything she might need.

Taking into account the great commute in the morning, where the most taxing delay would be dodging a dozy bee on the way through the rose trellis, it was the most perfect, heavenly place, and almost too nice to work in. But then she'd close the door behind her and take a seat at her antique waxed desk on the reclaimed swivel chair she'd reupholstered in a red gingham, turn her face to the huge windows looking out onto the garden, take a breath of contentment and start another day that would hopefully bring in enough money to keep this dream lifestyle afloat.

She was so lucky, she'd once said to her mum, but then her mum had reminded her that she'd fought and worked and saved hard for all she had right now so luck didn't really come into it, and Lara had to agree.

But working from her own home also meant that she would have to trust the assistant she'd eventually found she needed to come and go freely, and know they would never snoop where they weren't supposed to.

If luck hadn't come into setting up her business, it had definitely played a part in finding Betsy. Lara had been hurrying to the gym for a spin class one day as Betsy was leaving, and they'd almost knocked each other over. The next few times Lara went to a class, Betsy had been there, and eventually they'd started to chat whenever they saw each other. Lara had soon learned that Betsy had almost finished her travel and tourism course and didn't really know what to do with herself after that, and as soon as Lara had mentioned that she'd been thinking about getting help, Betsy had been only too happy to offer her services.

She'd started as an intern but had quickly become indispensable, and Lara had taken the financial gamble and put her on the payroll. It was another fated decision, as if karma had decided that perhaps Lara needed a break after what had happened with Lucien, because she loved working with Betsy and life was good now. The only thing missing was a man, but you couldn't have it all.

She'd always been a romantic at heart and, despite the disaster of her last relationship, had believed fervently that a perfect someone was out there for everyone. But these days she wondered if things were really that simple. They might be out there, but that didn't mean you'd ever cross paths with them. Maybe a happy life on her own was the best she could hope for, and what she had now was pretty good, even without that perfect someone to share it.

As Betsy disappeared from sight, Lara wandered over and picked up the Millington file she'd been complaining so vocally about. There were magazine clippings littering the desk but yet more stuffed into the file. Betsy was right about one thing – this couple really didn't know what they wanted. By the looks of things, the bride, at least, had been scouring wedding magazines since she was a little girl.

Lara smiled as she went through them. A couple who were this excited about their upcoming wedding was a lovely thing to see, but it could make the planning more difficult because they often found it hard to focus on any kind of cohesive vision for their big day. That was where Lara and Betsy came in, of course, and Lara liked to think that she was good at helping couples realise a vision they might not even have been aware they'd had all along.

Looking at the scraps of images spilling out of this file though, Lara could see why Betsy was struggling. This bride didn't know what she wanted and simultaneously seemed to want everything. There was no trend, no single style or aesthetic to pick out, just a mad, eclectic set of photos that showed everything from decorated barns to stately homes. The themes for flowers, food and décor weren't much better, ranging from shabby chic to country living to millionaire decadence. Figuring out what would turn this couple's wedding day into a dream come true was going to take some creative thinking. Often she could look at a collection of ideas and quickly get a sense of what that client was trying to achieve, but not this time. This time she was as much in the dark as Betsy.

Going over to the window, she stood, gazing out at the garden, turning over the problem in her mind as she did. The flowerbeds were bursting with colour; all the pruning, weeding and attention she paid to them had certainly rewarded her with swathes of fragrant lavender, delicate jasmine, fire-red poppies and sugar-pink roses.

As she took stock of her handiwork, her face lit with an amused smile. Fluffy was skulking around, patrolling his kingdom, and he'd just taken a swipe at a sparrow that had been silly enough to fly too low. Not quite low enough though, as it turned out, which was lucky for the sparrow but not quite so lucky for Fluffy. He didn't look too perturbed at his miss and, not to be beaten, had turned his attention to the little wooden bug hotel Lara had attached to the wall of the main house. It currently housed a bumblebee nest, and a few of the furry residents were circling the entrance in a lazy landing queue. Fluffy watched them now, his keen stare fixed on their movements.

Lara perhaps should have been more worried than she was, but she'd had the foresight to fix the box far too high for Fluffy to reach – at least she was as certain as she could be that she had. She'd never yet seen him leap that high anyway. And Lara didn't think that he'd be daft enough to try and grab one either, although as Fluffy could be a spontaneous and unpredictable creature, you could never be quite sure. It wouldn't be the first time he'd got himself into a pickle since arriving on Lara's doorstep that fateful stormy night.

Of course, being spoilt rotten had ensured he wouldn't want to leave, and he looked a lot sleeker and fatter than he had that first night. Betsy said he ate better than Lara did – certainly he fussed over his food bowl almost as much as many of Lara's clients did over their catering. But then, he was the *true* love of her life, the only male she'd ever been able to rely on – though a procession of useless boyfriends and a dad who'd deserted the family while Lara had still been a baby hadn't provided much in the way of competition.

Perhaps her theory about there being the perfect someone for everyone wasn't so far off the mark – she'd just forgotten to include cats in the equation. If she looked at it that way, she'd already found hers. Which perhaps wasn't saying a lot, because sometimes Fluffy was as fickle and secretive as any man who might be trying to have his cake and eat it. She didn't know where he went on his night-time forays, and perhaps it was better that way. If she found herself shaking a pack of biscuits and calling his name at the front door later that night, or walking the streets to see where he'd got to, it wouldn't be the first time.

It was a relatively recent thing that had started to happen over the last six months or so, and Lara could only attribute it to the fact that he was far healthier and happier than he had been when he'd first arrived, and perhaps that had made him more confident to wander too. If she looked at it that way, she ought to see it as a good thing; she only wished that she could. The fact was, whenever he was missing for too long, she hated it. She worried too much – everyone said so – but she couldn't help it. Somehow, because of the manner and the exact moment he'd arrived in her life, she felt as if they were fundamentally bound in a way she couldn't explain, but in a way that mattered, like she and this ordinary little cat were two lost souls who'd found each other for a reason.

Fluffy made a sudden leap for a low-flying bee. He only just missed and Lara decided that it was time she stepped in before he got himself in real trouble. Crossing the garden in sunshine that would soon be too strong to sit out in, Lara gathered Fluffy into her arms. Despite immediate purring as she scratched behind an ear, she could tell that he was vaguely annoyed that she'd ruined his morning's fun.

'Tough, mister,' she crooned as she nuzzled the soft fur of his neck. 'It's for your own good. I don't think chomping on a bee is particularly good for your health.'

While he wriggled, she carried him across the garden, back to the summer house, closing the door behind her before letting him down. As he stalked the room with an air of mild vexation, she produced a bag of cat treats from her desk drawer.

'Here you go,' she said, sprinkling a handful onto the desk. Fluffy leapt up and began to nibble, this scene obviously well rehearsed and all thoughts of hunting entirely inappropriate prey seemingly forgotten. Lara smiled. 'It'll keep you good for ten minutes at least, you daft cat.'

Fluffy took no notice. It seemed that cat treats drove all thoughts of hunting from his mind – and all thoughts of the person who'd provided them. Lara didn't mind. He was an ungrateful little monster, but he was *her* ungrateful little monster and she loved him.

Leaving him to his treats with a last fond smile, she took up the Millington file again to have another look before Betsy returned from her lunch break.

Chapter Three

It was a well-worn family joke but it never got old. At five feet five, Lara was no giant but she still towered over her mother. Everyone said it was because Lara's mother, Fay, spent so much of her days racing around, finding it impossible to sit still for more than a second, that she must have simply worn her legs down.

Fay was probably no more than five feet tall, though even that was an optimistic estimation, and she certainly didn't have time to stand around long enough to be measured. She was slim too, that kind of slimness that comes from being constantly busy, her dark hair threaded with highlights of auburn that she went to the hairdressers to get topped up every month; an appointment that proved to be about the only time she ever sat still and the only appointment she could make without some kind of drama. As Lara watched her now, a set of tall ladders wobbling dangerously beneath her as she struggled to reach an ornate plaster ceiling rose that she'd insisted – despite Lara's protestations – that she could reach, she'd never been more keenly aware of her mother's diminutive stature.

'She's going to come off there,' Betsy said in a low voice. Lara turned to see her assistant with an armful of ivory satin ribbon; she was watching Lara's mum now too.

'I know, but when my mum says she's going to do something it's hard to stop her,' Lara said. 'I told her no, but the minute I turned my back she was up there like a terrier up a pipe.'

'Do terriers go up pipes?' Betsy asked in a slightly bemused voice. Lara shrugged.

'Mum!' she called. 'I think that'll do it! You can come down now…'

'It's not quite straight,' Fay replied.

'Honestly, Mrs Nightingale—' Betsy began.

'I keep telling you it's Fay!' Lara's mum interrupted. 'There's no need for all this formality, you— Oh!'

The ladder swayed and Lara could only race across and try to grab it, heart in her mouth. But, by some miracle, it steadied before she got there.

'Please, Mum,' Lara insisted, now clinging to the bottom, 'that'll do. You're going to give me a heart attack!'

'And me,' Betsy said. 'And I'm too young to have heart attacks.'

'So I'm not?' Lara squeaked. 'Cheeky mare!'

Betsy grinned, and then both women turned back to Fay and watched with expressions of profound relief as she began to clamber down to the ground. Only Fay seemed oblivious to the palpable stress in the room – stress she'd caused. She simply looked up at the garland she'd secured with a satisfied smile.

'There. Looks alright, doesn't it? I might be knocking on a bit but there's use in me yet.'

'Yes,' Lara said a little faintly. 'It looks lovely, Mum. Do you know what though? I could really do with you starting on the table arrangements. I can't get them right at all and I know your eye is better than mine on these things.'

'Oh yes, it always has been,' Fay said cheerfully, glancing over at the crates of creamy roses and blush peonies waiting to be put out onto the freshly laundered linen of the guest tables. 'People have always said I ought to have been a florist or an interior designer or something. But I was so busy bringing up you and your brother and, well... it's too late for that sort of thing now, isn't it?'

'Never too late, Mrs... Fay,' Betsy said. 'What are you, like forty or something?'

'Oh, you!' Fay laughed. 'I can't be forty, as well you know, otherwise, how could I have Lara's brother, who's thirty-two, and Lara, who's twenty-nine?'

'Well, you don't look old enough to have a son who's thirty-two,' Betsy said. Fay shot her a look of faint disbelief but didn't argue, clearly a bit pleased with the compliment even if she pretended not to buy it for a second.

'I'd better get on,' she said. 'Those flowers won't leap onto the tables by themselves.'

'Nice segue,' Betsy whispered, turning to Lara now with an impish grin. They watched as Fay bustled off, away from the ladder and out of danger. Lara didn't grin though; she simply looked at Betsy as if hoping to find divine strength there. She needed it too, because a moment later there was an almighty crash and both women whipped their heads in Fay's direction to see that she'd already managed to drop and smash a crystal vase full of flowers. Lara had ordered a couple extra for just such an eventuality, but she hoped now that she wouldn't need more than that, otherwise she was going to be in trouble.

'I could lock her in a cupboard?' Betsy offered. 'They've got plenty of massive ones in this place, and she might just think we've given her another room to decorate. By the time she figured it out we'd be done in here.'

'Tempting as that is, I think not. Mum wants to help and I love that she does – God knows I need as much help as I can get – but sometimes...'

'It's more hindrance than help?'

'Hmmm,' was all Lara said in reply.

Her gaze swept the room they were currently decorating, the stunning ballroom of a vast Georgian mansion out in the Cheshire countryside. Although Lara had to wonder, looking at the marble and gilt splendour of the furnishings, the sympathetic period colours of the paintwork and the ornate ceilings that seemed to reach into space, whether their efforts to dress it for tonight's wedding celebration were really just a bit pointless. It was so magnificent, so beautiful just as it was, that she almost worried they were ruining it. But they were doing exactly what their clients had asked for, and that, of course, was what they were paid to do. They were a lovely young couple too, barely out of their teens. They'd told Lara that they'd been together since school and had always been convinced that one day they'd be married. They'd chosen this venue, the church, the flowers, the catering and the myriad other little details with very little fuss and extreme enthusiasm that it was hard not to be affected by. Lara had always looked forward to their consultations and had always been left with a smile on her face when they'd left, and she thought they might just be her favourite clients ever.

'Abbie and Matt are going to love this,' Betsy said, echoing just the thought Lara had been having.

'I hope so,' she said. 'They're so lovely. I want to get it right for them.'

'I think they're just happy to be getting married.' Betsy looked wistful for a moment. 'It must be amazing, being so in love, knowing that you've found the one, the person you were made to be with.'

'It must be.' Lara knew that Betsy was probably referring to her own lack of a boyfriend, but she wasn't necessarily thinking about only Betsy's status as a singleton.

Betsy looked guilty now, perhaps realising this, and was just about to reply when Fay's voice came from across the room.

'I saw Mandy Squires at the post office yesterday,' she called over. 'Getting a new passport she was. Hasn't been abroad since 1992, she says. I told her I hadn't been abroad since 1990 and to see if she could beat that and she said she couldn't. Told her it was down to being a single mother, of course, because how could I afford it? I said that if it weren't for school trips you would never have been anywhere at all.'

'True,' Lara acknowledged, though it had never bothered her in quite the same way it had her mum. She could understand why Fay might sometimes feel she'd missed out, though she never complained and Lara didn't think she was quite as bothered by it as she made out. As for herself, she was perfectly old enough and capable enough to take herself on holiday if she really wanted to go. Not that she had time for holidays since she'd started Songbird Wedding Services.

'She asked how you and your brother were getting on,' Fay continued. 'I told her you were both doing well. Her oldest is courting, she says – I told her to look you up if they decided to tie the knot, but she said she didn't think that was likely. She says her nephew is marrying a man; I said I had no idea he was gay and she said neither did they until he brought this fella home. I didn't offer your services for that because I'm not sure if they have normal weddings.'

'Of course they do!' Lara said, and she couldn't help but laugh now. 'A wedding is a wedding no matter who it's for. I planned one for two women only last week. They're tying the knot on Christmas Day.'

'What are you going to do for them?'

'What they've asked for, which is not a million miles away from what we're doing today for Abbie and Matt.'

'Oh…' Fay was thoughtful for a moment. 'Mandy asked if you were courting.'

'Did she?' Lara said, her good humour evaporating now. She had a feeling she might know what was coming and that she wouldn't like it.

'I think she was angling to fix you up with her Brandon but I wouldn't if I were you – there's something about him that's a bit shifty.'

'He's not my type anyway,' Lara said, glancing across at Betsy to see her stifling a grin.

'Although nobody would be as bad as that last one you had,' Fay said.

'Lucien? Thanks for bringing him up *again*, Mum.'

'I still can't believe what he did to you. With your best friend too! Poor Siobhan…'

'Poor nobody,' Lara said shortly. 'Siobhan knew exactly what she was doing. She was hardly an innocent led astray.'

'Yes, but he was that sort – you could see it a mile off. I never expected it of her though. When I think of all the times she stayed at our house and I cooked for her—'

'Mum,' Lara said, a warning tone in her voice that said to drop the subject and drop it quick.

'I knew he was shifty,' Fay continued, ignorant to any kind of danger.

'Perhaps you could have told me at the time then,' Lara said.

'I did!' Fay said, sounding mortally offended. 'I said I didn't like him. He never could look me in the eye!'

'Mum…' Lara pinched the bridge of her nose and squeezed her eyes shut. 'Could we not talk about this now?'

'Well, I suppose it's good riddance that they're getting married now, isn't it?'

Lara opened her eyes, hoping to find that she'd been transported to another time and place in the second that they'd been closed. But there she was, still in the grand ballroom of a country estate, somewhere in Cheshire, being verbally tortured by an oblivious Fay. She held in an exasperated sigh.

'And Mandy says to tell you how sorry she is for you. She says it must be heartbreaking to know that your friend and your—'

'I don't care about Lucien!' Lara slapped the clipboard she was holding onto the nearest table. 'I don't care if they marry each other twenty times over! I don't care if they televise it! I don't care if the Queen is the guest of honour – they can do what they want, but I don't want to talk about it!'

Fay threw a wounded look at her daughter, and then another at Betsy, which pleaded for some moral support.

'I was only saying—'

'Well don't!'

Lara stalked off, heading for a set of French doors. They opened out onto a balcony that overlooked immaculate acres of Italian gardens. She let the doors close behind her and gripped the handrail, pulling in a lungful of fragrant afternoon air as she struggled to calm her temper.

'A bit harsh, maybe?'

Betsy's quiet voice came from behind her. Lara turned round.

'I think you're in the wrong career. Judging by how silently you've just followed me out here, perhaps you ought to be a spy.'

Betsy gave a sheepish smile. She didn't know what to do or say, of course, suddenly finding herself in the middle of a family spat, and

Lara wished now that she'd held her temper better. It wasn't fair on Betsy to subject her to the scene she'd just witnessed and it wasn't very professional either. Her gaze went beyond her apprentice to where her mum was inside, now industriously setting out the flowers on the tables.

'I know she doesn't mean it,' Lara sighed. 'I know that she's offended by the things Lucien did on my behalf more than anything else. But it was a horrible time of my life and I just want to move on. I lost friends and a lot of dignity too, and I'm only just getting over all that. But I can't because everywhere I turn someone is waiting to remind me.'

'Did you love him a lot?'

'I thought I did but now… I'm not so sure. I was hurt though, more than I've ever been hurt in my life. Imagine being slapped in the face as hard as you've ever been slapped, and then imagine that happening to your heart instead.'

Betsy looked confused, and Lara didn't blame her. It was hard to explain to someone who'd never been subjected to that kind of pain and humiliation. And for Betsy's sake, Lara hoped that she never would be in a position to understand.

'Want me to go and get coffees from down the road?' Betsy asked.

Lara gave her a fond smile. The world hadn't yet dulled Betsy's sparkle. She might have been confused and inexperienced, unable to empathise with Lara's experiences, but she was still wise enough to know that Lara needed a moment alone with her mum to fix the hurt she'd caused hitting back at hurt she herself was feeling.

'It's not exactly down the road,' she said.

'Well, I know, but there is a Starbucks at the petrol station we passed a few miles back.'

'You feel confident enough to drive it on your own?'

'Oh yes, I've been driving loads since I passed my test; I'll be fine.'

Lara nodded. 'That does sound lovely.'

'The usual?' Betsy asked, turning to go back inside.

'Yes please, and ask my mum what she wants before you go. There's petty cash in the pocket of my satchel.'

Lara gave her a few minutes to get the money and go, and then took a deep breath before heading inside to offer a grovelling and entirely owed apology to her mum.

Chapter Four

The evening's clients, Abbie and Matt, had employed her for the full wedding package, which meant that Lara was required to stay all day and into the evening, even after the reception had wound up and everyone had gone home. Besides making certain everything ran smoothly, she had to ensure that the wedding gifts were collected up and sent to the clients' home and that rented equipment went back to the suppliers.

Full-package weddings, where Lara arranged everything from the very start right down to the tiniest little detail, were a mammoth undertaking, and Lara tried not to do too many at a time because they could take months, even years of involvement from her. In fact, she'd taken one on in her first month of business and twelve months later the big day had still yet to arrive. It wasn't a case of resting on her laurels during that time either; there were regular checks to be made to ensure arrangements and bookings were still good and that the clients were still happy with what they had planned.

Many clients hired Lara simply to coordinate the actual day so that it was one less thing for them to worry about. All they had to do then was turn up and say 'I do', knowing that someone else would be worrying about where everyone sat in the church and whether the reception DJ stayed sober. In these cases, prior to Lara's involvement, the couple (or other family members) would plan and book the event and then pass on the details to Lara. These sorts of bookings were far easier for her to enact, although a lot less lucrative. When Abbie and Matt had asked her to plan everything from scratch for them she'd almost turned the booking down because she was stretched as it was. But with them being so sweet and lovely, and with the timely arrival of Betsy, she'd eventually decided to take the job.

Tonight, as she hovered behind the scenes taking care of every little detail, she was glad she had. She'd sent Betsy home – the girl had worked a long-enough day as it was, and Lara was more than able to cope with whatever needed to be taken care of now. She kept a close eye on the party, but it hardly needed intervention from her because it was ticking over rather nicely all by itself. Drink flowed, food was enjoyed and old uncles embarrassed themselves on the dance floor to the sounds of seventies disco classics. Most wedding reception traditions were observed, including emotional speeches from friends and relatives and the happy couple, leading to the post-food debauchery when things would get less genteel and a lot more raucous.

It warmed her heart to see Abbie and Matt take to the floor for their first dance, and if nothing else bolstered her now often failing belief in true love, that did. She'd never seen a couple more connected, more at one. They seemed to lose everyone else in the room as they swayed to the music, lost in a universe where only they existed, where they didn't need air or food or money, only each other. *Maybe*, Lara thought as she watched them, embracing so closely that they almost fused into the same person, Abbie's dress fanning out behind her in a swirl of rustling ivory silk as Matt spun her round, *maybe this is still out there somewhere, waiting for me to find it.*

It hadn't been that hard to smooth things over with her mum and Lara had waved her off, thankful for her help with the venue and equally thankful that they were on good terms. But it had been harder to forget Fay's words, because, regardless of the intent, they'd hurt like hell. They'd cut like a rusting, careless old razor into Lara's soul, her pride, everything that she was. She'd always believed in true love and, to some extent, she still did, but she'd never imagined it could be such a slippery customer. One thing she'd learned was that she hadn't found it with Lucien and that was OK, but the experience with him had made her realise that it might be harder to recognise than she'd ever thought possible. How would she know? How could she be sure it was the real thing when it finally came her way?

In the end she'd been forced to put all her doubts and fears to one side. She had a job to do and lots of people relying on her to make this day perfect; she wasn't going to let Lucien get in the way of that.

It was as she was collecting up the cards and gifts while the DJ packed up his equipment that Abbie and Matt came to speak to her. They looked radiant and desperately in love, their hands clasped tight together and their cheeks flushed. They were both a little tipsy too, but that was hardly surprising considering how many guests had pushed drinks into their hands throughout the evening.

'We wanted to say thank you,' Abbie said. 'It's been so perfect and it's all down to you.'

'It's my job,' Lara said cheerfully.

'You do it brilliantly,' Abbie insisted. And then, taking Lara so completely by surprise that she almost dropped the glass coffee pot she was holding, Abbie threw her arms around her in an enthusiastic hug. 'You're just the best!'

'Thank you,' Lara said, her light laugh edged with a tone of bemusement as Abbie let her go again and snapped back into Matt's arms, where she seemed to fit as perfectly as a dovetail in a joint. She leaned her head into him and let out a sigh of contentment. 'You still want all the gifts sending to your mum's house, Abbie?' Lara asked.

'If that's OK,' Matt said. 'We've still got boxes everywhere at our new place from moving in so there's nowhere really to put all this until we're organised. We'll pick it all up when we're a bit more straight.'

'No problem,' Lara said, brushing a lock of ash-coloured hair away from her face.

'My friend's getting married,' Abbie said. 'I've told her all about you – she really wants you to do her wedding too.'

'That's brilliant,' Lara said. 'I'll wait to hear from her then.'

'Chloe, her name is. She was here tonight but she had to go early so there wasn't time to come and find you. I've given her your number. She's done quite a lot of it herself so she won't need everything like we did – is that OK?'

'Of course it is,' Lara said with a smile and a vague sense of relief that it sounded like a fairly straightforward job.

'Taxi's here!' someone yelled, and both Abbie and Matt spun round to acknowledge a guest standing at the doors of the ballroom.

Matt turned back to Lara. 'We have to go.'

'Of course, don't let me keep you. I'll get all this stuff delivered first thing in the morning to the address you gave me.'

'There's a lot – will you be alright?' Abbie asked, eyeing the gift pile doubtfully.

'Of course I will – now stop worrying about me and get your taxi before it drives off!'

'Thanks again,' Abbie said, pulling Lara into another drunken hug. Matt merely grinned before leading his new wife away. Lara watched them go. They'd be alright, of that she was certain. As certain as she could be of anything, that was, which sometimes felt like not very much at all.

Chapter Five

At school, Lara had been taught a poem about a highwayman who'd fallen for a landlord's daughter. Lara had thought it impossibly tragic, but also impossibly romantic as the lovelorn girl sacrificed herself to save the man she loved from the soldiers out looking to hang him. Perhaps that was where her romantic streak had first begun to manifest itself, a questionable (she sometimes reasoned) image of what true love ought to be. There was no way to tell really, but it had stuck with her, despite not having read it for many years. And one line of the poem in particular had stayed with her, something about the moon that night, a ghostly galleon tossed upon cloudy seas. Often, even as an adult, she'd look up on a bright summer's night and see a generous moon buffeted by racing banks of cloud, and she'd think of that poem – that line – and the impassive beauty of a moon that would have looked on and not cared about the drama going on in the world below. To that moon, true love would have meant nothing.

Not that the drama was quite so epic tonight. There was the moon, round and bright, disappearing and reappearing through mountains of billowing cloud like a ship cleaving the waves. It was hardly making Lara feel romantic though. It had been a long day and, though Matt and Abbie's wedding had wound up sometime after midnight, there had been plenty to do long after they'd left. It was Lara's job to make sure everyone who still needed to be paid got paid, that no damage had been done to the venue, that all the gifts were accounted for and sent on, and a million other little tasks that she'd been employed to worry about so that Abbie and Matt didn't have to.

Now, in the early hours of the following morning, all she wanted to do was crawl into bed. Instead, she was walking the streets and, as beautiful as they were in the pearly glow of the moon, it was the last place she wanted to be. She was chasing Fluffy, of course, which seemed to be a regular occurrence these days. *Stupid Fluffy*, she thought, and though she loved him dearly, that was what he was.

She hitched up her pyjama trousers. The elastic on this particular pair had given up the ghost months before but Lara was making them last. As long as she didn't have to run anywhere in them, she reasoned, they were still perfectly serviceable. They'd go in the bin eventually, once the seat had worn through entirely and there was a severe risk of showing a full moon of her own, but not until then. Still, she'd known even as she ventured out in them that she was taking a risk, and she had to hope that luck was on her side. Despite the fact that she'd thrown an oversized sweatshirt over her top half, it would still be mortifying for any of her neighbours to catch her out looking like this – after all, she was a respected businessperson. At least, that was the image she worked hard to project. Sadly, these pyjama trousers betrayed the reality. Right now, Lara was less a respectable young professional with a perfectly ordered life and more a young woman who was one piece of pyjama elastic away from laughing stock.

At least the streets were likely to be deserted at this time, apart from the odd drunk rolling home from a night out or Selina, the neighbour Lara often saw on this street while she was out on her nocturnal cat rescues. She'd found out that Selina was a nurse who worked shifts and, if Lara bumped into her tonight, chances were that Selina was returning home from a long day at work herself. She was hardly going to have the energy to judge Lara's tatty pyjamas.

There was a good reason why she was out in her bedclothes. It wasn't until she'd been ready to turn in that she'd realised Fluffy hadn't eaten the food she'd laid down for him that morning. A quick search of the house told her he wasn't home either, which wasn't really unusual in itself. However, when she'd thought about it properly, she realised she hadn't seen him that morning when she'd left for work either. And, judging by his untouched food, he hadn't been back at all that day, which was a longer absence than she'd like, even though she knew perfectly well that cats came and went as they pleased. He was a cat, but he was *her* cat, and she wanted to know that he was safe.

'Fluffy!' she hissed as she walked the street now, rattling a bag of his favourite cat treats. 'Where are you? Come on out, you great stupid lump! I've got goodies!'

The street was silent and empty, illuminated in pockets by old yellow street lights and the glow from the odd upstairs window. There was no sign of Fluffy and it was beginning to feel like a wild goose chase. Lara inwardly chastised herself for overreacting. Fluffy would come back in his own sweet time. She always ended up going out to look for him, seldom found him, and then he'd turn up a few hours later as if nothing had happened. Which, in his world, it hadn't. He was certainly smarter than to fall for the old rattling pack of cat treats trick. Lara considered heading home to her bed, but she decided to call out one last time.

'Fluffy! Come on!'

And then, from the corner of her eye, she spotted movement and she tracked it, expecting to see her wayward cat. Instead, she was startled to find herself looking at the biggest urban fox she'd ever seen.

It was out in the light for a moment before slinking back into the shadows, and Lara's blood ran a little cold. If Fluffy got into a scrap with something like that she didn't fancy his chances. The sight only filled her with new resolve to find her stupid cat and take him home, whether he liked it or not.

'Fluffy!' she called again, daring to raise her voice a little now. 'Where are you?'

'You've lost someone too?'

Lara spun round at the sound of a man's voice. She hadn't heard footsteps, despite the quiet street, and all at once her senses were on red alert. No footsteps equalled stalking, which equalled danger. She hadn't attended a jujitsu class since her teens, but everything she'd ever learned there flooded back now in a manic instant. Before she'd had time to fully process the situation, instinct had kicked in. Grabbing the man by the wrist, she twisted sharply and flung him to the floor.

'What the—' he gasped, clearly winded as he stared up at her. She stared back. Even she was a little shocked she still knew how to do that, especially now that she saw the size of him. He was no muscleman, but he nonetheless had the sort of build that made her flooring of him all the more impressive.

'You shouldn't creep up on people like that!'

The man pushed himself to sit and clapped a hand to his chest. 'I wasn't creeping up on you!'

'I didn't hear you – were you stalking me?'

'Stalking you! You're a maniac! You shouldn't be on the streets without supervision!'

He still sounded badly winded, but he'd fallen heavily on his back and so it was no wonder. Somewhere, in the corner of Lara's brain where common sense prevailed, she had to feel a little sorry for him.

He looked genuinely a bit scared by her, and she supposed she had reacted a little strongly...

'You shouldn't creep up on people in the dark,' she insisted, choosing not to listen to common-sense Lara. 'That's what you get when you do!'

'What if I'd been a little old lady? Would you have assaulted me then? I only asked you a civil question!'

'But you're not old and you're not a lady.' Lara folded her arms.

'For all you knew I was. You didn't have a clue; you just flung me across the road regardless!'

'Well, I knew you weren't a little old lady,' Lara fired back. 'Unless her HRT had gone really wrong, there was no way a little old lady was going to have a voice that deep!' She gave him an obvious once-over. 'You look like a mugger to me. Or worse. Creeping around the streets at night with your hoodie and your silent shoes... What else was I meant to think?'

He got to his feet and stared at her as he brushed himself down. 'Well, I'm not a mugger. *Or worse*,' he said, mimicking her voice on the last phrase. 'Jesus, what's wrong with you? Innocent people do go out at night, you know.'

He paused for a second, but when he spoke again Lara was shocked to find the hint of a smile. Surely not? She'd imagined it, hadn't she?

'Or are you saying that because *you're* a mugger?' he continued, rubbing at the base of his spine. 'Should I be hiding my wallet? Although, if the way you just floored me is anything to go by, I should probably just surrender and give you my wallet right now, because you've given me enough bruises as it is and I don't fancy a broken collarbone to go with them.'

'You could have been anyone,' Lara insisted, though she really was beginning to feel she'd overreacted. And the fact was, she was softening ever so slightly because, now that she looked closer, this guy was around her own age, seemed like he might have a good sense of humour and was very attractive. At least, the dim glow of the street lights was making him look good. And there was no dim glow that could make someone's voice sound that soft and velvety, so that had to be real, and it was ever so—

'I had to defend myself,' she added, her thoughts brought back to the moment as the sensation of her pyjamas sliding down her hips gave an unwelcome reminder of what she was wearing and how much she needed to get home. Hurriedly, she shoved a hand beneath her sweatshirt to hitch them up and tried to look like she didn't care.

'Well,' he said, and there was definitely a smirk there. 'You certainly did that.'

'Look, I didn't mean to overreact and I'm sorry. I just want to find my... Oh!'

In a pool of light a few lamps away could be seen a little feline figure, padding towards them.

'There he—'

'Satchmo! There you are!'

Lara looked on in bewilderment (and not a little indignation too) as the man walked over to what she now saw clearly was Fluffy and lifted him into his arms.

'Blimey,' he said, cradling the cat, 'you haven't half caused me some aggro tonight.'

'That's my cat!' Lara cried.

The man turned to her in confusion. 'This is my cat.'

'No... I think I know my own cat when I see him... Fluffy!' She clicked her fingers. 'Come on!'

'You're mistaken – this is my cat.'

'It's mine!'

'It's mine! And I feel sorry for your poor cat. Who calls a cat Fluffy? Are you too busy to think about names because that must have taken you all of a nanosecond to come up with?'

'Well it's better than Sasquatch or whatever your cat's called,' Lara returned sourly.

'*Satchmo*. And it's a great name. Not that it's any of your business what I call my cat.'

'It's none of your business what I call my cat either!'

If Lara had been warming to this guy, this new complication had well and truly chilled things again. He stared at her now, looking perplexed.

'What's your problem?' he asked. 'First you try to break my arm and now you're trying to take my cat?'

'It's my cat!'

'You're wrong.'

'And you're a weirdo, sneaking up on people at night.'

'Weirdo? And you base this assertion on the fact that I walk around after dark?' he asked, a bit too smugly for Lara's liking, who was now beyond tired and getting a bit cold and desperate to get her cat and go home. Not to mention the rogue pyjama bottoms heading south again. The first thing she was going to do when she got home was bin them – something she should have done months ago.

'Look,' she said through gritted teeth, 'I just want my cat.'

'Well, you'd better go and look for your cat because it's not this one.'

'I'm telling you he's mine! Bloody idiot!'

Lara sprang forward and made a grab to take by force what she was absolutely sure was Fluffy. The man dodged her easily, but in the ruckus the cat leapt from his arms and landed nimbly on the pavement a few yards away. They both bent to retrieve him at the same time, their joint efforts achieving nothing but annoying the cat so much that he streaked off, tail wagging as he went.

'Now look what you've done!' Lara hissed, a hand shooting downwards to rescue her pyjama trousers again.

'Me? You're the psycho cat abductor!'

'What!'

'If you hadn't been trying to grab him like a lunatic he wouldn't have run off!'

'If you hadn't been trying to take him I wouldn't have had to!'

'For the last time, he's my cat!'

'He's mine! Besides, yours, mine… neither of us is getting him back now, are we?'

The man looked as if he was going to continue the argument, but then he simply sighed and broke into a jog, heading in the direction the cat had taken. Lara was about to give chase when her attention was caught by a car turning into the silent street and pulling up close to where she stood. The engine stopped and the headlights went out. Selina got out, waving at her. Lara could see the nurse's uniform peeking out from beneath her jacket. It looked as if she'd just finished a shift.

'You're out late,' Selina called as she walked over. 'After your cat as usual?'

'Well, yes,' Lara said. And then added with new indignation in her voice: 'But some guy is currently hunting him down insisting he belongs to him.'

An idea occurred to her. She could get to Fluffy much quicker if Selina took her in the car. With a bit of luck they could spot him from the road, scoop him up and be home so fast the man wouldn't be able to do anything about it. And fair was fair, you couldn't go around taking people's cats, so Lara had every right – didn't she? This was her cat, wasn't it? She shook away the sudden doubt. Of course it was – how would she not know Fluffy?

She was about to voice the request, cheeky though it might sound, when Selina spoke.

'I expect that'll be Theo,' she said cheerfully.

Lara looked at her sharply. 'You know him?'

'Oh, I see him around a lot looking for that cat, just like I sometimes see you. I expect half the neighbourhood goes looking for that cat of an evening,' she said airily, pulling her bag from the car and digging into it for her house keys.

'What?' Lara asked, mouth wide open and feeling rather huffy She couldn't believe that Selina had chosen this moment as the first time to mention this to her. If someone else had been out looking for her cat, she wanted to know about it. How come Selina would take any opportunity to gossip about things that didn't matter but never mention that someone else was feeding her cat? Lara could only assume that she didn't see an issue with it. Perhaps it was understandable for someone who didn't have a pet, but it irked Lara just the same.

'Theo feeds it; has been for a few months now. I'll bet half the street feeds it – you know what cats are like.'

'Well yes, but…' Lara's sentence trailed off. She suddenly felt very stupid. She watched as Selina walked to her front door.

'Goodnight, Lara.'

Half the street feeds it… That might be some cats but not mine, Lara thought as Selina's front door opened and she went inside. *Not my Fluffy. He's mine; he's not fickle like all those other cats.*

But he was. The proof of that was playing out on a nearby street as this stranger tried to claim him. Well, Lara wasn't going to be beaten and she wasn't going to give up her beloved Fluffy to some lanky... what was his name again? Theo?

So you want to fight me for Fluffy, eh, Theo? Lara folded her arms tight across her chest and stared along the dim street towards where Fluffy had gone and Theo had followed. Well, if it's a fight you want then it's a fight you'll get!

Chapter Six

Betsy set a paper bag down on the desk in front of Lara.

'Will that do?' she asked. 'I went to the market – thought it would be cheaper.'

'Oh, thanks.' Lara picked up the bag and peered inside. A second later she took out a tiny silver bell. She turned it over in her fingers.

'It's not what you wanted, is it?' Betsy frowned, hands going to rest on her hips. 'I'm sorry – you want me to take it back and swap it?'

'No – of course not – it's fine.' Lara looked at it again. It had been sweet of Betsy to offer to dash out to the pet store for her and she didn't have the heart to tell her that, actually, the bell was far smaller than she'd wanted. She'd wanted something obvious, something that would tell the world that Fluffy had a loving owner and was not in the market for a new one. At the same time, a big enough bell might make enough noise to help alert Lara to his whereabouts a lot quicker the next time she was out looking for him. Like, before a certain Theo had a chance to get to him…

'It's not fine,' Betsy said, taking the bell from her and dropping it back into the bag. 'I can tell. I'll take it back and get a refund.'

'Honestly,' Lara said, grabbing it back. 'It's a few pounds' worth – hardly worth taking it back. I'll give it a try; I'm sure it will do the job.'

'I can tell it's not right.' Betsy snatched the bag from Lara but not with anger. 'The woman in the market said it was OK to return it if it wasn't what you wanted because I really wasn't sure. I mean, it's just a cat bell but—'

'I know.' Lara smiled. 'I'm probably over-egging the pudding, as my mum would say.'

'My mum says that too, but that's probably because she's always making puddings.' Betsy tucked the paper bag into the pocket of her denim jacket.

'No… but I am; I know. It's just…'

'I don't have a cat but even I know that cats wander. It doesn't mean he wants to go and live with someone else; he just likes to visit.'

'You say that, but my aunt's cat went to live with someone else.'

'Come on – Fluffy would never leave here. He's got it too good.'

'Try telling that to Fluffy,' Lara said with a wry half-smile. 'I'll pop to the pet shop after work. Thanks for trying anyway.'

Betsy sat at her own desk and hung her jacket over the back of her chair. 'It's OK – I thought as I was going that way for lunch anyway I could save you a job. I'll take this one back on my way home.'

'Thanks.'

Betsy nodded as she logged back into her laptop. 'Wouldn't it be funny if that guy was doing the same thing right now?'

'What?'

'The guy from last night. Wouldn't it be funny if he was buying a cat bell too? So that he could keep Fluffy instead of you?'

'Fluffy's not his cat. He can buy as many bells as he likes for his own fleabag. Anyway,' Lara sighed, 'I don't suppose for a minute that a bell will stop Fluffy from wandering all over the neighbourhood every night.'

'He must have always wandered so you might never stop that,' Betsy said mildly. 'He came from somewhere when he came to you.'

'But he didn't come from a home.'

'How do you know?'

'He was so thin,' Lara said defensively. 'If he'd come from a good home he would have been well fed. And I even took him to the vets to make sure he wasn't chipped or registered in any way and they had nothing, so...'

'Maybe he got lost and they looked for him but they couldn't find him because you had him.'

'Cats don't get lost. And they couldn't have looked hard because as well as checking he wasn't registered on any pet database I also put posters up all over the place to say I'd found him and nobody came to get him back.'

'But still, my mum says cats go where they want and love nobody.'

'Fluffy loves me.'

'But he goes missing all the time.'

'Not *all* the time...'

'But a lot. Why don't you just let him go on his way – he'll keep coming back if he really likes you.'

'I don't know... because it's better than doing nothing at all? It may be a pathetic attempt to keep him, but I don't have anything else. I just don't want to lose him; I know he probably likes to visit other people, and I might be in denial about that, but he's still my cat even if he does. I just don't want him to like someone else's house so much that he doesn't want to come back to mine.'

'He would never do that. Like I said, he's got it too good here.'

'But what if this Theo guy gives him better food or a comfier bed, or lets him scratch the sofa as often as he likes? What if he decides to stay there?'

'I thought you just said Fluffy wasn't his cat?' Betsy raised her eyebrows and Lara had to give a rueful smile.

'You and I both know that's probably not true.' She shook herself. There was work to be done and she was getting sidetracked by something that, ultimately, was probably pointless. She could no more stop Fluffy from wandering than she could stop the earth from turning.

She handed a scrap of paper over to Betsy. 'Would you be able to call this lady and ask her whether she wants champagne at the lawn reception or if she'd rather keep the costs down with Prosecco?'

'No problem.' Betsy took the note. 'Anything else?'

'There's a bit of filing to do and some expenses to record. Otherwise, if you could just man the phones until I get back that would be fabulous – I shouldn't be longer than a couple of hours.'

'Where are you going?'

'I've got an appointment with that friend of Abbie's, the bride from last weekend – Chloe. She called this morning and wanted to discuss a booking but she's struggling to get over here so I said I'd go and see her at work during her lunch break.'

'Righto, boss.'

Lara grinned as she reached for her car keys. 'If you're not careful I'll start to like being called boss and I'll turn into some horrible monster and then you'd be sorry.'

'You wouldn't,' Betsy said with a laugh.

'Yeah? Try me!' Lara replied, laughing herself as she headed for the door.

Chester's city walls – or what remained of the ancient stones – stood proudly against a blue sky. Like much of Chester, their history had begun with the Romans, the city having been a major strategic base during their occupation of Britain all those centuries ago. Lara always found that aspect of her home fascinating and staggering in equal measure. It was hard to comprehend all those years – two thousand of them, in fact – slipping by one after another, all those lives, all those dramas. How many people had walked these streets before her? How many were to come after she'd gone? While the city had moved on so quickly and so far, along with the rest of the world, growing into a trendy shopping centre and tourist destination, it also felt sort of ancient and eternal, as if it had never not been there, as if the ghosts of its past still walked in its present.

Lara had parked up in a car park on the outskirts of the city and was walking to the solicitor's office where Chloe worked. It was far easier this way – not to mention far more pleasant on a warm sunny day in a beautiful place like this. So far it was proving to be an exceptional summer, day after day of blue skies and warmth, and Chester was busier than Lara had ever seen it, with shoppers, school parties and day trippers. There were people heading to the river for a walk or a pleasure cruise; people exploring the amphitheatre, the remains of the Roman baths or walking the ancient city walls; people mooching along the main shopping streets, lined with the distinctive black and white buildings that dated right back to Tudor times.

She'd already passed a teacher with a primary-school class taking rubbings of some old bricks at the remains of the Roman bathhouse, every child dressed in a neat scarlet V-neck – though she could see a lot of them probably wanted to whip their school sweaters off and get into a nice loose T-shirt. Poor things, she'd mused, though she understood that their teacher probably found it a lot easier to keep track of them if she could immediately see their little red figures. It had made Lara smile though. They were so cute and engrossed in their task, chatting excitedly amongst themselves as the teacher kept a close eye on the proceedings.

Lara had always loved kids and she often daydreamed about her own. How many would she have? What would they be like? How would it feel to be a mother? Of course, she also mused with some degree of irony, she'd have to find a suitable father first, though she always tried to push that rather major complication to the back of her mind, refusing to acknowledge it.

Fifteen minutes and a leisurely walk later, Lara arrived at her destination to meet Chloe. If she was being entirely honest, she wasn't altogether sure she wanted this booking, but she knew that she probably needed it. She'd spoken briefly to Chloe on the phone and found it difficult to warm to her, and she was even less enthused by the timing. Chloe's wedding was just over two weeks away. Lara had immediately checked she had the weekend free and been almost disappointed to find that she had. Two weeks didn't give her much time, though Chloe had reassured her that there wasn't a lot for Lara to do except be there on the day to oversee proceedings.

In the end, Lara's business brain had won the argument and she'd agreed to at least come and talk to Chloe for a more in-depth picture. If she still felt uneasy about her role she could always refuse the job at that point, even though she had to acknowledge that it would probably annoy the hell out of her prospective client. The way Lara saw it, though, better to refuse a booking than to take it and find she couldn't cope, because that might end up annoying the client even more and ruin Lara's slow-growing reputation into the bargain. People were quick to write up and share experiences of services they'd received these days and the last thing Lara wanted was bad reviews from a disastrous day.

The building where Chloe worked looked surprisingly rundown. The large external windows were tinted so that the interior couldn't be seen from the street, but the outside, where faded painted signage bore the name of the firm and mortar was missing from in between bricks in large chunks, gave clues to what the inside might be like.

Lara was proved right as she passed from the bright street to a drab reception furnished by a dark wooden counter and barely illuminated by a dull strip light. A woman looked up from her computer as Lara approached, though she didn't smile, even when Lara offered her brightest beam. Lara quickly concluded that she had met friendlier wasps. The law services offered here must be fantastic, she thought, because they certainly didn't stay open by trading on their modern and welcoming offices, and certainly not on the charm of their staff either.

'Yes, can I help you?' the woman asked, though she looked as if she'd rather chew off her own arm than help anyone.

'I've come to see Chloe,' Lara said. 'I'm Lara Nightingale – she's expecting me.'

The woman swivelled in her chair and yelled, making Lara jump. 'Chlo! That woman's here for ya!'

She turned back to Lara, whose fixed smile didn't slip for a second even as the woman glared at her. Quite what it was about Lara that offended her so much was anyone's guess, though Lara had to reflect that if she was like this with a total stranger she had no reason to distrust, what must she be like with people she really hated? Lara decided then and there that she'd never put herself in a position to find out.

A side door opened and a younger woman emerged. She was very slim, with poker-straight hair parted in the middle and dark eyes in a face that seemed far too small for the rest of her. She looked at Lara with perhaps even less warmth or humour in her expression than in her colleague's. Perhaps, when Messrs Squire, Smith, Parton and Co. interviewed for staff, it was a stipulation that they be as miserable as possible. Possibly it was their unique selling point – all businesses had to have one, after all – and maybe some clients liked the dour vibe the place was giving off. If the people tasked with welcoming new clients were like this, what must the solicitors themselves be like? If this woman was Chloe (and Lara had to assume she was) it was difficult to imagine how the vivacious and bubbly Abbie could be friends with such a polar opposite. Perhaps Chloe was different when you knew her a little better – it was the only explanation Lara could think of.

'Lara?' the woman asked, walking to the counter and holding out a limp hand for her to shake.

'Yes, hi,' Lara said as she took it. 'I'm a few minutes early, I know, but if it's a problem...' She shot a glance at the scary receptionist. 'I thought the traffic might be worse than it was... I could come back in ten minutes or so...'

'Oh, don't mind her,' Chloe said, waving a dismissive hand at the woman. 'She takes an extended lunch break every day and thinks nobody notices. It's my wedding and I think, just once, I can have ten minutes extra too.'

'I do not!' the woman cried.

'Oh, don't give me that, Joan,' Chloe shot back. 'Everyone knows it. In late, home early, long lunches... How you haven't been sacked yet is beyond me.'

She looked at Lara as the deeply offended Joan huffed, though she didn't argue with anything that Chloe had said. Lara didn't know what to do or say at suddenly finding herself in the middle of this – she simply gave Chloe a tight smile as she beckoned her to follow her round to the other side of the counter and through the side door from where she'd just appeared.

Lara found herself in a room every bit as dark and drab as the reception. There were three desks in there, though only one was occupied as Chloe sat at a chair behind it and gestured to a vacant seat standing against the wall.

'Pull up a chair.'

Lara took it from the wall and placed it next to Chloe's desk before sitting down. Her gaze caught a wire tray stacked with paperwork; if this was Chloe's in tray, she had to feel sorry for her. Next to the tray was a framed photo of Chloe with a man around her age. They were dressed formally – him in a suit and Chloe in a gown of clinging red satin that flattered her slim figure – and they were holding what looked like flutes of champagne, smiling for the camera. This Chloe looked a lot happier and relaxed than the one sitting across from Lara now. Perhaps working in this building was the problem, and Lara could hardly blame her for that. Her own disposition, for the most part, tended towards sunny optimism, but even she'd struggle to be anything but miserable if she worked here.

'That's Gez,' Chloe said, following Lara's gaze. 'We were at some posh do at the racecourse there. Something to do with his boss. I didn't want to go but it turned out to be a nice party – lots of free bubbly.'

'Ah,' was all that Lara could think to say. 'That's a lovely dress.'

'Isn't it?' Chloe grinned. 'Cost a fortune – but I managed to pin the sales tag back inside after I'd worn it that night and got my money back from the shop. No point in keeping what I'd never wear again, is there?'

Lara was at even more of a loss as what to say to this. Chloe reached for a mug from her desk and took a sip. She didn't seem too concerned with the usual convention of asking a guest if they wanted a drink, but perhaps she didn't think that Lara counted as a guest. In fact Lara was thirsty, but she simply gave a professional smile. She'd get something on the way back to her car – there was a lovely little coffee shop on Chester's famous Rows that did amazing Frappuccinos.

'So... you just need me for the wedding day itself,' Lara said, keen now to get down to business. Chloe leaned back in her chair.

'Yeah. Like I said on the phone, everything is all sorted but I can't be bothered with rushing about on the day.'

'I can understand that. It's not really for you to worry about things like that – it's your big day after all, and the only thing you should be expected to do is shine.'

'Huh?'

'I mean, be the centre of attention and enjoy the moment with...'

'Gez.'

'Yes.'

'Oh, right. Yeah. So Abbie says you could do all that other crap.'

'Everything is definitely booked?'

'All of it. There's nothing really for you to do but be on hand in case there are problems.'

Something told Lara this might not turn out to be true, but she simply held on to her professional smile.

'Really,' Chloe continued, 'it's like getting paid to go to a party, isn't it? Get pissed on our booze and get handed a wad of cash at the end of the night for the privilege. Nice work if you can get it – perhaps I ought to become a wedding planner.'

'Actually, I usually ask for a bank transfer the day before the event,' Lara replied, wondering if Chloe was going to follow her slightly disingenuous comment with a request for a discount. She really was having second thoughts about taking this booking now, though if Chloe had asked her why, she wouldn't have been able to give a logical reason.

'Could you do us cheaper for cash?'

How Lara's smile didn't slip even at this point she'd never know, but it didn't, and it was perhaps the greatest feat of diplomacy she'd ever performed. 'I don't deal in cash, I'm afraid – a bit too risky.'

'If it was me I'd take cash. You could slip a few extra dos in if you did cash and you wouldn't ever have to declare them for tax. Make a few more quid on the sly – know what I mean?'

Chloe put her mug down and looked at Lara as if she thought Lara was a bit slow on the uptake and she felt sorry for her, as if she'd just told her the most obvious thing in the world. And maybe it was if you were the sort of person prepared to take the risk. Lara wasn't. She didn't really do risk and, even if she did, she would never do anything that might jeopardise the business she'd worked so hard to build, no matter how tempting a fast buck on the side might be.

'In my line of business that's harder than you might think,' she said evenly.

Chloe gave a careless shrug. 'So you can't do anything for cash?'

'Not really. Sorry. I mean, if that puts you off then—'

'You think we can't afford you?'

'Of course not. I just meant that you seemed to be keen on the cash transaction and as I can't do it-'

'That's OK, we'll do it your way; Gez's family is loaded anyway.'

Lucky Gez, Lara thought wryly. 'So I'm assuming that most of your payments have also been made and that you've phoned ahead to your suppliers to check that the bookings are still good?'

'I thought that's what you did?'

'Well, yes, I *could* do that but that's not what you're booking me for. Those things would have to be done around now – if not earlier – and you're only booking me for the actual day…'

Chloe's brow knitted into a deep frown. 'So you're saying I've got to do it even though we're paying you?' She snatched up her mug again. 'Abbie said that's what you would do.'

'I did that for Abbie because she asked me to organise from start to finish and it cost a lot more.'

'It's only a few phone calls…'

'Look,' Lara said, wanting now to leave more than anything. 'I'm sure if you give me a list and it's not too extensive I can sort something out if that's what you want. But I wouldn't usually and—'

'I've got the list in my drawer somewhere,' Chloe said, brightening again. 'Stick us in your diary and send me the bill when you've done everything.'

'I would need that bank transfer before the wedding,' Lara reminded her, though she was certain Chloe couldn't have forgotten the terms they'd discussed only a few short minutes before.

'Course – whatever. Gez's dad's paying anyway. Can't stand the bloke but he's got to be good for something, right?'

Lara gave another of those smiles she reserved for particularly difficult clients. It looked as if she was going to have to take this job despite her doubts, but at least it was only two weeks out of her life and then she'd never have to deal with Chloe again.

'OK,' she said. 'So if you've got time now, we'll go through all the details and take a look at your supplier list and I'll get you booked in.'

'Plenty of time,' Chloe said. 'Just let that old hag on reception try to drop me in it and I'll spill her little secrets so fast she won't have time to collect her handbag before she's booted out on the street.'

Lara's smile, once again, was rock solid. Later she'd congratulate herself – she really was getting rather good at it.

Chapter Seven

Betsy had packed up and left work at around six. Lara had been telling her for an hour before that to go home, but Betsy had insisted on finishing the filing she'd started, and then she'd launched into a blow-by-blow account of every phone enquiry she'd dealt with in Lara's absence, just so she'd know what to expect if or when they called back. Lara loved that her assistant was so dedicated and efficient but sometimes it was a little unnerving when Lara considered that Betsy might just be better at this job than she herself was, despite it being her business.

Once Betsy had left and Lara had spent a few minutes tidying and locking up, she headed out to a late-opening pet superstore in a nearby retail park. With the work hours she kept, she'd often wondered during the past year what she'd do without late-opening shops. Her mum would always say she felt sorry for shop workers, who had to be on standby to work at any unsociable hour, and to a certain extent Lara did too, but she had to admit that her life would have been a lot more difficult without them. It was all very well ordering online, but some things she liked to get immediately.

Like the basketful she was currently carrying to the till. It contained the finest cat food money could buy, bags and bags of Fluffy's favourite cat treats and a much bigger bell than Betsy had bought to go with the snazzy silver collar she'd also picked up. Fluffy hadn't been very keen on collars before and had managed to somehow lose three in the months leading up to this point. Lara had always assumed that he'd somehow managed to free himself from them, but now she suspected strongly that a human had done the freeing. She also suspected she might know who that human was, though the idea of it made her blood boil. She'd spent a lot of money on those collars and nobody had the right to take them off and dispose of them but her.

'Oooh, this is nice stuff,' the grey-haired lady at the till said with an approving nod at the cat food Lara had picked up. 'There's going to be a very happy puss at your house tonight.'

'I hope so,' Lara said, glad that the cashier had endorsed her purchase. A very happy puss was the general idea, after all. If Fluffy wouldn't stay put of his own accord, then Lara was going to feed him so well that he wouldn't even think of going anywhere else for his dinner. Either that or he'd get so fat he wouldn't be able to wander – both scenarios were a winner as far as she was concerned. Although perhaps winning was the wrong way to look at it, she quickly reminded herself. Perhaps winning sounded a bit too possessive. *Keeping*. Did that sound any better? Maybe not, but even though she realised Fluffy was a free spirit who ought to be able to come and go as he pleased, she wanted him to go just a little less and stay with her just a little more... And when she said a *little* more, she meant always.

The cashier rang the last item up in the till and handed it to Lara, who packed it into a bulging bag.

'That'll be forty-five pounds exactly.'

Lara tried not to choke as she pulled out her payment card. She'd expected it to come to quite a lot of money but she hadn't been prepared for that. Forty-five quid on cat food? Still, she supposed it would be worth it in the end.

'Someone's got a lucky cat...'

Lara looked up to see the cashier at the neighbouring till talking to another customer. She was packing vast amounts of the exact same cat food that Lara was buying into a bag for him. Lara couldn't see his face but...

He turned round. He was tall, with a nice, athletic build, dark hair that was short and wavy, dark eyes. In a better mood, Lara might have considered him handsome.

It couldn't be? She'd only seen his profile in the dim light of a street lamp before but...

The surprise on his face was almost as great as Lara's.

'That better not be for my cat!' Lara said coldly, unable to help herself, despite the scene she knew she was causing. The cashier at her till looked at her in shock, and then looked at Theo in some confusion as she figured out who Lara was talking to.

'Actually,' Theo replied in an irritatingly level voice, as if to point out to Lara that she was the neurotic, unreasonable nutjob here, 'it's for *my* cat. Why on earth would I be buying food for your cat?'

'I know what you're doing,' Lara said, putting her payment card away before grabbing her bag from the checkout and rushing over to him.

The cashier at his till stared between them both, but he simply smiled at her and pressed his card against the reader to pay for his goods.

'You're trying to tempt him to stay with you,' Lara insisted.

'I don't need to do that,' Theo replied coolly, 'as he's my cat anyway.'

'OK... I've been thinking about this... How long have you had him?'

'None of your business.'

'No, but seriously?'

For a moment Lara thought he was going to turn and walk off. But then he replied. 'About seven or eight months. I don't see that it matters.'

'Well, I got him twelve months ago. So that makes him mine – see?'

'It makes him whoever's he wants to be. Have you ever considered that he might not have liked living with you and that's why he started coming into my house? To be honest, I can't say I blame him – I wouldn't want to live with you either.'

'He does like living with me!' Lara squeaked indignantly. 'He loves my house!'

'Clearly – that's why he just wandered into mine and made himself at home. I didn't exactly have to kidnap him, you know – he's free to come and go as he pleases, but he always comes back to me. So what does that tell you?'

'Then why the posh food?' Lara hurried after him as he took his bag and began to make for the exit. Both cashiers stared after the pair now. 'If he loves coming to your house so much, why do you need to make such an effort to tempt him back?'

Theo stopped and looked at the bag Lara was cradling in her arms. 'I could ask you the same thing.'

'And another thing!' Lara said, ignoring the fact that she'd been caught bang to rights. 'Where are my collars?'

'What collars?' he asked, walking again.

'You know what collars! The ones you've been taking off Fluffy!'

'I haven't taken any collars off him.'

'Well, where are they then?'

'I don't know. I haven't taken them.'

'You must have done.'

'Why would I lie about it?'

'Because you want to keep him.'

'You're mad.'

'I'm right.'

'Look.' He stopped at a red car, some vintage sports model, and took a set of keys from his pocket.

Typical, Lara thought, hating him more than ever. Why would she have expected him to own anything else? She was sorely tempted to utter the phrase 'penis extension' but at least her brain still had enough sense rattling around in there to stop her, even if she was feeling totally unreasonable about everything else right now.

'We're going to have to agree to disagree on this. You think Satchmo is your cat—'

'He *is* my cat, and it's *Fluffy*—'

'And I say he's mine. We're going to have to accept that he's decided he wants to belong to both of us. Or maybe he really belongs to neither of us and just visits when he feels like.'

'So, why bother with the super-expensive food then? Why not just admit defeat?'

'The same reason you're doing it, I expect.'

Without giving her an opportunity to reply, he threw his bag onto the passenger seat and got in at the other side. Lara threw him a look of pure fury, but his eyes were fixed firmly ahead as he started the engine.

As he drove away, she marched back to her own car, fuming. If she'd been determined to keep Fluffy before, the battle lines were well and truly drawn now. Let Mr-Midlife-Crisis-Car try and tempt Fluffy away with swanky food because it wouldn't work. Lara knew better than anyone what her cat liked and it would take more than a few nice dinners. She was going to win in the end.

It was gratifying to see Fluffy curled up on the sofa when Lara got in from the store. He stretched out with a sweet little mew and went to greet her. She stroked him fondly as he purred and wound around her legs, and it was hard to believe that this innocent little face could be the cause of so much trouble.

'You'd better like this food I've bought,' she cooed. 'It cost more than mine does.'

He looked up at her and gave another little mew, as if to say he was listening, and then she pulled the collar from the shopping bag. Might as well try and get it on now while he was a more willing victim – later she might not be able to catch him so easily. But he was far quicker than her and as soon as he laid eyes on it he stalked off, heading for the cat flap. Hurriedly, she grabbed a bag of cat treats and shook it.

'Come on, Fluffy – I've got your favourite!'

He looked back once, seemed to decide it wasn't worth the risk and then headed out, the cat flap banging behind him.

'Stupid cat,' Lara muttered. Maybe she was going to have to abandon the collar and bell after all.

'You do realise it's starting to sound as if you fancy him?' Betsy gave an idle grin as she set a mug of coffee down on the desk in front of Lara. 'You were moaning about him before I went to make a drink and you're still moaning about him now.'

'Don't be ridiculous.' Lara snatched up the mug and took a swig, wincing as the freshly made brew burnt her mouth.

'You might want to watch that,' Betsy replied, her grin spreading and looking smugger. 'It'll be hot.'

'Funny,' Lara said. 'You know, during your probation period I can still sack you.'

'You wouldn't.'

'Hmm,' was Lara's only reply. She would never do that, of course; she loved Betsy to bits already and couldn't possibly manage without her, but she felt the sudden compulsion to remind her who was actually the boss around here. Perhaps it was the insinuation that she might be getting so uptight about Theo the Cat-Nabber because she was actually attracted to him, which was just about the most ludicrous notion she'd ever heard.

'So, is he cute?' Betsy asked, sitting at her own desk with her mug.

'I don't know. I wasn't taking notes – I was too busy trying to fend off his insults.'

'Sounds like he might fancy you too.'

'Well, if that's how people show they're attracted to one another in your world then it must be a very weird place,' Lara said stiffly, not daring to look up in case she caught another of Betsy's knowing smiles. That would have been very irritating indeed, and she was quite irritated enough without adding that to the mix.

'So how long did you spend looking for your cat last night in the end?' Betsy asked.

'God knows – at least an hour.'

'So the super-posh food was a waste of time?'

'I didn't even get a chance to try him with it. One look at the bell and collar and he was off.'

'I don't know why you bothered. I'd have left him to it; he would have come back eventually. And I wouldn't have bothered with all that expensive food either – it doesn't sound as if it's going to make a scrap of difference, especially if that bloke has bought the same food too.'

Lara knew this, but she wasn't going to admit that she'd gone out looking for Fluffy simply because she couldn't bear the thought of him settling at Theo's for the night. And she was well aware that his house probably looked just as inviting as hers did, except that Theo wasn't trying to attach a great big bell and collar to him.

'He did come back, after I'd given up and gone home to bed. I heard the cat flap go at around two this morning. When I woke up for work he was curled up at the bottom of my bed, all innocence.'

'Shame you didn't run into his other owner while you were looking for him…' Betsy said. She was all innocence too, but Lara knew what she was getting at. Did Lara's complaints really sound that hollow? Surely nobody would listen to her grumble about Theo and come to the conclusion that she fancied him? And even if she did think he was attractive (which she didn't), she could never date a man who was so infuriatingly cocky, a man who was so smug, who thought he was so clever and witty when, in fact, he was just plain annoying…

'Would you do me a favour and call Chloe Rowley for me?' she asked instead in a bid to change the subject and steer the conversation back to more practical matters. A bit of banter was fine but they still had work to do. 'Ask her to confirm that the list of suppliers I have here is everything she needs me to check for her wedding day. I don't seem to have anything down for entertainment and I've only just noticed.'

'Sure.'

'Thanks. I'd do it myself but I need to drive down to the river to look at the venue. I can see it being quite a difficult place to work, if I'm honest, but if I can get the lie of the land beforehand I can run any suggestions for alterations past Chloe in good time. That's assuming she'd be open to them, of course, and it would be enough time to change things with the venue.'

'What's she having?' Betsy asked, looking down the list Lara had just passed to her.

'An old boathouse. It's on the river, but slightly further out of town. I looked online and the parking looks a bit questionable for the amount of guests she's invited, though she assures me she's phoned to check and the owners of the boathouse say they can accommodate. I'm also a bit concerned about suppliers getting in and out as it's quite a way down some very narrow lanes which are prone to flooding. It's not really a wedding venue per se, but I can only hope Chloe has done her research to make it work for them.'

'Well, if she hasn't, what are you going to do?'

Lara shrugged. 'I honestly don't know. I suppose I'll have to go ahead and do the best I can, but it's going to be a learning curve for sure. I suppose it won't end up being the most awkward wedding I've ever worked.'

'Are you beginning to wish you hadn't taken the booking?'

'I was wishing that as soon as I'd left Chloe's workplace,' Lara said with a faint smile. 'Still, we can't be sniffy about these things – got to make a living somehow.'

'Are you going now?'

Lara looked at her watch. 'I probably ought to. I'll drink my coffee first and then head out.'

On the way to the boathouse, Lara called to pick up her mum. She'd phoned ahead, mindful that her mum might quite like an hour out in the sunshine by the river and that she still owed her big time for her outburst at Matt and Abbie's wedding. She was also aware that things were, perhaps, still not quite right between them. Lara hated the thought that they might still be at odds on some level, so she was only too glad to hear her mum's enthusiasm for the idea. Fay had agreed to be ready for Lara's arrival but, of course, she wasn't.

'Oh, you'll have to come in for a minute,' Fay said as she opened the front door. 'I've lost my beige shoes.'

'Can't you put some other shoes on?' Lara asked, standing in the hallway amidst the stacks of old newspapers and books that Fay kept just in case she decided to read them again (though Lara couldn't imagine she even knew what was in those piles, and if she didn't know what was in there, how could she know if she wanted to read it again?), rows of shoes and a rack full of coats that hadn't seen daylight since around 1987. As a child, Lara had never noticed how chaotic her home was – in fact, she'd rather liked it. But now, as an adult, it frustrated her. She could hardly tell her mum how to live – Fay had been alone ever since Lara's dad had left them not long after she'd been born, leaving her to bring up Lara and her brother as a single mother – and she'd got used to her own routine and lifestyle. But Lara couldn't help often reflecting on how much easier her mum would find day-to-day living if she could be a little more organised.

'It's not like you don't have another pair,' she added, angling her head at the row of shoes.

'I know, but my beige ones go with this coat and they're nice and cool.'

'I can see at least three pairs of sandals amongst that lot. Sandals must be cool enough, and they look as if they go with your coat.'

'They make my feet sweat.'

'Sandals make your feet sweat? I'm pretty sure that's the one thing they're designed not to do.'

'They do. I should know – it's my feet sweating in them, isn't it?'

Lara opened her mouth to reply, but then clamped it shut again. This was an argument she wasn't going to win. In fact, she rarely won any of them. It was hard to win an argument when there was absolutely no logic in it. Instead, she closed the front door and settled to wait while her mum disappeared into another room to, presumably, continue her search for the only shoes that would do. She'd tell her mum to hurry up, but there was no point in that either. Telling her to hurry up usually resulted in her taking longer than ever.

As she waited she checked her phone. Betsy had texted a photo of Fluffy lying out in the sun on her patio. She smiled, despite the fact that she ought to be annoyed with him for keeping her up late the previous night. God, she loved that cat, no matter how hard he made things for her.

A minute later, Fay returned. Still barefoot, she looked despairingly at the row of shoes in the hallway.

'I suppose it will have to be sandals after all,' she said. 'If you're getting all impatient with me...'

'Mum, if you need to find these shoes then I'll wait.'

'But you don't really want to. I suppose you could go ahead without me after all.'

'I don't want to go without you. I asked you to come so we could spend an hour together and I thought you might enjoy visiting the boathouse. You love the river.'

'I do,' Fay said ruefully. 'But I don't want to hold you up.'

'Well then, put some sandals on,' Lara said.

'But my feet will sweat.'

'Then look for your shoes.'

'I *have* looked for them and I can't find them.'

'Then...' Lara tried to smooth out the exasperation creeping into her voice. 'I don't know what to suggest. Perhaps you can go barefoot?'

Fay threw her hands into the air. 'Oh, right, I'll wear the sandals then. But don't blame me if I make your car smell!'

*

Ten minutes later Lara was driving. Fay was in the passenger seat, looking contented as the city passed by their open windows. The sun streamed in and the radio was tuned to Fay's favourite local station which played sixties and seventies classics. Fay was drumming her fingers on the window frame to Mungo Jerry's 'In the Summertime'. Lara was paying less attention to the radio and more to where she was going. Chester's one-way system was notoriously difficult to navigate if you didn't know it, and even though Lara, born and bred in the city, was well used to it by now, it took a little concentration as she tried to find the right road to take her to the wedding venue, which was outside the Roman walls.

'Jade Machin is still trying to get pregnant,' Fay said suddenly.

'Is she?' Lara asked vaguely.

'I don't doubt she's left it too late now.'

Lara didn't comment. She didn't really have a clue who her mother was talking about. Often she didn't have a clue who Fay was talking about when the gossip started. Fay was always saying that she had no friends and talked to nobody all week unless Lara or her brother visited (and Sean hardly made any effort at all). But for someone who led such a solitary existence, Lara was constantly amazed at just how much she knew of other people's business.

'But she couldn't find a man for ages, so I suppose that's it,' Fay said. 'Now she's married she's what doctors call a geriatric mother.'

Lara tensed in her seat. She waited for what she knew was likely to come next.

'I hope you don't do that,' Fay continued solemnly. 'Don't become a geriatric mother, will you?'

'I won't.' Lara's grip on the steering wheel tightened just a little. She didn't want to lose her temper today, not when the sun was shining and she'd had nothing but good intentions to spend the lovely afternoon getting along with her mum. She tried to bat the comment aside and think of something more positive, though she knew that Fay probably wasn't going to let it go that easily.

'I would like a grandchild from someone soon and your brother doesn't seem as if he's going to give me one.'

'Sean will settle down when he's ready. You can't hurry these things, Mum. The ideal partner comes along or they don't, and there's not a lot you can do about it.'

'Neither of my children seems to be having much luck in that department. Your brother's girl doesn't seem to want babies, and I fear you'll never find the right man. I'm never going to be a granny.'

'It's not for want of trying, Mum.'

'Not that your Lucien would have been good dad material. I can well imagine he'd have left you high and dry, just like your dad left me.'

'He definitely wasn't dad material – he cared too much about his clothes for a start. I can just imagine how he'd react to a baby being sick on him.'

'Well, what on earth is Siobhan going to do if she gets caught?'

'I'm sure she'll work something out,' Lara said tartly.

Fay looked out of the window, firmly chastised.

'I'm sorry,' she said finally.

'No, Mum, I'm sorry. I just don't want to talk about them if you don't mind.'

'I think about it all the time. I just can't believe what happened.'

'It's all old news now and I'm getting over it, but I'd get over it a lot faster and with less pain if I didn't have to keep discussing what they're up to. I don't mind chatting about anyone else you like, but not them, please.'

'Of course.' Fay gave a resolved nod. 'You're right.'

They lapsed into silence as the roads opened up into wider boulevards, and the black-and-white Tudor buildings that crowded the city centre gave way to more modern structures. A few minutes later Lara noticed the sign for the boathouse.

'Damson Tree Boathouse,' Fay read. 'That sounds pretty, doesn't it?'

'Very,' Lara said, taking a sharp right turn onto a stretch of road that could only be described as a track. Immediately the car began to bump up and down, jolting them around. Lara grimaced at the thought of the damage it was doing to the suspension. 'I hope it lives up to the name.'

They bumped along the track for another few minutes. The path was overhung by trees and shrubs, cooling the air and giving welcome shade from the glare of the sun. Eventually, they emerged from the tunnel and the road widened into a gravelled plot surrounding a large wooden building.

'This must be it,' Lara said, pulling up in a corner and killing the engine.

'Oh, it's lovely!' Fay cooed. 'Imagine having your wedding here! It certainly beats the British Legion Club where I had mine!'

'It is nice,' Lara agreed as they got out of the car. The gravel gave way beneath their feet as they walked, making it hard work, and Lara made a note of that. It was something that might or might not make access difficult for suppliers, especially coupled with the winding country lane that was the only way of reaching the location. But despite this, she couldn't deny that Damson Tree Boathouse was breathtaking. It wasn't a venue she'd used before, and not somewhere that any of her clients had requested, but if Chloe's wedding went without any technical hitches, then Lara was sure she'd be recommending it in the future.

The boathouse itself was built from whitewashed timber that gave it a sort of New England feel, with huge windows that looked as if they opened all along the front wall to bring the outside in. A veranda ran alongside, merging with a long jetty that led onto the river, the supporting columns garlanded by climbing roses and honeysuckle. All around the grounds grew lush trees: willows that dripped into the river, alder, poplars and river birch. Lara went to the windows to peer inside. There was more whitewashed wood in there, the ceiling high and beamed, and the floor was a honeyed parquet, the space flooded with natural light. It was currently empty and not dressed for any event, but Lara could see that it would look pretty spectacular for any wedding with the right décor.

Lara then walked the jetty, Fay following. She was here now; she might as well check everything out, including the river. One thing she hadn't asked Chloe was how many children might be attending, and she made a mental note to find out. If there were lots of little ones running about, it might be as well to find out what safety precautions the venue had in place, though the River Dee in this part was grand and sedate, winding its way through Chester itself and on over the border to Wales.

Lara looked out over the water; sunlight was sprinkled over the surface, the heavy branched willow trees fringing the banks and shimmering dragonflies racing overhead.

'I can see why Chloe's chosen it,' Lara said.

'Oh, me too!' Fay said. 'How come you haven't used the venue before?'

'I'll be honest, I knew about it, but I hadn't realised just how lovely it is. Although, I am still a little concerned about access. The lane we've just driven down to get here is very narrow and the only way in as far as I know. I worry about bigger vehicles or a large volume of traffic on it.'

'They must be able to do it or people wouldn't hire the place,' Fay said sagely.

'I suppose so,' Lara said. 'It's a shame I can't get inside, but it seems as if it's all shut up.'

'Didn't you phone ahead?'

'I left a message on a machine for someone to get back to me but nobody did so I thought I might as well at least have a drive up and get a rough idea of the layout. Time is of the essence with this one and I don't have enough to wait around for people to give me permission.'

'Oh!' Fay said, suddenly looking fearful now. 'You don't think we're trespassing, do you? Will we get into trouble?'

'There are no signs saying it's private land,' Lara said. 'I don't see that we would be.'

'Oh, but perhaps we ought to go,' Fay insisted. 'We could come back when someone tells you it's alright.'

'Well, if I'm going to be working here then it's going to have to be alright, isn't it?'

'I know but… if someone comes now, they won't know you from Adam. What if they call the police and we're arrested?'

'I don't think that's going to happen,' Lara said, almost laughing. But then she saw how genuinely worried her mum was and thought better of making light of her concerns.

'Come on, then,' she said, leading the way back along the jetty. 'Let's go.'

She looked back at the river once more with a faint twinge of regret. It really was beautiful here – the sort of place she could see herself getting married one day. A day that she was seriously beginning to doubt would ever come. Perhaps this was the best she could hope for; if she couldn't have it herself, at least she was able make the dreams of others come true. There was a lot to be said for the feeling of satisfaction she got from seeing others happy, if nothing else.

Chapter Eight

She'd had no time to get to the gym that week, so Lara laced up her old running shoes and headed out for a quick turn around the block. Betsy had packed up and left half an hour before, and Fluffy the troublemaking cat was nowhere to be seen. Perhaps Lara would spot him stalking the streets during her run, and perhaps seeing her he'd be reminded of home and follow her back. It wasn't very likely, but she couldn't deny she'd be pleased if it happened. Even better if that Theo guy was around somewhere to witness it.

Ugh, why did he have to keep popping into her mind? She'd had a lovely, productive day and then she had to go and ruin it by thinking of that loser. As she picked up the pace, the sun sliding down the sky but still hot enough to fry bacon on the pavement, she tried to empty her mind and concentrate on her breathing and the sound of her footsteps as they beat a steady rhythm on the concrete. Exercise was usually her happy place, when all she had to think about was technique and improvement, and she could forget for a short while about all the other worries that plagued her days. When she'd finished her session, she loved the sense of achievement and strength it gave her.

As she turned into the next street, she saw nurse Selina getting out of her car. She held up a hand in a cheery wave.

'Oh, Lara!' Selina said, gesturing for her to stop. 'Just the woman!'

Lara jogged over to her. 'Me?'

'I thought you ought to know – your cat came darting out onto the road a minute ago; I nearly hit him! You might want to see about that.'

'Right,' Lara said. 'Thanks for letting me know.'

'It's OK – he just scared me to death. I've never hit anything and I'd be absolutely devastated if I ever did – wouldn't be able to live with myself, especially if it was your adorable little cat.'

Lara nodded. 'I'm sorry, Selina. I'll see what I can do.'

'I'm not saying it's your fault – I just wanted you to know. Anyway... I'll let you get on.'

'Thanks, Selina.'

Lara waved goodbye as she began to run again. She'd told Selina she'd look into it, but if Fluffy was playing silly beggars on the roads then even though it was a worrying notion, there was hardly anything she could do about it. A dog maybe she could train and instil a bit of road sense into, but as far as her cat was concerned... well, she couldn't even get him to return to her house on a regular basis, let alone train him in any way whatsoever. As much as she might dislike it, Fluffy did what he wanted and there wasn't a thing Lara could do about it.

As she picked up the pace once again, the day's workload came back to her. Somehow, whenever her job presented problems, the time when she wasn't trying to solve them was when solutions often presented themselves. So, as she ran and emptied her mind, there seemed to be space, suddenly, for the conundrums that she hadn't been able to solve to work themselves out with very little effort from her conscious brain. It was just another reason she loved to exercise and why, when she came back from a long run, she felt completely relaxed and happy. Not about everything, of course, because no amount of running could work out the problem of her love life (or lack of it), but you couldn't have everything.

It was at this point she thought back to Chloe Rowley's upcoming wedding at the gorgeous Damson Tree Boathouse. A good look at the place had made her feel a little easier about the logistics, but it was a shame she still hadn't managed to speak to the owners about the booking. Betsy had told her that she'd managed to get hold of a very uncommunicative Chloe at work, who'd quite dismissively responded to Betsy's query about there being no sort of entertainment on their list of suppliers. She'd said that her husband-to-be was arranging a disco or something and she really didn't have time to talk about it because she had to type up notes on the divorce case from hell. Betsy, to her credit, had diplomatically but firmly pushed her on the matter, but Chloe had simply told her that there was no need to stress about it and everything that Lara and Betsy needed to know was on the list they'd been given.

Lara wasn't particularly happy with this information (or lack thereof) but she'd been left with no choice but to fall back on the old adage that the customer was always right and leave things at that for now.

At the corner of her vision she saw the shape of a cat streak across the road ahead and recognised it instantly as Fluffy. It was tempting to chase him down, but what was the point? He wouldn't go home with her if he didn't want to and she could hardly run far with him in her arms anyway.

She tracked his course and saw him head towards the gates of a house, slipping beneath them. A moment later the front door of the house opened, and Lara's expression hardened as she recognised Theo the Cat-Nabber, letting him in and then shutting the door again. Should she go and knock, get her cat back? It was doubtful he'd give Fluffy up that easily and, as Lara passed, she got a look at the house number. So, now she knew where Fluffy was going when he wasn't at her house, it might work to her advantage. Perhaps she could be subtle about this, cook up a plan to get her cat back without having to confront Mr Cat-Nabber.

With a small smile, Lara continued on her way, her brain now working furiously to take advantage of the new information she'd gleaned.

Chapter Nine

Damson Tree Boathouse was undeniably a charming building at any time but, as Lara pulled up on the gravelled car park, the effort that had been put into dressing it for Chloe's wedding almost took her breath away – and she'd seen plenty of beautiful wedding venues over the past year she'd been in business.

The columns on the old wooden veranda had white ribbon wound along their lengths, with frothing white bowls of rose and gypsophila at their bases. White bows garlanded the eaves of the vast front doors and inside was more of the same, with pristine white cloths and swathes of silk dressing the tables and chairs. Chalked onto a slate board at the entrance was a message welcoming guests to the wedding of Chloe and Gerard – something that seemed strange to Lara, as this was the first time she'd made the connection that Chloe's husband-to-be hadn't actually been christened Gez.

The sun was shining in a cloudless sky and the riverside was peaceful, save for the sweet chirping of small birds and the gentle lapping of the water against the wood of the jetty. Lara wasn't sure, but if someone had asked her what she thought heaven might look like, she'd be inclined to say this was probably pretty close. Not having any input herself in this instance – the venue having responsibility – it was a lovely surprise to see it all done too, without the worry of overseeing it herself.

Chloe was having the entire day there – from the service to the wedding breakfast and on to the evening reception – which made Lara's life a lot easier because she only had one location to worry about. All she needed to do now was go and find the boathouse's manager, Regan, to go through some last-minute checks with her before the wedding party began to arrive.

She hadn't been able to get hold of Regan until after her last visit, when she'd come with her mum in tow, but she'd had telephone conversations with her since and found her to be very pleasant and helpful. She only hoped that Regan would be just as agreeable in person. Not that Chloe had given Lara a massive list of things to oversee today – although Lara had a niggling feeling that Chloe was a bit lax on details and that something unexpected was going to come up and throw a spanner in the works. At least if the venue manager was reliable and approachable, Lara might have an ally if things did go a bit pear-shaped.

As she walked in through the large glass doors, the sun burning into her back, her footsteps echoing on the wood on an, as yet, virtually empty space, Lara saw a small team of young men and women who looked as if they could be the waiting staff. They were dressed in crisp white blouses and black trousers and were being briefed by an older woman in a charcoal trouser suit with dark hair done up in a classic and elegant twist. The woman turned as Lara walked in.

'Can I help you?' she asked, stopping her briefing mid-flow.

'I'm Lara Nightingale… the wedding coordinator. I'm looking for Regan.'

'Ah!' the woman exclaimed smartly and with some satisfaction. 'Give me one more minute and I'll be with you.'

Lara waited at the doors as the woman – presumably Regan – wound up the meeting and dismissed the members of the team to whatever tasks had been delegated to them. Then she made a beeline for Lara with a brisk smile, hands clapped together as if to congratulate herself on one job well done and ready herself for another. As she drew level, she offered a hand for Lara to shake.

'Lovely to finally meet you,' she said.

'You too,' Lara replied. 'And I have to say, you've got the boathouse looking incredible.'

Regan tipped her head. 'Thank you. I'd like to take all the credit but I have an excellent team here. Do you have everything you need for today?'

'I think so. I just wanted to introduce myself so that, obviously, you'll know me when you see me wandering around today.'

'Super. To be honest though, I'd have probably thought you were a guest. It's one of the things I find a bit disconcerting about these events – there are so many strangers milling about that I'd be hard-pressed to spot someone up to no good amongst them. It does worry me from time to time – and even with stringent checks, it's very hard to keep uninvited guests out.'

'I can imagine, but the one thing you have going for you is that you're out in the middle of nowhere. I've worked at weddings before where they've had a gatecrashing issue, but that's been when the venue was somewhere easily accessible to passing chancers. You know, like in the town centre where the pubs are. Hotels can be a nightmare for that too – random guests deciding to drop in and raid the free bar.'

'I suppose that's true enough,' Regan conceded with a brisk nod and a satisfied smile. She looked at Lara as if she approved of what she saw, which was reassuring for Lara too. It was far easier to work with someone who trusted and liked her – it wouldn't have been the first time Lara had found herself fighting the manager of a venue rather than working with them to make the clients' wedding perfect.

'Well, shall I show you where everything is while we have a minute?'

'That'd be great,' Lara said, following Regan as she headed towards a swinging door that Lara guessed might lead to the kitchens. As they went through it she was proved right, and they stepped into a pristine kingdom of stainless steel and ceramic tile, busy with waiting staff and chefs already preparing vegetables for the wedding breakfast.

'They won't start cooking yet,' Regan said, glancing at Lara as she watched one chef with interest. 'Don't want the smell to be hanging around during the wedding service, do we? Once the guests are out having photos and champagne by the river, our team will start on the lunch.'

'Brilliant,' Lara said. She could have done with a Regan at every wedding venue, but often that wasn't the case at all.

Regan shot her a brisk, professional smile. 'Shall we continue to the function room?'

Lara nodded, allowing herself to relax a little as Regan guided her to the next leg of her tour. She was in a beautiful old boathouse by a gorgeous stretch of river; the sun was shining and the birds were singing. Perhaps today wouldn't be so stressful after all.

As she wasn't really needed during the actual wedding service, Lara had stayed out of sight, though she'd been able to peek in every now and again to see what was happening. Chloe looked radiant, as all brides did, in an off-the-shoulder cream satin gown that fitted close to her slim figure, the skirt spilling out into a mermaid tail at the base. She wore her hair in a ballerina-style bun dressed with a diamante tiara, so that much of the flawless skin of her deeply tanned neck and shoulders was exposed. It was a very formal look, reminiscent of classic Hollywood glamour, and it suited her perfectly. One of the perks of Lara's job (in her opinion) was that she got to see all sorts of brides wearing all sorts of wedding outfits, and she always thought that, even if they were wearing something not to her own personal taste, they looked beautiful regardless.

Female guests were dressed for the glorious weather in summer dresses and light trouser suits, but Lara had to feel sorry for the poor men, most of whom were in formal, dark-coloured, heavy three-pieces. Regan had come to check on her once or twice as she went about her own duties, kindly asking Lara if she needed refreshments. Lara took her up on a cold soda water with a twist of lime, a welcome relief in the hot weather. Regan also told Lara to come and find her if she needed anything else, and Lara thanked her, though it was unlikely she'd want to bother her. In fact, Lara would do her utmost to deal with any problems herself – the last impression she wanted to give was one of incompetence.

Then it was time for the marriage register to be signed, followed by champagne on the lawns behind the boatshed and photos around the building and down by the river. While most of the main wedding party was busy with that, Lara noticed the venue staff swinging into action on the wedding breakfast. The guest list for this part of the day was far smaller than Lara knew it would be come the evening reception, and so it was all fairly quiet and good-natured as they sipped their drinks in the sunshine. Lara knew from experience that the evening, when the bulk of the friends, acquaintances, colleagues and plus ones arrived, would be a lot livelier.

As the guests finally sat down to their meal, Lara went down to the river – again, wanting to stay out of sight and to eat the sandwich she'd brought for herself. As she sat in the sunshine with her lunch, her phone rang. She smiled as she saw the name on the display.

'No... I don't need you, Betsy! Why aren't you enjoying your weekend like any sane person would be?'

'I was bored,' Betsy replied in a mildly offended tone. 'I thought maybe you might need me after all.'

'Bored? Surely you've got better things to do than worry about work?'

'I'm not worried; I just thought you might want some help.'

'It's very sweet of you but I'm fine. There's really not that much going on here at the moment if I'm honest.'

'It's all under control?' Betsy asked, sounding vaguely disappointed.

'All under control. There's a venue manager here who's amazing – so organised. To be honest – though I wouldn't say it, of course – I don't really think Chloe ever needed me. I think it would have gone swimmingly with just Regan in charge.'

'So, are you going to tell her that and give her money back?'

'No, I'm not!' Lara said with a light laugh. 'I've got a business to run and, besides, I'm here now. I'm sure there will be lots for me to do later on.'

'So, what's happening now? What does Chloe look like? Does she look gorgeous?'

'I'm having a sandwich while they all eat their lunch, and yes, Chloe looks stunning.'

'Awww, I wish I could see. I could start coming with you to the weddings, you know.'

'I know you could but that would mean giving up a lot of weekends and I wouldn't wish that on you.'

'I wouldn't mind.'

Lara's smile spread. She took a sip of water before answering. 'I know you wouldn't, and maybe soon if you really want to.'

'I could do them instead of you so that you get a weekend off sometimes.'

'Maybe...' Lara replied, less certain about this arrangement. It wasn't that Betsy wasn't intelligent and capable, but Lara... the truth that she couldn't deny, even to herself, was that she often struggled to relinquish control of a project. That was just the way she was. Perhaps that particular personality trait was well suited to running her own business, where she had to have a finger in every pie, but perhaps also worryingly conducive to eventual burnout. Her mother had said as much in the past, and though Lara had dismissed the idea, secretly she thought that Fay was probably right. 'With a bit more training,' she added. 'You'd have to come to some with me first.'

'I know – but you don't have to worry about asking me; I'd love that.'

'I love that you'd love that. So, now that's all out of the way, you can go back to enjoying your weekend and you don't need to worry about me at all.'

'Being bored, you mean.'

'There must be some shop that demands your patronage somewhere?' Lara laughed. 'Some salon that needs your bum on one of their seats? Some pub that you need to drink dry?'

'I'm skint,' Betsy said bluntly, and Lara had to laugh at that too, because Betsy had only been paid a week before and there were three more to go until her next pay cheque. Typical teenager – Lara had been exactly the same at eighteen. She was hardly better now, when she thought about it, though being self-employed for the past twelve months had been a steep learning curve in that regard.

'What did you do with it all?'

'All what?'

'Your money?'

'I don't know… it was my dad's birthday. And then some other stuff happened…'

'Ah. Stuff. I know what you mean. Do you need a sub?'

'If I have a sub that just means I'll be short next month too.'

'Very wise answer, but I thought I'd better ask. Remind me on Monday to talk to you about overtime and more training. It looks as if we're going to have to find a way to pay you more money.'

When Betsy replied, Lara could hear the new excitement in her voice. 'That would be amazing!'

'OK, well, if you're happy I'm going to let you go back to your boring weekend while I finish my sandwich.'

'Right, boss. See you Monday then.'

Lara gave a light chuckle. 'Bye, Betsy. Thanks for checking up on me!'

With the call ended, Lara swatted away a wasp before going back to her lunch with a huge smile on her face. There really were worse ways of making a living than this.

Once the wedding breakfast had wound up, a few of the daytime guests – older relatives and those who couldn't stay for the evening reception – left. The others retreated to a glass-walled garden room situated at the back of the boathouse for drinks and to relax until it was time for the evening reception to begin. Chloe had come to find Lara just to check that everything was OK, and Lara had reassured her that it was.

She had also taken the opportunity to tell her how beautiful she looked, but to Lara's shock, Chloe had begun to cry, telling Lara she'd had so many doubts that morning as she got into her dress and, even though everyone had said it, hearing it from Lara convinced her that, perhaps, her family weren't just telling her little white lies. Lara couldn't imagine how Chloe could have looked in the mirror that morning and doubted that she looked stunning, but wedding-day nerves were a funny thing; Lara had witnessed enough of those in the last twelve months to know that.

The sun was still high enough to be sitting just above the treeline as the evening guests started to arrive, but its ferocity was gone, leaving it mellow and pleasant. Lara had been to see Regan, who, once again, seemed to have almost everything under control, and so Lara was much happier as she turned her attention to her own little list of tasks. She'd typed up the instructions Chloe had given her as a handwritten list and now had it on a clipboard as she went about her business. She could have used the notes app on her phone or taken an electronic tablet, as Betsy had often commented, saving her the bother of typing up a list beforehand, but Lara always thought there was something about the clipboard that told people she was someone on official business, someone there to work. When she had her clipboard, she was largely left alone by guests. She'd gone to a wedding once without it and spent half the night being questioned by random guests on how they knew her and which of the wedding couple she was connected to. Nobody paid her much attention today and that was just fine – as long as the suppliers took note, nobody else even needed to know she was there.

Half an hour after the last carful of guests had arrived, Lara was outside at her own car, grabbing a moment to check her phone messages while she got a little air. It was getting hot and stuffy already in the main function room of the boathouse, despite pretty much every window and door being opened to let the balmy evening air blow through. It was just as she was getting ready to go back in to ensure that the cards

and messages of congratulations from absent friends were to hand for
the speeches that she saw a rusting old van coming down the lane.
She watched it for a moment, convinced that it was going to turn off
somewhere – though she couldn't imagine where. As far as she knew,
that lane only led to one place and that was the car park where she was
currently standing.

It pulled up there a couple of minutes later. Lara gave it a final
glance, and then dismissed it. She supposed that not all guests could
afford swanky cars and turned back to her phone, listening to the
voicemail messages. But then she looked up again and frowned as she
noticed the driver of the van get out and walk round to the back to
open it up. She heard the voices of more than one man, followed by
scraping and grinding that sounded like someone moving something
heavy across the van floor.

Lara rushed over. The driver, a young hipster type, was coming
back round to the cab. With him he had what looked like a guitar
case and an amp.

'Have you got the trolley?' he called round to the back. 'Save us
taking it in bit by bit?'

'What's going on?' Lara asked. He looked round at her blankly.

'What do you mean?' He nodded at his guitar case. 'I'm here for
the Bake Off – what does it look like?'

Lara waved a hand at the guitar case. 'You've got an instrument in
there?'

'Yes.'

'What for?'

'Well, traditionally they're for playing music on.'

'Music! This is a private function and you can't just turn up and
start busking here!'

'*Busking?*' he asked incredulously. 'We're not busking, love.' His hair was a bright copper, his face a mass of freckles. There was a sort of careless humour in his grey eyes – at least, there might have been if he hadn't looked so clearly offended by what Lara had just said.

'What are you doing then?'

'We've been booked to play.'

'Not here you haven't. Are you sure you're in the right place?'

'Of course we're in the right place – I'm not thick.'

'Nobody said that but I don't have you…' Lara checked down the meticulously typed list that she currently had tagged onto her clipboard. 'I don't have anything about a band on here.'

'Maybe you need to look again because we've definitely been booked.' A second man joined in the conversation now as he hauled a box of leads from the van. He looked a little scarier, with a beard that almost obscured his entire face, but Lara wasn't to be intimidated.

A third man leapt down from the van and came to join them. 'What's going on, Chas?'

The freckly man shrugged. 'She says we're not on her list.'

'Does that mean we won't get paid for tonight?' the third man asked. 'My rent's due tomorrow.'

'I'm sorry,' Lara insisted. 'I don't know who's booked you or where you're supposed to be, but I don't think it's here.'

'Well,' the third man said. 'Maybe your list is wrong.'

Lara shook her head as she turned back to her clipboard. 'This is the list the bride gave me and there's no mention of a band on here.'

'That's because Ged booked us.'

'Gez,' Chas corrected. 'Lucien's mate.'

'Lucien?' Lara asked sharply. Surely it couldn't be *that* Lucien? She suddenly felt faint at the idea that he might turn up at the reception.

Worse still, that he'd be here with Siobhan and she'd have to watch them playing the loving couple all night.

'Look,' she snapped, her patience suddenly a lot thinner than it had been a moment before. 'I don't have you down to play here tonight. I'd need to check with the bride and groom before I let you set up.'

'Won't they be a bit busy getting married around now?' the third guy asked, and his expression was just a bit too smug for Lara's liking.

'Love, if you don't want us to set up then we'll go, but you'll have to explain to Gez why we're not here.'

'Don't "love" me!' Lara fired back.

'It's Lara, isn't it?'

They all turned to see the fourth member of the band get out of the van with a long black case. To Lara's horror, she instantly recognised Theo. 'That's your name, isn't it?'

'How do you know?'

'You forget – I chat to Selina too. You know, when I'm trying to find out who's taken my cat...'

'Ugh!' Lara threw her hands into the air. Why was this man so bloody infuriating? And why did he seem to be everywhere these days? Was he deliberately following her around to annoy her? She only had to look at his face and she wanted to throw something at it. First Lucien and now Theo; this day just kept getting better and better...

Chas looked from Theo to Lara and back again. 'You two know each other?'

'Yeah,' Theo said. 'This is the girl who karate-chopped me and then tried to make off with my cat.'

'My cat!' Lara squeaked.

'So what's going on now?' Chas asked. 'Are we playing or not?'

'She said we can't play,' band member number two said.

'I said you're not booked to play,' Lara corrected him. 'There's a difference.'

'Ask Gez – he'll clear it up,' Chas said.

'If you'd just shut up and give me a minute I will,' Lara replied through gritted teeth. Then she paused. 'Does anyone have a phone number for him?'

'Very organised,' Theo scoffed. 'And what, exactly, is your job here? How come you've got the clipboard and the attitude?'

'I happen to be the wedding planner,' Lara said haughtily.

'Well, I hope they're not paying you a lot,' Theo said.

Lara clenched her teeth. 'I've been dealing with the bride and so I haven't needed the groom's phone number,' she said, struggling to keep her temper.

'So phone her,' Chas said.

'I…' Lara hesitated. She had to admit that she really didn't want to phone Chloe with this. It would look like she couldn't handle the situation, and Chloe struck Lara as the sort of woman who'd take great pleasure in spreading that opinion to any prospective client she might meet.

'So can you phone her?' Chas asked again. 'We're running out of time to set up.'

Lara grudgingly dialled the number she had for Chloe. It rang out, but then, Lara supposed that it had been a bit optimistic to expect Chloe to answer when she really thought about it. After all, who carried their mobile phone in their wedding gown?

'Look,' Chas said, 'you're going to have to give us a straight yes or no – do you want us to play or not?'

'I need to check; I have something completely different on my sheet—'

Theo leaned against the van, regarding Lara with a look that bordered on amusement. 'I vote we go and get a pint somewhere. We'll be in the Emerald Lounge if the karate kid here decides she wants us.'

At this Lara went from red to white. The Emerald Lounge was the very same jazz bar she'd been in with Lucien the night he'd dumped her just before the truth of his betrayal with Siobhan had come out. This was one reason, amongst many, that she hated it and hated the music that was played there. She'd taken a vow never to set foot in there again, and the news that Theo was heading there now only served to steel that resolve. And did that also mean that Theo's band was a jazz band? Ugh! If she'd hated him before she doubly loathed him now.

'Couldn't I have someone's phone number so I don't have to drive all the way into town to fetch you?'

'You'll see that we can be awkward too,' Theo said carelessly.

Lara narrowed her eyes. 'So what does that mean?'

'It means no; you can't have anyone's phone number.'

Lara resisted the urge to stamp her feet like a toddler.

'We might get a turn in there,' the unnamed third member of the band said to Chas. 'At least we won't have dragged all this equipment out for nothing.'

'Fine then!' Lara said, and even as she did she was aware of how stupid she was being letting them go. But they were winding her up to such an extent that she'd almost be glad to see the back of them. Besides, what else could she do but let them go? The fact remained that Chloe had given her no information on this part of the evening. When Betsy had phoned to query the entertainment she'd been told that they were having a disco. Her assistant wouldn't have got that wrong, would she? It could have been a simple mistake on Chloe's part, of course, or a lack of communication between her and her fiancé, and that happened more often than Lara liked. But if Chloe hated jazz as much as Lara did then having this band play would quite possibly ruin her entire wedding day.

'Right, let's move this lot,' Chas said, and Lara looked on with deepest misgivings, despite her decision to let them pack up. What if she was making a huge cock-up here?

'Wait,' she said suddenly. 'Let me try Chloe again…'

'Try her, but we're going to carry on loading this back on the van while you muck about,' Chas said airily. 'Like Theo said, you'll know where to find us when you realise you're wrong.'

'I'm not wrong, I just don't have—'

'Us on your precious list – we know.'

'It's not my fault!' Lara slapped her hand on the clipboard. 'I'm hired to take care of what's on here and it's not my fault I wasn't told about you!'

'We're telling you about us – right now,' Theo said in such an irritatingly mocking tone that Lara really was on the verge of risking arrest for GBH. 'Though it's clear you're not very good at admitting you're in the wrong about anything.'

'What does that mean?' Lara fired back.

'I think you know full well what it means.'

'Fluffy is my cat!' Lara cried but, to her chagrin, Theo only gave her a lazy smile before turning to lug his case back onto the van.

'Ugh, I hate that man!' Lara hissed, and when she got a reply, she was shocked to discover that the intensity of her feeling had caused her to say it out loud.

'I don't think he's overly keen on you either,' Chas said.

Lara turned sharply to him. 'What's he said?'

Chas gave a low chuckle. 'You really don't want to know. I tell you one thing though, I quite like a feisty girl. I'm not giving you my phone number, but you can give me yours if you like.'

Incensed at what she was quite certain was Chas taking the piss, Lara was about to show him just how feisty she could be when her phone rang. As she saw the contact info on the screen she immediately smoothed her features into something more professional. Not that Chloe could see her, of course, but a smiling face meant a smiling voice – that's what her years as a customer-service advisor had taught her and she firmly believed that now she worked for herself.

'Hello… Chloe?'

A woman who didn't sound like Chloe answered. 'It's her mum – I've got her phone for her. Is there something wrong?'

'Well, not really, but I do need to check something with her.'

'She's a bit busy right now. Maybe I could help?'

'It's just that I have this band here…'

'Jazzy Chas and the Anglo-Sax-ons,' Chas supplied, dropping in on Lara's side of the conversation. 'And it's Sax-ons… like Sax and Ons… because of the saxophone, you know, and we're Anglo-Saxons…'

'Right… Jazzy Chas and the Anglo-Sax-ons,' Lara repeated, staring at Chas's smile, which showed obvious pride in the pun, though Lara was convinced that it was quite the most ridiculous name for a band she'd ever heard. 'They say they're booked to play but I don't have them on the list and Chloe said she was having a disco when we phoned to ask.'

There was a deep sigh at the other end of the line and Lara could just imagine Chloe's mum's face. 'I'll see if I can get her attention for a minute and ask her.'

Lara stayed on the line as Chloe's mum apparently went to find her daughter. Lara could hear muted snatches of conversation and laughter as the woman moved through the guests inside the boathouse. Lara watched the band, still packing up, feeling as if the situation was racing away from her control second by second. Bloody musicians – why did they have to be so temperamental and unreasonable? She was simply asking them to wait while she checked if they were meant to be there at all.

Then a voice came back on the line.

'Chloe says she didn't book them.'

'Oh,' Lara said. She looked up at Chas, who was winding a hefty cable along the length of his arm. 'Chloe didn't book you, so…'

'I told you it was Gez,' Chas said.

Lara spoke into the phone again. 'Is Gez close by? Could you ask him? They're telling me he made the booking.'

'I'll go and look,' Chloe's mother said. Lara sighed and glanced at her watch. She had a million things to take care of without this unwelcome addition. There was the champagne toast to organise, she had to make sure everyone knew who was reading wedding cards and that they, along with the gifts, were where they were supposed to be, then there was the cake-cutting… and all that was even before the entertainment started. And while Chloe's mum – as well-meaning as her help was – pottered to and fro trying to get to the bottom of this particular conundrum, the band were close to being packed up and on their way. Lara would have liked to think that they wouldn't really make good on their threat to retreat to the Emerald Lounge for the night if she asked them to unpack again to play the gig, but she wouldn't have bet any significant money on it.

'Hello…'

Chloe's mum was back on the line. 'Gez says he asked them. Says his friend recommended them. Are they any good?'

'I have absolutely no idea,' Lara said, glancing back at the band members, who were now busy moving equipment like a platoon of soldiers on a mission. Theo and Chas carried a speaker between them. 'Hasn't he heard them play?'

'I don't think so, but he said his friend said they're very good. That should be alright, shouldn't it?'

Lara wanted to ask who this friend was, but she was afraid that the reply might confirm her worst fears about potential guests. Two in particular that she really would find it difficult to acknowledge with any degree of professionalism if their paths should cross during the course of the night. Knowing that Siobhan and Lucien were an item was one thing, but having her face rubbed in it was quite another. Besides, she supposed that Chloe's mum was hardly going to know the answer anyway.

'OK, thanks,' Lara said, pushing all her doubts to one side and recognising that she needed to act quickly if she was going to stop the band from leaving. Ending the call, she rushed around to the back of the van where they were securing the equipment.

'They want you to play,' she said.

'Bloody hell – we're packed up now,' member number three said.

'You did it so fast—' Lara began to protest.

'Because you told us to,' he replied.

'I didn't tell you to pack up,' Lara squeaked. 'You started to pack up because you were going to that crappy jazz bar!'

'You told us we couldn't play – what else were we meant to do?'

'I said I needed to check you were booked! That's not the same thing at all!'

'So you want us to unpack again?'

'Yes.'

Theo folded his arms, joining the conversation again now. 'Yes what…'

Lara blinked. 'What?'

'What's the magic word?'

Lara frowned. 'Really? We're playing this game?'

'We can just as easily head off to the Emerald Lounge. I'm up for a pint—'

'OK, OK! *Please*!' Lara hissed. 'Better?'

Theo looked at Chas, who shrugged. 'We'll have to get a move on if we're going to be ready for eight thirty.'

Lara had really wanted to hate Theo's band. Her hunch had been right about it being jazz (though their name, on reflection, was a fairly obvious indicator), and she'd wanted them to be as awful as most of the jazz Lucien had played during the time they'd been together, but the fact was that Theo's band was pretty good. Nobody was more annoyed than Lara to have to admit that, but nobody could argue with the way they got the wedding guests on their feet to dance.

They fitted the ambience of the evening perfectly too. Somehow, against the backdrop of the lanterns strung through the trees that reflected onto the gently chattering river and the beautiful old boathouse, alive with conversation and laughter, the usual old disco didn't seem quite right. But Theo's band had a sort of elegant coolness about them, every member had obvious talent and charisma (even though offstage they were massively irritating) and it just sort of worked with the mood of the evening, which was relaxed but classy.

Even more annoying was that Lara found herself searching for Theo every time she looked at the stage. Just as she had for most of the day, she tried to stay as invisible as possible. It was a policy of hers when she oversaw a wedding day like this – she wasn't a guest and didn't want to get in the way of people enjoying themselves. To Lara, it was something like not seeing the strings of a magic trick – everyone wanted to marvel at it but nobody wanted to see how it was done.

Tonight, really, she had more reasons than usual to stay behind the scenes because she absolutely didn't want to keep catching Theo's eye, but somehow she kept finding things that took her to the room where the stage was set up. Every time he saw her he got this small, smug grin on his face, and she felt sure he was enjoying a private joke at her expense. She really hated him for it. She had to be impressed that he could play keyboard *and* saxophone, which he demonstrated by swapping from one to the other even part way through songs, though it was not remotely sexy at all and no reason not to continue hating him. In fact, every time she met him she couldn't help but feel that he was inwardly laughing at her; even during full-on arguments (i.e. basically every time they met) she felt that beneath the sarcasm and the jibes, he found her massively amusing. And not in any good way.

It was on one of these occasions, when she found herself wandering over to take a look at what the band was doing even though she didn't know quite why, that she heard a voice from behind her.

She spun round to see Gez, Chloe's new husband, nodding up at the stage. 'They're good, aren't they?'

'Yes,' Lara agreed, though she still wished she could say otherwise. There was no denying to anyone with ears that they sounded good, even if it wasn't your sort of music. And it definitely wasn't Lara's sort of music. But, even if they were terrible, she was hardly going to say that to the client who'd booked them and clearly liked them.

'Took a chance on a mate's recommendation – lucky they weren't total shit, eh? Chloe would have murdered me.'

'You'd never heard them play before?' Lara asked, assuming the mate was the Lucien that Chas had mentioned before and wondering – if it was – whether it was *her* Lucien. Not hers, of course, but the lying, cheating ratbag from her previous existence as a woman who got upset about these things. Not now, of course, because now she was a strong and independent woman who didn't have time for that sort of nonsense. Still, it was a name rare enough to give her some serious concerns. And if it was her Lucien, she couldn't help but wonder if he might still turn up at some point tonight and how she'd react if he did. So far he hadn't and it was getting late. As time went on, Lara had been quietly building her hopes that it would turn out to be a complication she'd worried about unnecessarily.

'Nope,' Gez replied. 'If I'm honest I don't know all that much about jazz. I wasn't even sure I liked it before tonight.' He sniffed. 'This lot are OK though, not like that weird jazz that proper fans listen to – this lot plays proper tunes. They're OK.'

'They certainly know how to get the room on their side,' Lara said.

'Yeah, but then most everyone is so pissed now they'd probably dance to the sound of a washing machine on the spin cycle.'

'Maybe,' Lara said, and she couldn't help a little smile. 'So you're having a good day?'

'Cracking! The only thing wrong with it is that I'm still sober.'

'That sounds a bit out of order.'

'Someone's got to look after Chloe – she doesn't know when to stop. She was pissed as a fart by five thirty.'

'Right. Where is she, by the way?' Lara asked, scanning the dance floor and the room beyond, suddenly aware that she hadn't seen the bride for some time.

'Last I heard one of the bridesmaids was helping her throw up in the toilet.'

'Oh God! Is she OK?'

'Oh yeah!' Gez said cheerfully. 'Normal Saturday night for Chloe is that. She'll get that lot out of her system and be ready to start again in an hour.'

Lara smiled. For some reason she suddenly felt very old and staid. She couldn't remember the last time she'd had a mad night out like that – not cool for someone who wasn't yet thirty. But it just seemed as if she always had something else to think about these days: important decisions to mull over, accounts to do, paperwork to file, research and bookings to make, big days that needed her to be focused and sober. Things like socialising and nights of wild abandon had disappeared slowly from her calendar until she'd quite forgotten what they were like. It hadn't helped that there was always a very real fear that being out and about in the clubs of Chester would bring her face to face with Lucien and Siobhan too. And all those worries were without the added stress about her mum, who was perfectly capable of living by herself but still gave Lara plenty of headaches anyway.

The song that had been providing the backing track to their conversation came to an end and, on stage, Chas announced that they were going to slow things down.

'It's a shame your new wife isn't well enough for a slow dance right now,' Lara said.

'No chance!' Gez grinned. 'I'd be waiting for a month of Sundays.'

'Seems a shame to waste the slow songs.'

Gez looked across the room to a table where an old lady was sitting alone, watching the party go on around her. She looked frail and, although she was smiling, her gaze on the dance floor, her smile was melancholy. She looked so sad, so unutterably lonely, that Lara was annoyed with herself that she hadn't noticed her before. If she had, she'd have tried to do something to make sure she was feeling a bit more included. Quite what, she wasn't sure, but something had to be better than nothing.

'My great-aunt Emma,' Gez said in answer to Lara's silent question. 'She lost my uncle a few months ago. He would have loved this band – they were big ballroom dancers. Any party, they'd be on the dance floor as soon as the old-time songs were on; loved it. Regional champions when they first got married.'

'Poor thing,' Lara said, hardly realising she'd said it out loud.

'Makes you think, doesn't it?' Gez said. 'I'll bet when she was celebrating her wedding day all those years ago she never imagined a day when she'd be sitting at someone else's wedding and her husband would be gone.'

Lara looked up at him and smiled. She liked Gez a lot more than she did Chloe.

'Would you excuse me?' Gez said. 'You're right – it's a shame to waste the slow dances. I'm going to see if my aunt would like to dance with me.'

Lara's smile spread, and she nodded, watching as he left her and went to speak to his elderly relative. He leaned in and said something, and his aunt's face lit up in a beaming smile, then he led her carefully and slowly to the dance floor. It was lovely to see how caring and considerate Gez was and how much pleasure the dance was giving to the old lady. Lara wondered if she was thinking about her husband now, imagining him rather than Gez whirling her around the floor, and Lara could only hope that the brief daydream was bringing some comfort to her, that it might go some way to soften the pain of her loss, even if only for a few short minutes.

They'd barely been on the dance floor for two minutes, however, when a pink-satin-clad bridesmaid raced across and grabbed Gez by the arm. Lara watched them have a brief, urgent conversation, and then she saw Gez looking apologetic as he explained something to his great-aunt Emma, leaving her standing alone on the floor a second later as he followed the bridesmaid out of the room.

'Everything OK?' Lara called as he passed.

'Yes,' he shouted, not looking particularly worried despite the speed at which he'd left his aunt. 'Chloe's a bit drunker than I thought. I'd better go and see what I can do.'

He sounded cheerful and relaxed, and so Lara allowed herself to relax again too. Her gaze turned back to the abandoned great-aunt, who was still standing alone in the middle of the whirling throng, looking more melancholy and lost than ever. Feeling that none of the other guests had really noticed her predicament, Lara made a snap decision, and was about to go over and fetch her, when she was stopped in her tracks by something peculiar and completely unexpected. Theo had abandoned his saxophone and leapt down from the stage onto the dance floor. Chas saw it and, despite Lara's distance from the stage, she was certain she saw him roll his eyes at one of the other band members, although he didn't look particularly shocked by the fact that Theo had stopped playing mid-song.

Her gaze flicked back to Theo, who was making his way through the dancers until he reached Emma. He bent low to speak to her and her face lit up, then he took her hand and led her in a dance. Lara stared at them, though nobody else seemed to think it was odd – at least, they didn't seem to be taking any notice. He wasn't really very good either, and it clearly wasn't the sort of dancing he was used to, but Emma didn't seem to mind at all when he got the steps wrong. She beamed, like the sun bursting through a cloud as she looked up at him, and he smiled down at her.

Lara found herself conflicted as she watched, strange and unexpected feelings sweeping over her. This couldn't be the same man who had been so scornful the night they'd argued over Fluffy. It couldn't be the same man who'd mocked her earlier as she'd tried to iron out their booking. This was someone kind and gentle, thoughtful and concerned. Lara didn't know another man alive who would have seen so clearly Great-Aunt Emma's loneliness and who would have been considerate enough to do something about it.

The song finally came to an end, and a laughing Chas requested that their saxophonist join them back on the stage for a song that absolutely required him to play a hefty solo. With a broad smile, Theo tipped an imaginary cap to the stage. But before he returned, he offered Great-Aunt Emma an arm and led her back to her seat. Then, with a quick grin, he left her to jog back to the stage and pick up his saxophone, the band immediately launching into a more uptempo song.

Lara took the opportunity to hurry over to Emma. She didn't know why she felt the need to go over and talk to her; she only felt an overwhelming curiosity about what had just happened. Not that she had a clue what she'd ask Emma. *Does he smell nice? Do his arms feel as good as they look? Do you feel like you're melting when he looks at you too?*

She shook her head to shake the questions. Wrong questions and very annoying questions. Not the sort of questions she ought to be asking about Theo the Cat-Nabber.

'Are you alright?' Lara asked as Emma looked up at her approach. 'Having a nice evening?'

'Oh yes, lovely, thank you.'

'You're not too lonely? I mean, I saw...'

'I was a little bit, to be honest. I lost my husband this year and he did love to dance. He'd have worn my feet off on a night like this. But I've just had a lovely dance with a very nice boy.'

Lara glanced at the stage. Theo was in the zone now, his eyes closed as his fingers raced back and forth over his instrument.

'Do you know him?' Lara asked, suddenly finding that she was unable to take her eyes off him and not knowing why.

'No – not from Adam,' Emma said. 'But he's lovely, isn't he? Quite a dish. Not a very good dancer,' she added in a loud stage whisper, but then, most of the conversation had been a bit like that anyway. 'But that doesn't matter,' she continued. 'It was nice of him to dance with an old lady. I'm sure he'd rather have danced with someone young and pretty like you.'

'You're not that old, surely,' Lara said automatically.

'Tsk, I'm eighty-five next week,' Emma said with a chuckle. 'Old enough to be his great-grandma. Mind you, if I'd been sixty years younger he's the sort of boy I'd have been happy to take home to meet my papa... And then we'd have done things Papa wouldn't have approved of...'

Lara looked down at Emma now and caught her winking quite violently, which was a little disconcerting to say the least.

'Well, I'm glad you enjoyed your dance,' Lara said, not knowing what else to say.

Emma began a response but had only got about two words of it out when Lara stopped listening. Because she'd seen new people arrive, and a great wave of dread and nausea rushed her.

Just as she'd feared: Lucien and Siobhan had entered the fray.

Lucien strode in like the cock of the walk he'd always regarded himself to be, while at his side Siobhan was looking a little nervous. She was wearing more make-up than Lara had ever seen her wear, her long blonde hair curling luxuriously around her shoulders.

Lucien stopped and scanned the room, and Lara felt herself instinctively duck into a chair at Emma's table and lower her face. When she dared sneak another look, his gaze had gone off in another direction. He seemed to recognise someone he knew and raised a hand in greeting, Siobhan still attached to the other one like a prize he'd won in a raffle. With some unwelcome bitterness, Lara had to admit that they both looked incredible and were a handsomely matched couple. They were like the sort of celebrity couple you saw in Hello! magazine, showing off their country house with its spot-lit kitchen island and hot tub in the garden. Lucien wore slacks and a pink shirt, open slightly at the neck, while Siobhan had gone for a classy black number that showed off her hourglass figure.

'... don't you think?'

Lara looked down at Great-Aunt Emma, whose insistent voice had pulled her back to the room. She looked up again at Lucien and Siobhan. Lucien seemed to be scouting for a table they could sit at, but they hadn't seen her yet – at least, Lara didn't think so. They certainly wouldn't be looking for her either – as far as Lara was aware Lucien didn't know anything about her new career as a wedding planner. Well, maybe he had been told by someone at some point, but he was so self-absorbed that he probably wouldn't have remembered. It would have to be some pretty seismic information to have registered, when so much of his thoughts were consumed by the things that were important to him – namely him.

Siobhan… would she have known? Lara's business had been fairly well advertised on social media and so Siobhan surely knew it existed, but perhaps, even if she'd been apprehensive, she wouldn't necessarily expect Lara to be here because there was more than one wedding coordinator in Chester, after all, and not every couple would hire one anyway. But regardless, would she be feeling anxious now, nervous, as Lara was? Would her eyes be skimming the room, just in case this happened to be one of Lara's bookings, just in case Chloe and Gez were one of the couples using that kind of service? How well did they know the bride and groom anyway? Would they have heard from Chloe or Gez that they'd hired Lara in particular? Was that why they'd arrived so late – hoping Lara would have left by now? Perhaps not – perhaps Chloe and Gez, if they had said anything, had only mentioned the company name and perhaps Siobhan wouldn't have made the connection even then.

These and a million other questions too vague and half-formed filled Lara's head. And then she looked down again at Emma, who was still waiting patiently for a response to whatever question she'd just asked. But Lara couldn't focus on that now. She didn't think she could focus on anything now.

'I'm sorry,' she said. 'I need to…'

No suitable lie sprang to mind, and so Lara simply hurried away, excusing herself with a brief apology, desperate to get out of sight before Lucien or Siobhan saw her. She couldn't leave, of course, but perhaps she could head off and stay behind the scenes; with a bit of luck she'd be able to skulk around unnoticed until everyone went home.

Throwing one last glance towards the doors as she left Emma's table, she saw Lucien put up a hand in greeting to Gez and Chloe, who were now back in the room and partying hard once again. Chloe was swaying on her feet and looking decidedly grey, but she was doing her best to dance, her dress a lot more creased and a lot less elegant than it had been that morning. There were a few ominous stains on it too, but Lara couldn't think about that now.

They made their way over and Lucien shook hands with Gez while they exchanged a few words. Then Lucien took Siobhan by the hand once more and led her onto the dance floor, and Lara was shot by an arrow of jealousy, a dart of betrayal that lodged right in her heart.

She was hurting but, more than that, she was furious at her reaction. She'd imagined herself well and truly over this – so many times – but it seemed she'd been wrong. Fighting her emotions with every ounce of strength she had, she made a dash for the doors, out towards the river. If she could just have a few minutes to collect herself, steel herself, she might just get through the rest of the night. Perhaps a few minutes would be enough. But then, perhaps no amount of time would ever be enough. The idea that she might always feel like this threatened to overwhelm her. She hated that she still cared, and she hated that she was this weak – that she couldn't seem to put it behind her.

She sucked in a breath and turned her face to the sky. No – she *could* do this. A few minutes were all it would take, and surely nobody would miss her? The party was in full swing and everything was going well.

The evening air was fresh and the moon was rising, a huge creamy orb, just visible above the treetops. At any other time, Lara might have marvelled at the brightness of it, at how she could see the seas and canyons that marked its surface even from millions of miles away, and how magical it was as it appeared, haloed in a clear sky not yet bothered by any but the brightest stars. But she didn't see it, nor did she see the gnats that hung in a lazy cloud beneath the canopy of trailing roses on the veranda, or the fuzzy moths that fluttered and bumped against the yellow lanterns. And she certainly didn't see Regan, coming the other way. She had no idea the other woman was there until she almost ran into her.

'Steady on!' Regan laughed, hands out to stop her.

'Oh... I'm sorry,' Lara began, sniffing hard but hardly daring to look her in the eye. She hadn't wanted anyone to see this, but if she'd had to choose a witness, the last person on her list would have been Regan. Well, perhaps not the supremely irritating Theo either, or Lucien, of course, or Siobhan... Well, basically, she hadn't wanted anyone to see, though her reasons for not wanting Regan involved were entirely different. She had developed the greatest professional respect for Regan as she'd worked with her today, believing her to be smart, organised and capable, and Lara hoped that Regan might leave tonight with the same impression of her. That was hardly going to happen if she found an emotional jellyfish dashing about the place and wailing about every little upset.

'I just have to check something...'

But then a pair of firm hands settled on her shoulders to put a stop to her escape, and Lara looked up to see Regan regarding her with concern in her brown eyes.

'Is everything alright?'

'Yes.' Lara gave a brisk nod. 'Of course.'

'Well, it doesn't look that way to me. Is it something I can help with?'

Lara shook her head.

'I'm a good listener,' Regan insisted.

'It's really nothing.'

'It doesn't look like nothing. Come for a walk...'

'Please,' Lara said desperately, 'I'd really rather not talk about it. If you get me talking, the floodgates will open and you might regret asking.'

'Let them open if it helps,' Regan said firmly.

Lara only shook her head with more force, clinging to the last vestiges of her control and hoping against hope that she could do it for long enough to get away from this situation without a complete breakdown. If she needed to cry (and the thought that she did made her boil with anger once more at her own weakness) then at least, if she could keep it in until she got home, she could cry everything out of her system then and the incident wouldn't affect her night's work.

'Lara…' Regan said. 'Let me get you a drink – wait here.'

'Honestly,' Lara began, and then she paused. Regan wasn't going to give this up; perhaps Lara ought to tell her something just to get her off the case. A half-truth… it wouldn't hurt, would it?

'Look, it's nothing. Someone just came in – a guest – and I was shocked to see them. We had… well, we were together once and it didn't end all that well. I'm not upset, you understand, and once I've had a moment to compose myself it will be fine. It was just seeing him walk in… the shock… I wasn't expecting it and it threw me.'

Regan took a moment to digest what Lara had told her, holding her in a steady gaze as she did.

'I understand,' she said finally, and something in the way she said it told Lara that perhaps she understood a little too well. Had Regan experienced something similar in her past? What secrets were hidden behind that professional, capable exterior?

'Please… I don't think you do. I mean, I know you do, but… I appreciate your kindness, but I really do cope better if I can just ignore the thing that's bothering me and get on. Being nice to me will only make things worse.'

Regan stepped back and gave a vague shrug. 'Whatever works for you. If you need me don't hesitate to come and find me.'

Lara's smile was a bit on the damp side, but it was a smile nonetheless. She'd meant what she'd said when she'd told Regan how much she appreciated her concern, but this wasn't a burden she wanted to foist on someone she'd just met. For that matter, it wasn't a burden she'd willingly foist on anyone. 'Thanks.'

Regan left her with a little nod and went inside. Lara turned back to the dark shapes of the trees that lined the riverbank and let out a long sigh. At least most of her duties were over now, so she shouldn't need to be in the main room very often – not until the end of the night at least. Then it would be up to her to oversee that all the gifts and cards were collected and sent on to Chloe and Gez's home, and that all suppliers not answering to Regan were happy and had cleared away after themselves. Which meant dealing with Theo's band, though Lara wasn't going to think about that just yet. A few minutes ago she'd have been concerned by the idea, but now she had far bigger worries.

Lara didn't think she'd ever seen anyone look as drunk as Chloe did by the end of the night, and she'd seen some impressive states since starting her business. Lucky for Chloe, she had her lovely new husband to look after her, and he'd taken his duties in that regard very seriously.

Lara had seen them to a car and had a brief word with Gez before they'd left for home, and he'd seemed very happy with how the evening had gone, which had made Lara feel a lot better considering how trying it had been. Their honeymoon was to follow in a week or so, which was probably just as well, Lara thought, because Chloe was in no state to go anywhere and would probably need a week to recover.

She'd spent the following hour wrapping things up and chatting to various suppliers and contractors, some of whom she knew from previous weddings. All the while, at the back of her mind, was the thought that if she was backstage with them, she was far less likely to bump into Lucien and Siobhan. With a bit of luck, they'd already gone, though she lingered a little longer with Regan just in case. By the time Regan started to pack up, almost all the guests had left and Lara felt safe enough to go back into the main room, though she wished she hadn't when she found Theo and Chas, sitting at a table drinking whisky.

'Don't worry – it's only one for the road,' Chas said as he glanced up to see Lara looking at him. Perhaps her face was showing a particular disapproval, but she certainly hadn't asked for an explanation. Her gaze flicked to Theo, looking to see if she could find the man who'd danced with Gez's great-aunt when she'd been left all alone. But he wasn't there now and Lara had to wonder whether she'd dreamt him after all. The only Theo she found now was the one she didn't like at all, the careless, almost mischievous cockiness back in his expression. He downed the contents of his glass in one go and slammed it onto the table.

'Want another?' Chas asked.

'I think the bar is closed now,' Theo replied.

'The venue is about to lock up,' Lara said.

'Yeah; the van's packed,' Chas said. 'We were just having one for the road, but I'll go and see if I can't persuade the bartender to sneak us one more before we head off.'

Lara pursed her lips but said nothing. She was sure her expression said it all for her – not that Chas seemed to care. He just grabbed the two shot glasses from the table and sauntered off, whistling to himself.

Lara was left alone with Theo. As she looked at him now, the image of him dancing so chivalrously with Great-Aunt Emma flashed into her brain and she felt, even then, a softening towards him. She wanted to say something encouraging, something about how nice she'd thought his gesture. But instead, her brain beamed in another image that chased that one away: Lucien and Siobhan smooching at a table when she'd been forced to walk that way, when she'd been half-mad with panic that they might break off and see her.

And then they had. Lara must have looked almost comical as she'd frozen, mid-stride. They'd looked straight at her, but neither had made any move to come and speak to her. Nor did they at any other point during the night. She still didn't know whether to feel relieved about that or hurt that they cared so little that they weren't even going to attempt any kind of truce – especially Siobhan. Had Lara really meant so little to either of them? Had their years of friendship counted for nothing?

'You've been paid?' was all she could think to say.

'I think Gez has sorted something with Chas.'

'That's good. Thanks for... well, not buggering off when I couldn't find your booking.'

'Thanks for saving your bacon, eh?'

Lara's forehead contracted into a frown now. She did not need her bacon saving by anyone, least of all a smug little cat-nabber. Was he implying that she was incompetent, unable to do her job? It hadn't been her fault that her list of bookings wasn't right. She looked at Theo, and the man who'd danced with Great-Aunt Emma definitely wasn't there. No, she decided, the man she'd hoped to see again really hadn't ever been there at all. She must have imagined him.

'If you'll excuse me,' she began stiffly, 'I've got a lot to do before I can go home.'

'Are you OK?' he asked.

Lara stared at him, caught off guard. 'Of course. Why wouldn't I be?'

'Only… I couldn't help noticing you seemed upset earlier.'

'Oh? Earlier when?'

'I don't know… I'd just got back on the stage after I got off for a dance and I saw you rush out.'

'Really? Well I wasn't upset. I had something that needed seeing to urgently.'

'You're sure?'

'Of course I'm sure.'

'But if you needed—'

'I don't. I don't need anything other than to get finished up here so I can go home to my cat.'

At this, the concern he'd worn lifted and he changed into someone that Lara recognised only too well. '*Our* cat, you mean.'

'Whatever,' Lara returned sourly. She didn't want to admit it, but it was becoming more and more difficult to deny that he had a point. Whether she liked it or not, it was obvious they were sharing the same cat. She couldn't imagine how Fluffy could have chosen two less well-suited people to throw into this co-ownership arrangement though. If cats thought like humans, then Fluffy was probably having a good old chuckle on a nightly basis over his little prank.

'We're done…'

They both looked to see Chas walking back towards them.

'No chance of another drink,' he continued. 'They've already cashed up and I couldn't persuade them to open the till again.'

'Probably because it's illegal,' Lara said coldly. 'There are licensing laws for a reason, you know.'

'Whatever,' Chas sniffed. He looked at Theo, ignoring Lara. She couldn't decide at that moment which of the two men she wanted to punch the most.

'Are you coming or what?' he asked, jerking his head at the doors. 'The van's packed up – Sam and Joe are just sharing a ciggie by the river.'

'I think they lock the gates any time now,' Lara said crisply, just in case they were thinking they might spend the night messing around by the river, *sharing ciggies* or whatever other juvenile activity they were planning on doing. Probably swapping football cards or poring over grubby porn magazines that one of them had stolen from their dad or something.

Theo got up from the table. 'Yeah, ready for the road if I'm honest.'

'Got to go home and feed your cat, eh?' Chas said with a broad grin. Lara ground her teeth and internally counted to ten. Theo turned to her.

'See you around then.'

'I'm sure,' Lara said.

She watched them walk away. What an arrogant, smart-arsed, smug little… *No, Lara!*

She chased the image away. Why on earth would she want to kiss a man like that?

Chapter Ten

The following Monday morning Lara rammed the last corner of toast into her mouth and chewed rapidly. It was lucky that a work commute for her meant walking the length of her garden because any further and she would never be in on time. She could never figure out how it had happened that her morning routine had become so lax; she'd never been like this when she'd had a proper job where she had a boss to answer to and a desk to be at by nine. Somehow, being her own boss had changed all that, and not always in a good way.

She had to be disciplined, of course, otherwise there lay a slippery slope, and, if she wasn't careful, in a year's time it would be rolling into work in pyjamas with a bowl of cereal in her hands. And what kind of example would it set for Betsy if Lara swanned in whenever she felt like?

Pouring the last of her coffee down her throat before the toast had even left her mouth, Lara grabbed her phone and the keys to the summer house before heading out of the back door.

It was as she was tucking the phone into the back pocket of her linen trousers that it pinged to announce a message.

'Tough,' she muttered. 'Whoever you are I don't have time for you now.'

There wasn't anyone she could think of who would need her that urgently – apart from a client, of course – but they'd more likely call the business number to speak to her. It was probably her mum, fussing about something she'd lost and hoping that Lara would know where the offending item was. She often did this, and yet Lara had more hope of finding the Loch Ness monster than she did of finding whatever it was that had disappeared into the sea of her mother's clutter.

Whether it was or wasn't, it would have to wait for a few minutes because she had to be at her desk before Betsy arrived so that she could divide up the tasks for the day into things that Betsy could do and things that she herself needed to take care of. Before she could do that she had to unlock the side gate to the garden so that Betsy would be able to get in, and without giving the text another thought, she hurried out to open up.

Fluffy was on the patio, stretched out in the early morning sun. Lara had felt unnecessarily triumphant that he'd been around for most of the weekend; to imagine Theo out looking for him gave her a certain pleasure that she was well aware was unbecoming. Still, it was there all the same, whether she liked it or not, and she decided not to let it spoil the fact that she got to enjoy her cat for most of her lazy Sunday.

She paused and crouched to give his belly a tickle, causing him to open his eyes and give her a look of the vaguest vexation before deciding that she wasn't so annoying after all and settling back to sleep. Lara smiled and stood up again. He probably wouldn't go far for the next few hours, and maybe she could persuade him to take up residence in her office for the remainder of the morning with a few cat treats once she'd got the workday up and running.

Even at this early hour the sun burned Lara's neck as she walked through the garden, every corner crowded with dazzling, fragrant flowers. They really had been blessed this summer – or cursed perhaps, depending on what you thought about climate change. Though Lara was as concerned about such things as anyone else, she also saw the fabulous summer from a purely selfish point of view. It was very good for the wedding business. Couples who had the weather on their side were more likely to be happy with their big day as a whole and more likely to give Lara a glowing review for her part in it, while couples who attended such a glorious occasion might just be seduced into setting their own date, hopeful for the same. There was no scientific evidence for Lara's thoughts on this, of course, but she felt certain that it all made perfect sense as a hypothesis. Either way, she certainly hadn't been disappointed with the bookings in her diary this year, nor with the feedback she'd been getting. If that was to do with the excellent weather, then long may it continue – she'd take it all any way it came.

She'd just put the key into the lock when Betsy arrived at the gate.

'You're keen,' Lara said.

'Yeah, I was up early. Dad woke me up going fishing. Couldn't get back to sleep and didn't see any point in hanging around at home once I was ready to come out.'

Lara smiled. She hadn't forgotten their conversation about giving Betsy more responsibility and a pay rise, and she was sure her assistant hadn't either. It might have explained the eagerness, though Lara felt that to cite that reason alone might be a little unfair. Betsy was always keen and seemed to love working with Lara as much as Lara enjoyed having her there.

'Have you had breakfast?' Betsy asked as Lara let her in and shut the gate again.

'I've just scoffed a slice of toast. Why – do you want some? I'm sure I can—'

'No, no… it's just that my mum has sent some breakfast muffins for you. She was trying out a new recipe or something. They're a bit nice, actually – I've eaten about twenty already! I don't know why, but I'm just so hungry these days and I really can't stop eating them!'

Betsy grinned and held up a paisley-patterned tin.

'Well,' Lara said with a grin of her own, 'if they're that good I'm sure I can take a couple off your hands. Shall I put the kettle on so we can have tea with them?'

'Coffee for me please.'

'Oh yeah, you're the weirdo who hates tea. I mean, who doesn't drink tea? I don't know how I ever managed to employ someone who doesn't drink tea, but it isn't right.'

Betsy laughed. 'I probably don't hate tea but I'm not used to drinking it so I don't. We're just a coffee house, that's all. My mum and dad both drink it all the time – they only keep tea in for visitors.'

'OK then… I suppose as an explanation that'll have to do. Get yourself settled in the office while I put the kettle on.'

As Betsy went over to the summer house Lara went back to the main house. She looked up at the door to see another little queue of bumblebees circling the entrance to the nest and guessed that maybe the queen was ready for a little love action. She couldn't be sure, but when she'd been on the national bee website to research her little guests she'd read something about it and this seemed to fit. They weren't hurting anyone and certainly not bothering her, though she knew that it always made Betsy a bit fidgety when there was a larger than usual crowd hanging about. Fluffy was still sleeping and didn't seem to have noticed them, which was probably just as well. Lara was pretty sure he was far too crap to catch any of them, but she would rather not find out. She really didn't fancy trying to extract a sting from the roof of his mouth today – she had far too much else to do.

But the sight of nature simply doing its thing cheered her a little. Despite her bright greeting of Betsy and delight at another morning of sun, she'd struggled to get the image of Lucien and Siobhan arriving at Chloe's wedding out of her mind over the weekend. Whenever she did manage it, it was replaced by recollections of Theo dancing with Gez's great-aunt, or how he'd looked at her at the end of the night when he'd seemed to be genuinely concerned for her welfare. And if she wasn't dwelling on either of those things then she was replaying her conversation with Regan, when she'd caught Lara crying like a ridiculous pre-pubescent girl.

What made it worse was that she was certain Regan thought it was because Lara was still in love with him. But it wasn't that at all. In fact, that couldn't have been further from the truth. The truth was far simpler. It just felt to Lara as if whenever she finally managed to turn the page on that chapter of her life, up he'd pop again to remind her of it, though as long as he and Siobhan both stayed in Chester, Lara had to suppose that chapter of her life would never be fully closed.

It had certainly been wide open all weekend. Lara had found herself wanting to message Siobhan, simultaneously wounded and incensed that her ex-best friend had made no effort to speak to her, despite obviously noticing her, and then she'd wanted to message Lucien, too, to demand an explanation. In the end, she'd forced herself to recognise that although these actions might provide temporary satisfaction, in the long term there was just no point in opening up all that hurt again.

She'd thought about going to see her mum to tell her all about it, but Fay could always be relied upon to say exactly the thing that would make Lara feel worse and so she didn't do that either. She'd settled instead for a five-mile run, although, disappointingly, even that only offered a temporary respite.

Still, as she crossed the threshold this morning, out of the bright sunlight and into the cool shadow of her kitchen, Lara reminded herself that just because she couldn't entirely eradicate Lucien from her life, it didn't mean she had to let him keep on getting to her. She could still win by making him irrelevant – she just had to figure out how to do that. Her mum would have said the answer to that question was easy – that Lara just had to find another man. That was easier said than done when she was so busy though, and, besides, she wasn't sure that it was the catch-all answer her mum seemed to think it was. More than that, the one thing Lara absolutely did not want was to settle for an almost-there relationship again. Next time it was the real thing or nothing at all – she was far too busy to waste her time on anything less than perfect.

With that thought, she got busy making their drinks.

A few minutes later she was carrying two mugs back to the summer house. Betsy had already taken the lid from the paisley tin of wonder and had left it on Lara's desk. Lara could smell the muffins as soon as she came in, all fruity and sugary sweet. She handed Betsy's drink over and peered inside the tin. Betsy's mum really could bake – so far this month they'd been treated to chocolate cupcakes, Victoria sponge, cherry scones and red velvet cake. If there was no other reason to keep Betsy on, Lara thought wickedly, then she might have been tempted to just for the cakes.

'They look amazing,' she said, taking her seat. 'What's in them?'

'I think some are banana and oat and some are apricot or date or something. I think she went for the healthy things, trying to make me eat more fruit.'

'There are worse ways to get your five a day. Tell me again why your mother hasn't been on Bake Off yet.'

'We keep saying that to her but she doesn't think she's good enough.'

'If she's not good enough then I don't know who is. I'd give her a Hollywood Handshake for sure.'

'I'll tell her that,' Betsy said. 'It'll make her day.'

'These have certainly made mine.' Lara bit into a muffin and sighed as a large, tangy chunk of apricot exploded onto her tongue. If ever a cake tasted like summer, this one did.

'Do you like it?' Betsy asked.

'So good...' Lara mumbled, crumbs spraying across the desk. She didn't care – this was worth it. 'Better than good. Better than anything...'

Betsy giggled, clearly proud that her mum could bake the kind of cakes that did what they were doing to Lara. Lara threw her a wink.

'Just ask your mum when I can move in. I think it's time I sacked my mum and employed another one who can bake like this. My mum can't bake at all.'

'But she's lovely,' Betsy said.

'I suppose she has her moments,' Lara acknowledged. She took another bite of her muffin and made another rapturous face, which made Betsy laugh again. 'You do realise this means a twelve-mile run tonight?'

'There can't be that many calories in a breakfast muffin?'

'Maybe not in one, but I intend to eat the whole tin before lunch.'

Betsy's broad grin almost broke free of her face. Lara popped the last of the cake into her mouth and pushed the tin across her desk, out of her eyeline.

'God help me, I will eat the whole lot if I can see them.'

'Want me to put them away somewhere until tomorrow? Mum says they'll keep for ages in the tin.'

'I need you to lock them up in a vault or I'll be sneaking in for a midnight snack and there'll be none left tomorrow.'

Betsy took the tin to her own desk and sealed it again. Lara licked her fingers before taking a large gulp of her tea and turning to her diary.

'Oh bugger!' she said after a moment. 'I forgot Terry was coming.'

'The accountant?'

'Hmm. He's in the diary for ten and it's nine thirty now.'

'Does it matter?'

'Not especially. It's just that I'm not really ready for him. I hate feeling not ready for him – he can be scary when he starts scrutinising my receipts.'

'He is scary – I'm glad it's not just me who thinks so. It's when he looks at you over the top of those half-glasses.'

'I'm sure he'd say thorough, rather than scary,' Lara said. 'And he is thorough; there's no doubt about that. I just wish I didn't feel like a naughty school pupil being told off by the headmaster whenever he's going through my stuff.'

'I could see him,' Betsy said brightly. 'You could pretend you have a client to see and go out.'

'Now that's throwing yourself under the bus for me,' Lara said, laughing lightly. 'It's very loyal of you but I'd better do it. I know what's what and he might ask things you can't answer. That's not to say that you're not capable, of course, it's just that my accounts aren't always crystal clear to anyone else but me – I think that's why Terry comes down so hard on me.'

'That's OK,' Betsy said. 'I understand. I just thought I'd offer because we did say I could start doing more.'

'We did, and we'll definitely make time this week to talk about that properly. Let me get the Monday muck pile out of the way and we'll pencil some time in the diary for later in the week.'

Betsy nodded eagerly, clearly thrilled. Lara had to wonder if she'd ever looked like that about anything at eighteen and had to conclude that she didn't think so. But then, she knew Betsy loved this job and Lara had never had a job back then that she'd really loved. In fact, this was the first one she'd really loved too.

'Right…' she muttered, turning back to her diary. 'Terrible Terry… let's see if I can't be a little bit ready for you!'

Terry arrived on the dot of ten. They exchanged pleasantries and Lara decided, as the day was so glorious, she'd take the meeting outside on the patio. Fluffy remained stretched out, taking full advantage of the sun as it moved round the house and the heat intensified. Lara was often amazed at how contrary her cat could be – either stalking the streets for miles night by night or sleeping the day away, hardly lifting a paw.

Terry made a brief comment about what a handsome cat he was, which was quite unexpected as her accountant was usually silent on anything but business matters. And, more surprising still, by the time she'd offered him tea and one of Betsy's mum's divine muffins, he'd almost softened into a regular human being. Still, whenever he looked at Lara over those half-glasses, she had to hold in a little laugh, remembering what Betsy had said earlier, and she couldn't help but think her assistant might be right. She wondered, as he pored over her receipts and tutted loudly, whether he might look like a regular human being if he would only wear a different style.

By the time they'd wound up the meeting and Terry had unlocked the puzzle of Lara's terrible account keeping, it was almost twelve. The sun was high overhead, and Lara wondered how Terry wasn't fainting in his expensive but thick woollen suit as he shook her hand and she saw him out through the side gate.

As she walked back to the summer house, she happened to look down and was certain that her arms had tanned since she'd been outside. She'd always known there were perks to working from home, and this was another to add to the list.

'How's it going?' Lara asked as she went into the office.

Betsy looked up from a bridal magazine she'd been trawling through. Lara loved going through those too; every page was just filled with beautiful things to sigh over – it was yet another perk of her job, and a necessary one. Though it often felt like a luxurious distraction, she had to keep up with the latest bridal trends, and there was no better way to do that than to buy regular piles of magazines that would have everything in one place, rather than the more time-consuming task of visiting website after website to see what was new there.

'It hasn't been too busy.'

'Nothing urgent for me to look at?'

'That nutty woman from Nantwich rang again.'

Lara raised her eyebrows as she sat down. 'The one who's convinced she's getting married but doesn't actually have anyone to marry?'

'Yeah.'

'What did she want?'

'The usual. Wanted us to recommend somewhere nice for her to have the service.'

'And what's the theme this time?'

'Frozen.'

'As in "Let It Go"?'

'Yup.'

Lara let out a sigh. 'Anything else?'

'Oh, yeah; I took a call from a Mrs Wilson. She was at the wedding on Saturday. Says she thought it went really well and says Chloe gave her our number for her daughter's wedding.'

'That's good,' Lara said, absently taking a sip of an old cup of tea and grimacing as she realised it was stone cold. She'd make another one for them both, just as soon as she'd gone through the messages with Betsy. 'What does she want?'

'Same – just the day, I think.'

'My favourite sort of booking.'

'You say that but you might change your mind when you find out when it is.'

'Don't tell me it's another short-notice one.'

'A month's time.'

'On a Saturday?'

'Yes.'

'Honestly! People think they can click their fingers and everyone will come running. Did you check the diary?' Lara pulled it towards her. 'I feel certain the Pettifer wedding is around then.'

'It is, but the Pettifer wedding is only a day service with no evening reception, isn't it? I could… I mean, if you wanted, maybe I could do that? This booking is all day and night so it would be more money, wouldn't it? But if I do one and you do the other, we can take both. I didn't say yes to the lady because I thought I ought to ask you first…'

Betsy looked hopeful. Even though they'd yet to have their conversation about her taking on more, and even though Lara wondered whether sending her to a wedding alone was a bit too much of a leap, deep down she had a certain faith that Betsy would probably do a good job. How was she to learn if she never had a go? Lara also knew if she could learn to delegate then it made good business sense in the end. Like now – two bookings had to be better than one. She knew what Terry would say had he still been there. She'd have to pay Betsy overtime, of course, but still…

Finally, she spoke. 'Did you take Mrs…'

'Wilson.'

'… Wilson's phone number?'

Betsy passed over a sheet of paper. 'I took a few notes about the wedding too.'

'Brilliant,' Lara said, reading it. 'I'll have a chat and see what she wants.' Then she looked up and noticed again the mug with the layer of cold tea sitting in the bottom. 'But first things first – drinks.' She collected the cup and went over to get Betsy's.

'Thanks, boss!' Betsy reached into her desk and grabbed the paisley tin. 'Think we need something to go with it?'

Lara laughed. 'We're, like, an hour off lunchtime – we won't want our lunch!'

'Lunch is right here,' Betsy said, lightly tapping the tin.

Lara's laughter trailed out of the office as she went back to the house to make drinks.

As Lara crossed the garden to the house, she noticed that Fluffy was no longer in his sunbathing spot. A quick inspection of the kitchen showed he wasn't there either; nor was he in his other favourite sleeping place on Lara's bed. She had to suppose that he'd eventually decided to go about his usual daily business, whatever that was.

She went back to the kitchen, deep in thought about the day's work so far. If Betsy was going to take on a wedding for her, it really was time they had their chat about increasing her role generally and also increasing her pay. Perhaps they'd get a few minutes to do it before Betsy went to lunch.

As she stood and waited for the kettle to boil, Lara gave the worktops a quick tidy and took the spare moment to empty the leftover food from Fluffy's bowl ready for a fresh serving when he eventually decided to turn up again. She tried not to let the idea that he might have gone to Theo's bother her. More likely he was out stalking the streets, terrifying baby birds and squirrels, like any self-respecting moggy would be. Once she'd done that it occurred to her that she hadn't actually checked her phone all morning and she now recalled that she'd had a text message first thing that she'd never opened. Once she'd unlocked her phone and looked, however, she wished she hadn't bothered.

The number was one she didn't recognise, not stored on her phone under anyone's name. She didn't usually get messages from numbers like that unless it was some kind of cold sales text from a company that had somehow managed to get her details. Either that or a client, though she rarely gave her personal number out to them and she certainly couldn't recall doing that recently. Forehead faintly creased, she opened it up.

Wedding planner? I always thought that was a fantasy. I guess I was wrong. Well done for making it happen.

Lara's breath caught in her throat, her limbs tingling and her gut heavy.

Lucien: it had to be. Who else would it be?

But then Lara paused. Perhaps she really was too hung up on the fact that she'd bumped into him the previous weekend and she was seeing his hand in everything everywhere, even where it wasn't. Maybe it was someone else, someone she'd lost touch with, someone else whose number had been lost from her phone. She searched her brain but she really couldn't think of anyone else it might be; she wasn't generally in the habit of deleting numbers from her phone, especially those of people she liked.

She read the text again, but it was hard to judge the tone. If it was Lucien, was he being patronising or genuinely pleased for her? Was he impressed with how far she'd come since they'd split? Or was he sneering at her life choices?

More to the point, what gave him the right to message and comment at all?

But then she thought about it again for a moment. She'd deleted both Lucien's and Siobhan's numbers from her phone after the truth had emerged around their affair – so what if this was not Lucien, but Siobhan? Did that change her feelings about the message? Did it make it one of affection if it had come from Siobhan, rather than one of derision or idle curiosity? In which case, how did Lara feel about that? Did it make it some kind of olive branch offering, perhaps in recognition of the fact of a shared past and that their paths had crossed lately? Did it mean that Siobhan had been thinking about what they'd lost as much as Lara had?

Thanks, she replied.

What else? Her finger hovered over the key to send the message. How could she find out who it was without making it obvious to the sender that she didn't know who was talking to her? But then she decided that whoever it was – Lucien or Siobhan – it didn't matter. Neither of them deserved that courtesy anyway.

Who is this? she added before sending.

She watched the screen for a moment. When no immediate reply came, she put it down and turned her attention back to the drinks she'd come to make, her thoughts firing off in all directions.

A few minutes later, when still no reply had come through, she shoved the phone back in her pocket and went to take the drinks out to the office.

But as she walked the length of the garden she heard the text tone ping faintly.

'Thanks, boss,' Betsy said as Lara swept in and put a coffee on her desk before setting her own down. She pulled out her phone and took her seat.

You don't know? Does that mean you deleted my number from your phone?

Lara tapped a reply: *Clearly. If this is who I think it is then why would I keep your number?*
  I thought we might be able to stay friends.
  You're actually joking, right?
  Maybe. 😊 *I've got to say, seeing you again on Saturday was weird. I've been thinking about it all weekend. It brought back feelings…*

What does that mean? Lara asked, now almost certain that she was talking to Lucien. If she had an ounce of sense she'd end this conversation now, but it seemed that at some point during the last few minutes she and sense had quite irreconcilably parted ways.

You looked good. It reminded me how hot you can look if you try.

'Slimy bastard!'

Lara slammed her phone onto the desk, and Betsy looked up, eyes wide at the outburst.

'Is everything OK?'

'No, it bloody isn't!'

Lara took a breath and fought for some composure. He was winding her up for the hell of it, he had to be, and there was no need to get upset over such a juvenile game. However, that was easier said than done where Lucien was concerned. 'But it will be when I've had a few minutes to calm down.'

'Right…' Betsy looked doubtful. Lara could see why – she was quite certain she didn't look calm, because she felt a million miles away from that state of mind. 'Is there anything I can do?'

'I wish there was. There's nothing anyone can do – unless you can find a brick to whack me over the head. It'll either knock me cold so I won't have to think about it or knock some sense into me.'

Betsy was silent for a moment, almost as if she was giving the request some consideration.

'Ignore me,' Lara added. 'You'd think I'd be past all that bullshit by now, wouldn't you? Apparently not.'

'Um… Lara… is this…?'

'My ex was at Chloe's wedding reception on Saturday.'

'Oh God!' Betsy stared at Lara. 'Not the one with the hair!'

Despite herself, Lara gave a small smile at Betsy's description. Her apprentice had never met Lucien, but apparently the mental picture Lara had painted of him had informed her perfectly of his most prominent features.

'Yes. He of the coiffured hair and limitless vanity.'

'Did you talk to him?'

'No. He was with Siobhan. It would have been weird and awkward to talk to them together at the best of times but even worse when I was meant to be working.'

'Oh, I bet it was horrible. I don't know how you didn't throw a drink over them both.'

'Neither do I,' Lara said ruefully.

'So he's texting you now?'

'Looks like it. I don't know the number, but as I deleted him from my contacts, it's hard to tell. Judging by what he's saying it's him though.'

'And what's he saying?' Betsy asked, leaning forward almost eagerly.

'Just some bull about how he's been thinking about me. I'm probably overreacting. He's probably pulling a stunt.'

'He's been thinking about you. Like *thinking*? In *that* way?'

Lara nodded.

'Creep,' Betsy said with sufficient outrage and disgust to make Lara smile again.

'That's one name. Quite a generous one, really. I can think of far worse.'

'I bet his girlfriend would be thrilled to know he's sending texts to his ex like that. What a player…'

Lara paused, reaching absently for her mug. Whatever had happened between Lara and her ex-best friend, Betsy was right – Siobhan didn't deserve this. Surely she didn't know that Lucien had messaged Lara? Did Lara have a duty to tell her about it? But then, even if she felt compelled to, would Siobhan believe her? Would Lara sound like a bitter, spiteful, wronged ex who'd been reminded of old wounds and took some great masochistic delight in opening them up again?

Lara shook her head, dismissing the idea. 'It's her lookout,' she said, 'not mine. Not now, at least. I suppose, if anything, I ought to thank him for finally proving to me that I had a lucky escape.'

'Do you think he was texting other girls when he was with you?'

'I don't know, and I don't want to know. I suppose he must have been texting Siobhan if no one else, considering what happened, but I don't want to think about that. Some things are better left buried.'

'I'd want to know,' Betsy said, taking a sip of her coffee and regarding Lara over the rim of her cup.

'Well, perhaps you're a stronger woman than me then. Knowing Lucien, he probably thinks it's funny to see if he can play me. If I replied with some invitation to start up again, I'm sure he'd find it hilarious to think that I might be hung up on him still.'

Trying very hard to put the incident to the back of her mind and get on with the important business of earning a living, Lara reached for the sheet containing the new client lead that Betsy had taken that morning.

'I'd better give this Mrs Wilson a ring, see what she wants before she gets sick of waiting and decides to go with someone else.'

'You're doing it right now? Don't you want to wait until you're...' Betsy raised her eyebrows slightly as her sentence tailed off, but the action wasn't lost on Lara. Something about it irritated her slightly, like Betsy thought she was unstable, made of emotional china and liable to crack, but she tried to dismiss the thought. It was probably unfair of her to draw such a conclusion when Betsy was more likely just concerned for her welfare. But then she grabbed her mug and almost hid behind it. Clearly Lara's involuntary reaction had shown on her face and her assistant was now wondering whether she'd overstepped the mark.

'I *am* calm,' Lara said, filling in the gap of what had been left unsaid. She was calm, wasn't she? Didn't she look calm? Maybe not completely calm but she certainly wasn't going to allow Lucien to ruin her day any more than he already had, calm or not.

'Right,' Betsy said, bending her head to her work again.

The room was filled with a brief awkward silence, the likes of which had never existed between them before, and the instant Lara recognised it she felt sad about it. Even now Lucien's influence was being felt in ways that she just couldn't escape. She'd barely spoken to him for over a year, had thought she was done with him, but here he was again, interfering in her life. Lara's resolve hardened. She wasn't going to allow it.

'While I think about it,' Lara said into the silence that had descended over the office, 'I want to grab a few minutes with you sometime later today to talk about that pay rise.'

Betsy looked up with an uncertain smile, though she seemed brighter now. 'That would be good, thanks.'

Lara nodded. Then she dialled the number Betsy had taken earlier that day and waited. After half a dozen rings a lady picked up.

'Hello... this is the Wilson residence.'

'Oh...' Lara said, a little taken aback by the formality. 'Is that Mrs Wilson?'

'It is.'

'Right, well I'm Lara Nightingale... from Songbird Wedding Services. I believe you spoke to my colleague this morning about booking us for your daughter's wedding?'

'Oh, I did! Thank you for calling back!'

'It's no problem. Could you tell me a little bit more about what you want from us? You have a date for the wedding... the eleventh of next month? And you have suppliers in place?'

'Oh yes, that's all quite correct.'

'The date is very soon for us,' Lara said. 'Normally we'd want a little more notice than that, but we could—'

'Oh dear, is it going to be a problem? I did think it was a little short notice myself but Chloe told Fiona – that's my daughter; they're old school friends, you know – that you were perfectly fine with her short notice. She said you really only wandered around keeping things in order on the day so there shouldn't be much of a problem as everything else is sorted.'

Lara gave a stiff smile and held in a sigh. Good old Chloe. Lara was thankful for the business, of course, but she hoped that Chloe wasn't going to be telling too many people that she wandered around all day doing not much at all and that Lara could work for them at the drop of a hat. If she did, Lara's schedules were going to be all over the place. Either that or she was going to have to turn down work, and she really didn't want to do that if she could help it.

'It doesn't work quite like that. I mean, I can do things fairly last-minute but even though I'm really just supervising the day, there are things I need to do during the run-up so that I can give the day the best chance of running smoothly.'

'But you'll be able to fit us in?'

'We do have another wedding that day but my colleague should be able to cover one while I cover the other.'

'That's the girl on the phone?'

'Betsy – you spoke to her earlier.'

'She sounded terribly young.'

'Well, she is,' Lara said cheerfully, 'but we won't hold that against her.'

'We'll have you, won't we? Fiona is very keen that we have you. We don't want a young girl…'

'I'm sure I can work something out. Forgive me for not remembering, but did I meet Fiona at Chloe's wedding?'

'I'm sure you did. She was wearing a blue dress.'

Well, that's helpful, Lara thought with no small degree of sarcasm. Now I know exactly who she is.

'Would it be useful if I came out to see Fiona for a chat? Obviously, you'd be welcome to sit in too, and her dad... or whoever wants to be involved. I know how some families like to be very hands-on, and that's completely understandable.'

'Well, her father's in Dubai and he wouldn't give a fig anyway – he'll just turn up on the day, get drunk and pay the bill at the end. But Fiona works a half-day today – could you come this afternoon?'

Lara was about to say that the afternoon was a little bit short notice, but then she looked across at Betsy, who was staring hard at the screen of her computer. Why was she worrying? Betsy was more than capable of holding the fort. In fact, extra responsibility was what she'd been asking for so why not take advantage of that?

'What time would you like me?' she asked.

'About two? It will give Fiona enough time to have one of her slimming soups before she sees you.'

'Sounds perfect. Let me just have your postcode for the satnav.'

Chapter Eleven

Fiona and her mother had proved to be time-consuming. The fact was, they both liked to talk… a lot. And often it was completely off-topic. Rather than discuss the wedding details (though they did talk about them too, mostly to make quite unrealistic requests), they'd both fly off on tangents where they discussed subjects as irrelevant and diverse as the state of the bins in the city centre, whether two of the dancers on Strictly were having an affair and how fast the Amazonian rainforest was burning or whether, indeed, it was actually burning at all. By the time Lara had fought her way back to the office through rush-hour traffic, Betsy was already packing up to leave, having finished for the day.

'I'm so sorry,' Lara said, 'I half-expected you to be gone already – it's late for you.'

'I didn't know what to do about locking up so I thought I'd better stay. I rang my mum and she's keeping some pie warm for me.'

'Thank you. How's everything been?'

'OK. Quiet really. Nothing to tell that won't wait until tomorrow.'

'I know we said we'd have that talk about your pay too, but—'

'That's OK,' Betsy said. 'I know you can't help being held up. I don't mind waiting until we have more time. How was the appointment?'

Lara raised her eyebrows. 'Let's just say Bridezilla has come to town.'

Betsy made a sympathetic face.

'I suppose we're due one,' Lara continued. 'It's been a while.'

'Can we cope with her?'

'I expect so. The only demand I'm really uncomfortable with is that she's decided to cancel her disco – in fact, she'd already done it by the time I got there when I would rather she'd waited and talked to me about it first.'

'Why would she do that? What's she having instead?'

'She wants Jazzy Chas and the Anglo-Sax-ons.'

'Who?'

'The same band that Chloe and Gez had playing at theirs.'

'Has she booked them?'

'Oh no – that would be far too easy. She wants me to do that.'

Betsy frowned slightly. 'Why would she cancel the disco herself but then not bother booking the band?'

'Because she'd already cancelled the disco before I arrived, and I suppose that once we shook on the deal she decided that she could hand everything over and that it was now my responsibility to sort out the replacement.'

'But it's not – we're only doing the day, aren't we?'

'Try telling that to Fiona Wilson.'

'So you said you'd do it?'

'I didn't see how I could say anything else in the end.'

Betsy was thoughtful. 'The band that Chloe and Gez had... isn't that...?'

Lara nodded. With everything else that had happened on their truly manic Monday, there'd barely been time for Lara to fill Betsy in on what had happened at Chloe's wedding – in particular the mix-up over the entertainment. Once she'd briefly managed to mention it, poor Betsy had taken it badly, feeling responsible for the mistake, having been the one who'd made the call to Chloe in the first place to confirm what entertainment she had in place for the reception. Lara had reassured her that it had been nobody's fault except possibly Chloe and Gez's, and they could hardly complain about it to them.

'Yes,' Lara said ruefully. 'The Cat-Nabber's band.'

'Oh God. What are you going to do?'

'I'll have to book them, won't I? There's nothing else I can do.'

'Do you have a number?'

'I'll google them – they must have a website where I can contact them. Let's just pray that they're available that night or I don't know what I'm going to tell Fiona. She was pretty set on having them.'

'Want me to have a look now? Won't take me a minute.'

'No, it's late enough already and you have a pie keeping warm at home.' Lara gave a tired smile. It had been a long day. 'Go home – I'll see you tomorrow.'

'OK.' Betsy collected her things and headed out. Lara followed her to lock the side gate before going back to the office. There was no point in putting off what she had to do so she logged back into her computer and opened up a search page. Theo's band was easy enough to find, and Lara could only assume from this that they were searched fairly regularly and so must be quite popular, though she'd never heard of them until the previous weekend. She supposed they must be in with all Chester's jazz luvvies.

Clicking the link, she scrolled through what were basically pages of posing photos of them all at various events. The site wasn't very well organised, and it seemed almost deliberate that a visitor would have to work their way through loads of these before they finally found contact details, which Lara did after about five minutes of searching. It really hadn't taken her so long to find it because she kept pausing at the ones where Theo was front and centre. That wasn't it at all, because she'd been distracted enough today by one posing git, without getting distracted by another.

Refusing to allow herself to look again, she started to compose a message briefly explaining (reminding them) who she was and asking about their availability for the date. It was a bit close to eating humble pie for her liking, but it was business and she did what she had to do – as she would always do – putting personal feelings aside.

Once she'd written the enquiry she clicked send before switching the computer off for the night and locking the summer house up. There was plenty of work still to be done, but what was urgent she could take home easily enough to do there later.

As she went through the garden back to the main house her eyes raked the undergrowth for a sign of Fluffy. She'd been busy all afternoon so if he'd been back since he'd wandered off earlier then she probably wouldn't have seen him, but she could never settle if she didn't know he was OK. She half-thought about walking to Theo's house to see if she could spot him on the streets around there, but that meant running the risk of actually bumping into Theo himself and she really wasn't in the mood for that, despite the fact that the direct communication would be useful in helping to book the band for Fiona's wedding. For now, however, she decided she'd go and get some food and give her wayward cat some time to come back of his own accord before she went searching. As for Theo's band, she'd emailed them and if any of them had an ounce of professionalism (doubtful, but a girl could hope) then she'd get a prompt reply via the magic of the internet soon enough.

Over a salad of cold chicken and couscous, Lara went through the details of Fiona's wedding day. Though she tried to concentrate, her attention wandered often, back to her phone and the message Lucien had sent earlier that day. She hadn't replied, of course, and she'd been too busy directly afterwards to give it all that much thought, but now that the day was almost done and Betsy had gone home she sat alone in her quiet house and questions began to creep into her head. Mainly: why now and what should she do about it?

Nothing, was the most sensible answer, but doing nothing wasn't in her nature. As a child, if she'd ever had a scab she'd have to pick it, and if she ever found a loose thread on her clothes she'd have to pull it, and if she ever got a loose tooth she'd always find a way to bother and bother it until it fell out. She was no different as an adult, except that the things that nagged her now weren't physical but mental and emotional. Lucien had messaged her and she ought to have been able to leave it at that, to ignore it – but she couldn't.

She opened the text and read down the message thread again. Then she closed it, pushed the phone firmly away and went back to her meal. She couldn't be that kid who picked at scabs, not this time. This time she had to leave well alone, because nothing would heal if she kept worrying at it.

Only one solitary morsel of food had gone into her mouth before she reached for her phone again. Her finger hovered once more over the message to open it. But then, with an irritated sigh, she forced herself to open her inbox and read her emails instead. It was a job that needed to be done and it would focus her mind on something more useful.

Checking down the list, she noticed one from the website of Jazzy Chas and the Anglo-Sax-ons and opened it up.

Thanks for your enquiry but we're unavailable on that evening.

Lara frowned. That was it – the whole message. No 'Dear Lara', no 'Yours sincerely', no 'Best wishes', no nothing. Well, there were certainly no charm-school graduates amongst the members of Jazzy Chas – not that Lara hadn't already seen that perfectly clearly first-hand, of course. Still, it was annoying and it gave her another headache. Fiona wouldn't be happy that she couldn't have her band, and although she ought to have half-expected it at such short notice, she wouldn't feel it was a bit her fault.

Lara let out a long sigh and pushed her plate away. Better to call Fiona now and let her know so they could figure out an alternative as soon as possible.

'Hello,' Fiona said as she picked up. 'Not calling to tell me you're not taking me on after all, are you? I was hoping that third time would be the charm.'

Lara opened her mouth to reply, a vague frown creasing her forehead, but then she stalled. Third time would be the charm? Did that mean Fiona had been dropped by other wedding planners before she'd engaged Lara's services? If that was the case, just how much of a Bridezilla was she? It was tempting to ask but perhaps better not to. Lara was sure she'd find out soon enough and at least the wedding was close; if Fiona proved to be as big a pain as Lara was beginning to suspect she was, at least Lara would only have to suffer it for a few weeks.

'No,' Lara said. 'I'm sorry to call so late but I just needed to let you know about something.'

'What's that?'

'The band you wanted to play at the evening reception… I'm afraid they're not available. Do you want me to see if I can find someone a bit like them? I'm sure there must be—'

'You mean Jazzy Chas?'

'Yes. That's who you wanted, isn't it?'

'That's funny. Are you sure they're not available?'

'Yes. Sorry.'

'Only I spoke to Chloe who spoke to Gez, who spoke to his friend, who called... I want to say Chas? Is that really his name? Like the band? Anyway, he said they'd do it.'

'What?'

'He said they'd do the wedding for us.'

'Are you sure?'

'Oh yes. It's a good job I asked, isn't it? I mean, if we'd relied on you then we would have had to settle for someone else, wouldn't we?'

'But they emailed me to say they weren't free. They definitely know it's the eleventh, don't they?'

'Of course they do.'

'Sorry, I don't mean to push this but you're absolutely sure they're clear on the date? It's just strange, you know, that they should tell you yes and me no for the same date.'

'Maybe they didn't realise it was the same reception.'

'Maybe. When did you speak to Chloe?'

'About half an hour ago, I'd say.'

Lara checked the time on the email. It had been sent over an hour ago. Did that mean they'd said no to her only to contradict that by saying yes to Fiona herself? Or had there been a huge mix-up? In which case, Lara needed to get it sorted before it got out of hand. To make matters absolutely clear and confirm whether they were getting the band that night or not, she needed to speak directly to someone from the band. But as they'd all refused to give her their phone numbers when she'd last met them at Chloe's wedding, and as she only had what seemed to be a very unreliable email contact, the only other course of action was to try and speak to someone on the social grapevine that Fiona had used to contact them.

But then, she thought, going cold, did that mean going through Lucien? He was the friend who'd connected Gez and Chas, after all, though Lara had since realised when she'd mulled it over that it must either have been a very distant friendship or a very recent one, because Lara had never come across Chas in all the time she'd been seeing Lucien and had never heard him mentioned. It seemed likely that he was more of a casual acquaintance; Lucien had always been better at cultivating those than real friendships.

Lara puzzled it for a moment before deciding that nothing that risked contact with Lucien was a viable option. But, maybe there was one more alternative. It would mean swallowing a hefty, choking slice of pride, but she could go and see Theo...

She knew where he lived, after all, and maybe she'd discover Fluffy's whereabouts in the process.

'So that's settled?' Fiona said into the silence. 'No need to do anything else? We've got the band so I can leave everything else to you?'

'Um... sure,' Lara said non-committally. 'Leave it with me.' She didn't want to say it was all settled for certain in case it wasn't, but she was feeling pressed by Fiona, who clearly thought she'd done a pretty good night's work.

'Fantastic!' Fiona said. 'Speak soon!' And before Lara could reply she'd ended the call.

'Fine...' Lara sighed as she watched the screen go black. Then she glanced up at the clock. It was a Monday evening so, with a bit of luck, no gigs for Theo and she'd catch him in. Abandoning her chicken salad, she grabbed her keys and phone and headed out to see him.

*

The evening was still warm, the streets bathed in the last mellow sunlight of the day, and the walk was pleasant enough, but Lara's mind was racing. She half-wondered whether she might have been more relaxed had she put on her trainers and leggings and jogged there, but she supposed that might not have looked very businesslike, even if it had helped to empty her mind and calm her thoughts.

As she turned the corner of Theo's street, she saw Selina, leaning on her front gate as she chatted idly to an older neighbour, a petite lady with huge spectacles and a shock of white hair. They both had a mug in their hands, though it must have been a bring-your-own party, as they were both on their own side of the low fence that split the two properties. She looked deep in conversation, and Lara wondered whether she ought to say hello or leave her to get on with it, but it seemed rude to pass without acknowledging her. Selina saved her the bother of ruminating further by noticing Lara and waving cheerfully.

'Here she is! Looking for your cat?' Selina asked, sipping from a mug.

'I'm certainly keeping an eye out for him,' Lara said, smiling as she walked over to them. It looked as if Selina was drinking an innocent tea or coffee, but Lara detected the whiff of something stronger lacing it. 'Although that's not necessarily what I've come for. Have you seen him?'

'Nope, can't say I have, but I haven't been home long. So what brings you along this way without your running gear if you haven't come to find your cat?'

'Well... I need to see someone,' Lara said. 'It's kind of urgent.'

'Urgent, eh?' the neighbour said with a chuckle. 'I wish I could say something was urgent. Since I retired I've got too much time on my hands and nothing is urgent at all. I have to say I miss having urgent things to do.'

Lara gave a patient smile, though she was itching to get on, and Selina made a sympathetic face to her neighbour. Then she turned back to Lara.

'So, who is it you need to see?'

'Um…' Lara began but, for some inexplicable reason, she suddenly felt very coy about telling Selina who she had come to see.

A brief silence followed while Lara thought about what kind of answer she could invent and why the hell she'd even want to invent an answer at all. She had absolutely no reason to, so this sudden irrational desire to cover up made no sense. Her reticence only made things worse, though, because Selina and her neighbour exchanged a look as Lara's gaze involuntarily darted along the street to Theo's house.

'I need to see someone about a work-related thing,' Lara said in a vain attempt to head off whatever gossip was possibly already forming in the minds of the two women.

'Oh,' Selina said again, though she was grinning now.

'I wanted to book Theo's band for a wedding,' Lara said in a very deliberate voice now, deciding that honesty was perhaps the best policy after all.

'Right,' Selina said. She tipped her mug towards her mouth before seeming to realise that she'd already drunk the contents a moment before and looking vaguely disappointed by the fact.

'So… it was nice chatting to you but I really ought to…' Lara hooked a thumb in the direction of her destination.

'Don't let us stop you,' Selina said.

'OK,' Lara replied as she started to walk. 'Enjoy the rest of your evening.'

'We will,' Selina called after her. 'Don't be a stranger!'

Lara turned to wave and found both women with folded arms, watching her go. As she once again faced her direction of travel, she was fairly certain that they were still watching her. At least, she had the distinct and irrational feeling of eyes on her back. Perhaps not so irrational, given what she knew of Selina and her love of gossip, which was almost as great as Lara's mum's – at least, there'd been plenty enough times when she'd tried to engage Lara in local gossip for Lara to guess this. Lara could quite imagine that Selina would be over there like a shot later to grill Theo on the visit, and that half the neighbourhood would know she'd been at Theo's house by tomorrow morning.

Outside Theo's house, she paused. The curtains were closed – though it was early evening and what kind of person would want to shut this glorious golden hour out? Did that mean he was asleep? She'd sort of assumed that, as he played with a band, he didn't have any other job, but perhaps he did. Perhaps he was a shift worker like Selina? He might not thank her for waking him if he was trying to grab a nap before a twilight shift. But then, wouldn't Selina have said something if that was the case? Lara had a feeling she would probably know. Despite the uncertainty, Lara steeled herself and knocked anyway.

She waited. And waited. She was just about to knock again when Theo finally opened the door. He looked deliciously rumpled, the dark waves of his hair mussed up and the hem of his denim shirt misaligned, as if he'd done the buttons up in a hurry and missed one out. Lara thought, as she gave him a quick once-over, that her hunch might have been right after all – if he hadn't just been sleeping then he certainly let himself go once he was home.

'Well,' he said with a lazy grin, 'if it isn't Hong Kong Phooey. What can I do for you? I haven't got our cat, if that's what you've come for.'

Lara ignored the jibe. 'It's strictly business tonight,' she said.

'Oh?'

'I don't suppose you have access to the band's calendar, do you?'

'The band's calendar… You mean the one hanging up in Chas's kitchen?'

'You don't all have… Never mind. It's just that I tried to book you earlier today for a wedding. I emailed the address on your website and someone replied to say—'

'That we weren't available.'

'That was you?'

Theo nodded, folding his arms across his chest and yawning as he leaned on the door frame.

'Why did you say you weren't available?' Lara asked, bristling at the arrogance of his body language. Did he think this was funny? The way he made his living might be come day, go day for him, but Lara was in it for the long haul. Her business was her life, and she wanted to run it for the rest of her life – and she wasn't going to be able to do that if she had to rely on no-good slackers like him.

'Because we're not,' he said.

'Are you sure?'

'Pretty sure.'

'But my client spoke to Chas and he said you were.'

'Right.' Theo shrugged. 'Well, if your client spoke to Chas then why are you here?'

'Because I need to check.'

'She's checked with Chas, right? So there's no issue, is there?'

'So… are you going to play at the reception or not?'

'I couldn't say…' Theo ran a hand through his hair and ruffled it some more. Lara narrowed her eyes. Was he deliberately trying to look sexy? 'You'll have to ask Chas,' he continued. 'As he seems to be the go-to guy.'

'I can't ask Chas because I don't know how to contact him. I'm asking you now because you were the one who sent me an email saying no to the booking.'

'That's true; I did.'

'Why?'

'Because it had come from you.'

Lara's mouth fell open. Of all the responses she'd expected, that wasn't one of them. 'I don't...'

'It's quite simple,' he said. 'You're rude.'

And with that, he began to close the door. Lara launched herself at it, sticking her foot between the door and the frame. The wood hit her hard and she might have broken a bone had he not pulled back looking slightly less cocky than he had a moment before. Though she was so angry right now that she wouldn't have felt a thing even if she had.

'Oh no you don't!' she hissed.

'Come on; let me close my door.'

'No. Not till you explain what the hell is going on!'

'To you? Why should I? You're rude. You're possibly the rudest woman I've ever met and, trust me, I've met some stinkers.'

'You're the rude one!'

'Yeah? Well, we could discuss all day who's rude and who's rudest and I'm sure it would be lots of fun, but I've got other things to do.'

'What? Like go back to sleep in the middle of the day like a weird jazz vampire?'

'Well, I've got to feed my cat for a start...'

'You said he wasn't here!' Lara squeaked.

'Because you'd have tried to take him away with you.'

Lara paused. She'd never wanted to hit someone as much as she did right now. She could smack him one, right in the middle of that handsome face. Let the police come, let him press charges – it would be worth it just to wipe that smug, arrogant grin away.

'Is this…' she began, puzzle pieces suddenly slotting into place. 'Is this all about Fluffy?'

'Satchmo,' he corrected.

'Whatever. This is about my cat?'

'*My* cat.'

'*Our* cat. *The* cat. Whatever. Is that what this is about though?'

The grin was gone as he weighed her up. 'Isn't it for you?'

'No!'

'So you won't mind if I decide I want to keep him?'

'Of course I do – I didn't say that!'

Theo nodded slowly, still regarding her steadily, as if he was trying to see where the next button was, where the chinks in her armour were, how far he could push before she'd snap.

'I'll do the gig,' he said.

Lara hadn't expected him to back down so easily, and a new set of insults were hanging from her lips when she was forced to swallow them back.

'Thank you,' she said instead, almost choking on words that were far more civil. It was worth it, she supposed, if she got what she needed from him.

'I'll do the gig,' he repeated, 'if you let me keep Satchmo.'

'What?'

'Let me keep him. For good. He's mine. You get your gig and I get the cat.'

Lara shook her head furiously. 'No! No way, absolutely not!'

'Then I'm afraid we have nothing else to talk about.'

Theo pressed himself forward, forcing Lara to step outside or to find her nose against his chest. Unwillingly, she stepped out into the evening sun again.

'But Chas said—' she began.

'I know, but I'm sure he'll come down on my side when I explain. It's not like we're short of bookings. I don't know if you noticed but we're pretty good.'

'I wouldn't have noticed,' Lara said coldly. 'Because jazz is literally the worst music ever invented! I'd rather listen to an elephant with a head cold. In fact, your saxophone sounds like an elephant with a head cold!'

Theo shrugged. 'Suit yourself. Obviously your client disagrees. Good luck with finding another band for them.'

He began to shut the door again.

'Wait!' Lara cried.

His forehead creased slightly as he paused. He looked now as if even he was bored of this game. But he waited and Lara spoke again. She took a deep breath.

'I'll level with you. Please…' She held up a hand as he looked ready to cut in and he nodded shortly for her to continue. 'I'm sorry if I was rude to you. I need you to do this wedding – I won't lie. I really need you to do it, and you could ask almost anything of me at this point and I'd give it to you, but… I can't give Fluffy up. I just can't, not for anything. If you said my business would go down the tube, I'd lose my house… whatever, I still wouldn't be able to give him up. You have no idea how much he means to me.'

'So he can only mean anything to you?' Theo asked quietly. 'What about me? I feed him too. He comes to my house and sits with me too.'

'I know and I'm sure you're fond of him and it's not even about that. I can't explain it, not properly. He came to me on the worst night of my life, just appeared from out of a storm as if by magic, as if he'd been sent to make everything better. And he did. When he was there I forgot all my pain; I was only happy when he was there keeping me company. I need him; I can't…'

Lara shook her head, eyes filling with tears. Selina and her neighbour might have been watching but it didn't matter now. She'd tried and she'd failed, and if the price of success was her beloved Fluffy then that was too high anyway. Without another word, she turned and ran for home.

Chapter Twelve

It was too late. Theo had seen her crying and she'd told him far too much about the night that Fluffy had arrived on her doorstep, and now she felt she couldn't go back to him again to ask about the gig. If Fiona wanted his band then she'd have to negotiate the deal and if that meant Lara losing Fiona as a client then this time she'd have to risk it.

She'd run for two streets and then she'd stopped and walked the rest of the way home, feeling like a miserable failure. On top of all that, the one little soul who could have been waiting at home to make her feel better was at Theo's house. The funny thing was that, despite her antipathy towards him and all that had been said, she didn't blame Theo for not wanting to play at Fiona's wedding. Lara probably had been rude and unreasonable and she only wished she could make him understand that the irrational way she behaved whenever he was around wasn't really her at all. Lara could barely understand herself where that woman came from but something about Theo just brought her out.

When she got back to her house and finally locked the world out, she felt so wretched that she couldn't even be bothered to drink wine. She spent half an hour pedalling furiously on her exercise bike, but that made her feel no better, and then she ran herself a hot bath, but that did nothing except make her feel floppy on top of her misery.

Her mum sent a text at around nine to say that she'd lost her birth certificate and could Lara go with her to the town hall for a new one, though Lara couldn't imagine why her mum would suddenly need her birth certificate and couldn't be bothered to ask. It was likely that Fay had simply realised she didn't know where it was and thought that she ought to. Lara would bet a substantial amount of money that this had happened maybe half a dozen times during the years that Fay had lived in her current house. If they had a few weeks to look, there'd be half a dozen birth certificates stashed in hiding places so safe they were undetectable, even to the woman who'd put them there.

The night was hot and muggy, and Lara changed into her thinnest camisole and shorts for bed. Before she went up, she still had work to finish, though she could barely keep her mind on any of it. Still, after clearing away the remains of her uneaten dinner, she sat at the kitchen table and tried.

By the time the knock came at the door, she'd read about the event facilities at the grounds of Chester FC three times and not a bit of it had stuck in her head. She frowned at the clock and at the interruption. It was a bit late for visitors, and most people sent her a quick text to make sure she was in and available before they turned up. Unless this was an emergency?

Racing upstairs, she grabbed a robe to cover up and went to get the door. She'd probably looked better, but there was no point in worrying about that now. If it was some kind of emergency, she didn't suppose they'd care if she looked a bit rough.

'Selina told me where you lived,' he said as Lara opened the door.

Lara stared at Theo, who stood on her doorstep with Fluffy in his arms.

'I couldn't stop thinking about what you'd said,' he continued. 'I had no idea that Satchmo had done all that for you and I don't have a clue what it might be, but clearly it's important... I mean, I'm fond of him too but I didn't know... Well, whatever it was that happened to you I guess now I understand why he means that much to you. So I decided to bring him back.'

Lara couldn't deny that this turn of events had shocked her, moved her, even softened her towards Theo. She couldn't imagine what it had taken for him to come and find her house after all that they'd said on his doorstep. But he was missing the point here. Fluffy would never really be hers and Satchmo would never be his. The cat that they both loved might go by a dozen different names and grace a dozen different laps around Chester and he'd never belong to any of them. Nothing was clearer to her now than that.

'He'll just go back to your house tomorrow,' she said wearily.

'No he won't. If he does then I'll bring him back here. I'll keep bringing him back here until he gets it – he's your cat now, not mine.'

'I don't understand... Why would you do that?'

Theo shrugged. 'I wanted to tell you I'll play the wedding too. No strings this time, promise.'

Lara allowed herself a small smile. 'I really appreciate that. Fiona will be thrilled too – she was really keen on you. In fact, you've got a fan there.'

'But not in you,' Theo said with a rueful smile. 'What did you say my saxophone sounded like? An elephant with a head cold?'

Lara blushed. 'Look, I didn't mean that, it's just that... well, let's just say hearing jazz music doesn't always bring back the best memories for me.'

'*All* jazz music?'

'I'm sorry, but kind of.'

'You think maybe we could change your mind on that?'

'I doubt it.'

'Wow,' he said, his gaze frank now as he looked at her. 'Someone did a real number on you, didn't they?'

'It's old news now. Listen…' Lara hesitated. He'd come all this way to bring Fluffy back and she owed him some acknowledgement of that. 'I know it sounds a bit weird after… well, after before, but do you maybe want to come in for a moment for a drink or something? Maybe we can finally talk about this stuff like adults?'

'Sure,' he said. 'It's probably a good idea to clear the air if we're going to be working together.'

He stepped inside and Lara closed the front door. As she led him down the hall, Fluffy leapt out of his arms and raced ahead for the kitchen.

'He might be hungry,' Theo said. 'I didn't feed him. Thought it might help – you know, if I didn't feed him and you did.'

'That's actually really nice of you.'

He shrugged. 'It's no big deal.'

'It is, though. I know it is. Thank you.'

'I figured you put forward a way better case than me. If we were in court for child custody, you'd have won hands down.'

Lara looked along the hallway to see that Fluffy was on his way back.

'His food's probably too old,' she said. 'I'll have to put fresh down.'

In the kitchen she went to the cupboard to fetch a clean bowl and tipped some dry food into it. Fluffy fell on the bowl as she set it down, purring loudly.

'You know what's funny,' she said as she watched him. 'He won't even eat that swanky food that I spent a fortune on now. Ate it for about two days and then no more. I have tons of the stuff left. It's rotting in the cupboard as we speak.'

'He was probably sick of the sight of it with both of us feeding it to him,' Theo said with a low chuckle. Lara smiled up at him. He had a nice laugh when he wasn't using it to mock her. She bent to fuss an oblivious Fluffy as he ate and, from nowhere, found that she was crying.

'Hey, I'm sorry...' Theo began, looking helpless.

'It's OK,' she said. 'It's just so sweet of you to... and I was so horrible, and now...'

She rubbed a hand across her eyes to dry them but the tears wouldn't stop. 'God... so annoying...'

'You're not,' he said. 'Look, I didn't mean to upset you. I'll go—'

Lara straightened up and took a deep breath. 'No, don't. I offered you a drink – at least let me get that for you. You've come over specially, after all, and you didn't have to.'

'I won't—'

'I've got tea, coffee... I could open some wine. It's nice wine – some fancy champagne stuff from one of my clients.'

'It's...' He seemed torn. He wanted to stay; Lara could sense it, though his next words denied that. 'I should go.'

'You can't stay for just one?'

He gazed down at her, the struggle clear on his face. There was something in the way he looked at her that made Lara feel... Her stomach flipped. She'd never felt so confused, so conflicted. Everything about this moment was wrong, nothing about the way she suddenly felt made sense, but there was a dark thought somewhere amongst the confusion that told her she'd always known this moment would come, that somehow, no matter what else happened, this would happen, that she wanted...

Him. She wanted him. She'd never wanted a man so badly, but she wanted him now and the need was almost mind-blowing. Something in his eyes told her he felt the same – something primal, some connection that went way beyond words.

'Stay,' she said. 'I'll try not to get violent.'

His voice was an octave lower when he replied. Dreamy, husky with promise. 'Maybe I wouldn't mind so much this time.'

Lara smiled, but her eyes didn't leave his.

'Are you…?' he began. He stalled. He began again. 'Are you…? This is so weird. Tell me I'm wrong if you want to, but are you feeling this tension too? You and me… I'm not dreaming this, am I?'

'No, you're not.'

'But we… we hate each other, right?'

'Yes, we do.'

'So, what's going on here?'

'I don't know,' Lara said, letting unchecked urges take hold as she moved towards him. She might regret this in a few hours. She would most certainly regret this in a few hours, but some moments were bigger than regret and consequences.

'Is this wise…?' Theo said in a low voice, simultaneously loaded with lust and yet hopelessly out of his depth. Lara knew it because she felt it too.

'Probably not,' she replied as she pulled his mouth down onto hers.

Chapter Thirteen

Lara's eyes opened. Someone was hammering at the front door. Then Betsy's faint voice drifted into the house, though it was hard to tell what she was saying. She rubbed her eyes, groggy and not quite awake, and pushed herself to sit. *Betsy…*

'Shit!'

Lara leapt out of bed and raced to the wardrobe, yanking out a pair of leggings and a T-shirt and pulling them on. Happening to glance back at the bed, she saw that Theo was awake now too. No, she hadn't dreamt it then – he'd stayed over and they'd slept together. She'd only just woken and this thought had only just occurred to her but already she was filled with a vague panic that she'd made a terrible mistake. Theo didn't look panicked at all, though. He looked ready to drop off again. Fluffy was curled up at his feet looking supremely smug as he slept on top of the twisted covers. Lara couldn't remember him coming up to the bed, nor could she recall exactly what time she and Theo had finally fallen asleep, though she was sure Fluffy hadn't been there when she'd finally drifted off.

Betsy's voice came up the stairs again, this time clearer and more insistent. She must've been shouting through the letter box.

'Lara! Are you OK?'

'Duty calls?' Theo asked sleepily.

If Lara had the time or inclination she might have taken a moment to appreciate how adorably dopey he looked first thing but she had neither. This was the worst kind of start to a working day. She was barely awake, barely firing on one solitary cylinder, let alone all of them. More importantly, how was she going to explain this to poor Betsy, who sounded worried to death? She couldn't, not without some creative thinking. Inwardly she cringed at all the times she'd lectured Betsy about falling in with unsuitable boys, had passed judgement on the lads she'd met at nightclubs and told Lara about, and now here was Lara, doing one of the things she'd very firmly warned Betsy not to do – a one-night stand. Although, did it count as a one-night stand if you'd done it three times that night? In some quarters that was practically a marriage.

Lara stamped on some trainers. 'I have to work.'

'That's one of the advantages of gigging,' he said. 'No early starts.'

'Hmm,' Lara said.

'No early starts,' he repeated dreamily, his words heavy with meaning.

Lara looked again and he was wearing the most innocent of expressions – but she knew exactly what he was talking about.

'Well,' she said briskly, 'I have early starts and I'm currently very late for one of them. There's bread, butter, jam, peanut butter… whatever you want in the kitchen. Cereal too. Help yourself to breakfast when you're ready.'

'Wait!'

Lara turned back, brush halfway to her hair, her body halfway out of the room.

'Will I see you again?'

'You know you will,' she said.

'Oh yeah, sure, I know that. I mean, why wouldn't you want to see me? I'm just checking because this… Well, I'm just checking – are we a thing now, you and me?'

Despite everything, Lara grinned. There hadn't been time to stop and think once they'd begun – there had only been instinct and lust and later contentment. Then maybe a little more lust until they were both exhausted. But now, as she looked at him, she realised that it had meant more to him than that. And maybe it had to her too. Yes, he could be cocky and smug and infuriating, but he could also be sweet and kind and unexpected. And he was sexy as hell.

'I think…' she said, on uncertain ground, not really sure what answer to give. 'We need to talk. Later.'

'Whenever someone says we need to talk, nine times out of ten that's a bad sign.'

Lara gave him a reassuring smile. 'This is the one out of ten where it's not bad. It's just sudden, and we need to establish where we are. I think you'd have to agree on that much?'

'If we agreed on that it would be our first agreement on anything,' he said with a quick grin. But in the next second it faded. 'I'm not one of those guys who use you and then don't call. There are some of us who don't do this sort of thing unless we really like the person we're sleeping with. There are some of us who'd only ever do it knowing there'll be more than one night.'

Lara flushed, a broad smile lighting her face. His admission was so unexpected, so sweet and sincere, it took her completely by surprise.

'I know that.' She stepped over to kiss him. 'I have to go,' she said. 'And we still have to talk later.'

'Yeah, I guessed that.' He smiled in a way that gave him tiny creases around his mouth. Lara had never noticed those before. They were cute.

'Don't be sleeping there all day,' she added. 'Not while I'm working downstairs – it's a bit rich. And leave by the front door, not the back; I don't want Betsy to see you.'

'Who's—' he began, but Betsy's voice cut across him.

'That's Betsy,' Lara said. 'My apprentice. She's young and impressionable and doesn't need to know the sordid details of my sex life. So if you don't mind…'

'Front door, not back. Understood. Is your sex life really sordid? Was I sordid last night?'

'Extremely,' Lara said. She threw him a last grin before rushing downstairs.

'What's happened?' Betsy asked as Lara unlocked the gate and let her in. 'Are you alright? I phoned you and you didn't answer, so I had to start shouting through the letter box… Have you just woken up?'

'My phone must have been downstairs. I think I forgot to take it up with me when I went to bed so my alarm wasn't set.'

'You didn't set your alarm? But you're OK?'

'I'm fine. I'm sorry if you were worried.'

'Honestly, I nearly called the police. I thought you might be dead or something.'

'I'm glad you didn't,' Lara said wryly. 'I don't think oversleeping counts as serious crime.'

Betsy threw her a sideways look. 'You look like a serious crime. You look like someone dragged you round a pub car park by your hair.'

'Thank you!' Lara laughed. 'Charming!'

'But you're usually so tidy with make-up and everything.'

'Well, I've just got up – what do you expect? If it's OK with you I'll go and get a quick wash and tidy up while you make a start in the office.'

'OK,' Betsy said, though she was still eyeing Lara with a hint of suspicion. 'What happened last night?'

'Nothing happened last night. Why?'

'You didn't set your alarm.'

'I know.'

'You always set your alarm.'

'I forgot.'

'You never forget. You've never forgotten all the time I've been working for you.'

'Well, it just goes to show that even I'm not perfect.'

'Yes you are.'

'I'm really not,' Lara said. 'You can trust me on that one.'

Lara meant her remark with heartfelt sincerity. She was far from perfect, and if Betsy needed proof of that, Lara would only have to point out the actions of the previous night. There had been vague, nebulous thoughts that she might later regret what she'd done with Theo. Right now, as she stood in the garden with the morning sun on her face, the bright light of that daytime star seemed to examine her more fiercely than even Betsy, and those thoughts came rushing back. And rather than whispering in the heat of the moment, they were now shouting for her full attention. He was there, in the house now, in her bed, and really she knew nothing about him. Sure, she knew every inch of his skin, how he tasted, the smell of him, what his breath sounded like as he drifted to sleep, but she didn't know him at all. Maybe regrets and consequences wouldn't be ignored so easily after all. Maybe, before this went further, she needed to address them.

'Want me to make some drinks while you get ready?' Betsy asked. 'We've still got breakfast muffins too.'

'No!' Lara said, though she was aware it perhaps sounded like an overly hasty response. 'It's fine. I won't be long – I'll make drinks and bring them out when I'm done. The muffins sound good, though – I'm starving.'

'Did you do a lot of exercise last night then?' Betsy asked. Her face was the very picture of innocence as Lara turned and gave her a sharp look. Was there really a subtext here, a subtle innuendo, or was Lara imagining it?

'I think I'm just having a hungry day,' she replied.

'Right,' Betsy said slowly. 'So it's nothing to do with that man at your kitchen window with Fluffy in his arms?'

Lara sucked in a breath as she spun to see a shirtless Theo wave at her. 'For God's sake!'

'He's cute,' Betsy said.

'He's in big trouble,' Lara shot back, marching towards the house.

'What are you doing?' she demanded once she was inside, glancing back to see Betsy watching them from the garden.

'You said I could get toast.'

'I also said not to let Betsy see you!'

'I didn't know she'd be right there when I came down. Anyway, I don't see what the problem is. And Satchmo wanted to say hello,' he added, picking up the cat's paw and making him wave at Lara.

Lara ignored the fact that he was still calling their cat Satchmo, because for all they'd said about him living exclusively with Lara, there was no way that was ever going to happen. Fluffy would certainly have ideas of his own, no matter what she or Theo tried to impose on him.

'It's just... well... it's not really a thing yet, is it?'

'I still don't see your point.'

'It looks bad, doesn't it?'

Theo raised his eyebrows. 'Does it? How? Even "things" have to begin somewhere. Even "things" start with a first night. And anyway, I thought we were going to talk about the "thing" thing later?'

Lara glanced out to the garden again. Betsy had apparently decided that watching them have a conversation that she couldn't hear was boring and had gone into the office.

'Is that where you work?' Theo asked as he followed her gaze.

'Yes.'

'It's cool.'

Lara couldn't help but smile now. It *was* cool. She loved her little garden office, she loved her little house and her business, and she was proud of what she'd built here.

'Can I look?' he asked. He let Fluffy down and dropped some bread into the toaster.

'Maybe later,' Lara said. 'If Betsy's working I don't want to disturb her.'

'OK. Later when?' He rested his elbows on the kitchen worktop, chin on his hands as he watched the toaster like a little kid waiting for grandma to finish baking his favourite cake. There was no doubt that when he wasn't being a smug pain in the arse he could be very sweet, his gestures endearing.

But none of this had figured in her plans and right now Lara didn't know how she felt about it. Last night she'd been more certain, focused on her needs, acting on her desires, but had that been a mistake? She was only human, and had it been so wrong to want to satisfy her needs? They'd had fun, hadn't they? They'd had a great time. But now it was all talks and relationships and it was moving way faster than Lara could keep up with. But she couldn't tell him not to come back later – not after he'd opened his heart to her, not after what he'd told her upstairs only a few moments before. He'd slept with her because he really liked her, that was what he'd said. God knew why, because even she had to admit she'd been vile to him, but she knew it was true nonetheless. The proof had been in his eyes, in the way he'd shown his true self when he'd turned up with Fluffy to give him up to her.

'You don't have any work tonight?' she asked.

'Not tonight. Most of our bookings are at weekends. Occasionally we do an open mic night midweek but it depends on who else is going. I don't think it's happening tonight.'

'Right…' Lara said. 'I'm just not sure how much work I've got on today and what time I'll be finished. To be honest, I had stuff on last night but I didn't get round to it for one reason or another.'

'Yeah?' he asked, straightening up and puffing out his bare chest. 'And why would that be?'

Lara laughed. 'Well, maybe the arrival of a certain man didn't help. I had other stuff going on too.'

Her mind went back to Lucien's text. Had it really only been twenty-four hours since she'd received it? So much had happened since then she almost felt like that version of Lara Nightingale was someone completely different living a strange, parallel life. Theo had arrived and she'd split into two people, and this new Lara had been created.

But Lucien's message still troubled her because of what it might lead to, because she could foresee complications and because – despite what Siobhan had done to Lara, despite what she might say to anyone else – she still didn't really believe that her friend deserved it. Siobhan had betrayed Lara in the worst way possible, but it had been for perhaps the best reason in the world – love. She'd fallen in love with Lucien – she'd said it and Lara had no reason to doubt it was true. What she often doubted was whether it was fully reciprocated. Lucien would have been attracted to Siobhan the way he was attracted to a designer jacket or an expensive watch – a shiny, glamorous accessory to show off. But did he love her? Lara doubted he was even capable of loving anyone but himself. Now, there was a love affair to rival the greatest of them all.

'You sound like a workaholic,' he said.

'It wasn't work.'

'Ah. If you tell me, will you be forced to kill me?'

'Something like that.'

'Can I ask questions and guess it myself?'

'It's not a game, Theo.'

'I know. I just want to know what I'm dealing with. Will it affect our "thing"?'

'I hope not.'

'It's to do with what you told me about the night Satchmo came to you?'

'Yes.'

'Hmm. Just one more question. Is there a man involved?'

'Yes.'

The toast popped up and he didn't say anything else as he took it from the toaster to butter it. Lara wanted him to say something. She wanted to know what he was thinking, but for once she didn't ask. Did she look like damaged goods now? Did she look like hard work?

'We're not together now, though, if that's what you're worried about,' she added. 'What we did last night wouldn't count as an affair or anything.'

'Right.'

'It's just…'

Don't pick the scab, Lara.

For once, she followed her own advice and resisted the temptation to open a conversation that might not end well. They'd had a great night and they were getting on well now – why spoil it by complicating what could be that simple?

'There's orange juice in the fridge,' she said. 'Help yourself. I'm going to grab a quick shower.'

As she made her way upstairs, she heard him shout from the kitchen. 'Need some assistance with the soap?'

'No!' she called back and had to laugh at the sound of him chuckling.

'Do you think he'll want one of my mum's muffins?' Betsy asked when Lara eventually reached the office.

'He'll be leaving soon,' Lara said briskly. 'He's eaten half of my bread already – I'm sure he'll be fine without a muffin.'

'But we have spare.'

Lara looked at Betsy. 'Are you just dreaming up excuses to get a better look at him? He's nothing out of the ordinary, you know – just a regular man.'

'Yes, but you don't date men. Ever. So he must be a little bit special.'

Lara cleared her throat loudly to signify that this topic was off limits.

'It's true,' Betsy continued. 'This is the first time I've ever seen you with a man.'

'You're not with me twenty-four-seven, are you?'

'No, but you don't even mention anyone. Apart from your ex and that cat guy…' Betsy's eyes widened. 'It's not your ex, is it?'

'No!' Lara fired back. 'How stupid do you think I am?'

At this, Betsy had the decency to blush. But immediately, Lara wondered whether she'd been too harsh. Perhaps if Betsy had been as preoccupied with an ex as Lara was forced to admit she had been with Lucien, she might have suspected the odd lapse in judgement in that regard too. It wasn't such a stretch of the imagination to suppose that there was a danger of Lara falling back into bed with Lucien – both figuratively and quite literally.

'It's not Lucien,' Lara clarified and she was going to leave it at that. But then she sighed. What was the point in trying to keep secrets when – if Theo was to start appearing there more regularly – Betsy would find out soon enough anyway? 'It's the cat guy.'

'No!' Betsy's mouth was a perfect circle of surprise. 'Oh my God!'

Lara turned her computer on, determined not to blush or squirm or show any kind of regret or shame or any of the other emotions that niggled at the back of her mind. She'd spent the night with Theo – so what? They were both consenting adults who happened to find each other attractive despite their very obvious personality mismatch and various past disagreements. Why shouldn't they have sex if they wanted to?

'What a legend!' Betsy exclaimed.

'No, it's an example I urge you not to follow,' Lara said.

Betsy frowned. And then it turned into a grin. 'Wait… This was a one-night stand?'

Lara put her head down to examine her keyboard more closely, her face glowing.

'Oh, Lara!' Betsy squeaked. 'That's—'

'That's enough,' Lara cut in. 'Private is private and work is work.'

She looked up to see Betsy's grin fade. If anything, she looked hurt now, but Lara was too embarrassed to care. She didn't want to discuss this with anyone, certainly not with Betsy, who wouldn't really understand. When she thought about it, Lara herself still didn't really understand.

'I'm sorry,' Betsy said in a small voice. Now she'd gone from looking a little hurt to genuinely mortified.

'Let's say no more about it,' Lara replied, feeling like a total bitch now. 'I realise it was a bit of a shock for you to arrive this morning and find Theo here and I… Well, it wasn't exactly professional of me not to be here for you. But we've got a busy day ahead and we need to get on.'

Betsy gave a silent nod and turned to her computer, clearly not daring to push the matter further now that she'd been put in her place, content that Lara had drawn a line under the matter for both of them.

'There's one good thing to come out of it,' Lara added in a breezier tone. 'Fiona Wilson will be getting her band.'

Betsy looked up again and Lara was smiling slightly. 'The things I do to make a client happy, eh?'

Betsy looked as if she wanted to laugh but wasn't sure if she was allowed. So Lara did it for her, and the tension lifted from the room like mist rising from a dewy dawn field.

But Betsy didn't laugh. She started to cry. Lara leapt up from her seat and rushed around the desk to put an arm around her.

'Oh, Betsy,' she said. 'I didn't mean to upset you! I'm so sorry!'

Betsy shook her head. 'It's not you.'

'Then what is it? You were fine not five minutes ago.'

'I… I don't know,' Betsy sniffed. 'I just… I can't help it.'

'Do you need to go for a walk? Take a break, get some air?'

'No thank you.'

'Do you need to go home? Are you ill? Is there something going on at home that's upset you?'

'No.'

Lara looked to the heavens for inspiration but found none there. Feeling helpless and confused by her sudden change in mood, she rubbed Betsy's back and tried her best to soothe her. One minute she'd been fine – laughing and teasing – the next minute inconsolable. What had brought it on? If it wasn't about what Lara had said then what else? Was this what it was like being eighteen? Lara felt like being eighteen was a million years in her past but she didn't recall it being quite that fraught.

'Is it work?' she asked, still trying to figure it out. 'Is it me? Is it because we haven't sorted your pay rise yet? Is it about this morning? Because if it's that I am sorry; you just caught me in a bit of an awkward spot and I felt as if you shouldn't have had to see that, and it really isn't your fault—'

'No,' Betsy said. 'It's not any of that at all. I think maybe I would have cried anyway, but you just shouted a little bit and that just set me off. But it would have happened anyway because I woke up feeling like I wanted to cry. If anything, you cheered me up really.'

Betsy had managed to contradict herself on almost every beat of her speech but Lara let it go at that. She made a sympathetic face. 'Some days we all feel like that.'

'I expect it's hormones or something,' Betsy said.

'How about I get us some drinks while you take a minute?'

'It's my turn to get them,' Betsy said.

Lara raised her eyebrows, prompting a watery smile from her.

'I wouldn't talk to Theo,' she added.

'No, but I'm afraid Theo would talk to you and he'd find it all very amusing. I'll get the drinks this time – you can do this afternoon's round when he's gone.'

Betsy nodded. 'I won't tell anyone about him if you don't want me to.'

'Just for now, I'd appreciate that. It's early days and I'm not quite sure of any future there might be.'

'So it wasn't just one night? You're going to see him again? I thought you couldn't stand him?'

'It's a funny thing, that,' Lara said as she made her way to the door. 'So did I.'

*

Theo had left her with a smiley face drawn into a dusting of sugar on her kitchen worktop. Lara should have been annoyed about it when she'd come into the kitchen at lunchtime to find him gone and his little message the only sign that he'd been there at all, but she wasn't. She smiled at it and couldn't bring herself to clear it away.

He'd also washed Fluffy's bowl and put fresh food out. Fluffy, of course, had completely ignored it and was currently curled up on a seat cushion, probably expecting Lara to throw Theo's food away later and put even more fresh out. She'd do it as well, because Fluffy was the real boss around here no matter what anyone else thought.

When Lara went upstairs, she found that the towels in the bathroom had been folded and the bed had been made. *Sexy and tidy*, Lara thought. *Have I actually dreamt up my perfect man?* But then she reflected that most of the time his irreverent humour and sharp-tongued quips drove her to distraction, and unless the deepest desires of her unconscious mind were also deeply masochistic, then no, she definitely hadn't dreamt him up.

In the rush (mostly to tear each other's clothes off) they'd never had a chance to exchange phone numbers, and so Theo had called the office phone late afternoon to see if Lara still wanted to meet that evening. Lara tried to keep the conversation and her tone neutral, certain that Betsy was doing her best to look as if she wasn't listening when she obviously was, and in this entirely casual way they'd arranged for him to arrive at eight. She'd put the phone down, still casual, even though there were fireworks going off inside her.

She issued a self-caution as she got ready to see him, taking care to wear something that was sexy (accessible) without looking slutty or desperate. They absolutely weren't going to have sex. Tonight was for talking – finding out where they were really heading, laying some ground rules and getting to know the real Theo.

What she hadn't foreseen was how easily and quickly he'd get her carefully chosen clothes off. As she lay in his arms, exhausted and dripping with sweat, she looked at the clock on her bedside table to see that it was only just eight forty-five.

Theo stroked a thumb across the tip of her collarbone as she rested her head on his chest. 'See, you are perfectly capable of being pleasant after all.'

'What does that mean?' Lara raised a faintly disbelieving eyebrow. 'Are you trying to insult me now you've got what you wanted?'

'I think you'll find it was what *you* wanted.'

'You took my clothes off.'

'You didn't have to help me.'

Lara giggled. 'Fair point.'

'I just mean, I'm sure if you'd told me this was going to happen a few weeks ago I would have laughed in your face.'

'Well, I didn't know you properly before, did I?'

'You're that rude to everyone you don't know then? How are you even still in business?'

Lara laughed lightly. 'You know what I mean. Anyway, you weren't exactly nice to me in the beginning.'

'That's because you did karate moves on me.'

'Jujitsu. And I thought you were going to mug me.'

'Then you tried to steal my cat.'

'*My* cat.'

'*Our* cat. Things like that can make a bad first impression.'

'So is that what you thought of me? A violent cat-stealer?'

'You said it, not me.'

'Well, I know you now.'

'*Very* well.'

Lara laughed again. 'I don't really though, do I?'

'OK, so what did you think of me when you first met me? You can say it – I won't be offended.'

'Honestly, I don't know. Every time I thought I had you figured out I turned out to be wrong.'

'But you thought I was handsome, right? I mean, that's pretty much the only thing that I need to know. That's all any man needs to know.'

'I'm sure it isn't. But yes, I did. Incredibly. I think that's what scared me the most about you – my last boyfriend…'

Lara's sentence tailed off.

'I don't mind if you talk about him. I'm not one of those jealous types who can't take hearing about the man before him. And we're just this at the moment, aren't we, so how can I get jealous?'

'I don't want to talk about him.'

Lara felt him stretch beneath her head. 'Screw him,' he said. 'I think he's a dick anyway.'

'But you don't know anything about… Oh… you do.'

'Chas told me about him. I don't know the guy personally. Never spoke to him. Chas knows him a little from the circuit. He's a big music fan. When he saw you at the boathouse wedding he told Chas he used to go out with you.'

'And what else did he tell Chas?'

'I don't remember.'

'Theo…'

'Honestly, I don't.'

'I don't believe you.'

'Does any of it matter?'

'Yes, it matters to me. Did he say bad things?'

'Do you really want to do this now, Lara?'

'Yes. If people are spreading rumours about me then I want to know what they are.'

'Before I tell you, I want you to know that I don't believe any of it – not now that I know you better.'

Lara tried to ignore the fact that, between the lines, Theo was saying that he'd believed the rumours at some point before he knew her better. That was an argument for another day; right now she had enough to worry about.

'What did he say, Theo?'

Theo sighed wearily. 'I suppose I'd want to know if it was me,' he said.

'Go on.'

'Your ex told Chas that you were unstable. That you made things up. That you tried to split him up from his new girlfriend. That you'd spread lies about him to try and make him look bad and to get mutual friends to side with you.'

'Lucien told Chas all that?' Lara stared at the wall. She'd known Lucien could be cruel, but this seemed off the scale. None of those things had happened. If anyone had been gracious about the whole Siobhan thing, it had been the one party who had every right to be anything but gracious, and that was Lara. The fact that he could do this was just another twist of the knife. She'd left them alone, even though them being together had caused her great personal pain. She could have screamed, shouted, caused a scene, spread the story all over town, but she hadn't. She'd got on with her life quietly, without fuss, and had tried to work her way out of the pain, focused on building her business.

'He's lying,' Lara said furiously. 'It's exactly the sort of lie he'd find funny because he's sick. I mean, I knew he was sick; I just didn't know he was that sick. Either that or he's trying to fool himself because he feels bad about what happened and wants to transfer the blame onto me so his conscience is clear. But I don't think he's capable of feeling bad about anything he's ever done. I didn't do any of those things, though, not a one. I mean, if anyone lost mutual friends it was me because he persuaded them all to side with him and now I know how!'

'It's all bull?'

'Of course it is! What do you take me for? Don't you believe me?'

'I'm sorry… of course I do.'

'But you believed his version before?'

'I didn't know you before; not like I know you now.'

'So that's what everyone thinks? That I'm this lying nutjob?'

'Of course not!'

'You don't have to pretend.'

'I'm not!' He took her face in his hands. 'I'm not.'

'Just everyone who talks to perfect Lucien then. Anyone who talks to Lucien will hear how I can't leave him alone, how I never got over him.'

Theo let his hands drop again. He looked awkward. 'To be honest, it did sound a bit like that when you mentioned him. I'm guessing that your attachment to Satchmo had something to do with your break-up? Is that what you were talking about when you said he'd come to you on the worst night of your life?'

'He went off with my best friend! It's bound to make anyone sound like that!'

'Now you're angry; I knew we shouldn't have had this conversation,' Theo said quietly. 'I think maybe I should go.'

'No!' Lara laid a hand on his chest to still him. 'I'm sorry for over-reacting. I don't want you to go, it's just… it doesn't matter. Lucien's in the past now. Let him say what he wants because I don't care anymore and nobody who matters will believe him anyway.'

'You're sure?'

'Sure.'

'So this thing… you and me. It's not… I don't know… a distraction?'

'Of course it's a distraction,' Lara said, her frown transforming into a smile. 'It's distracting me for sure. But it's a nice one that I hope can become more. Is that OK?'

'That sounds OK. So I can tell people now?'

'About us?'

'Yeah.'

'Are you sure you'd want to? I mean, considering the conversation we've just had – and yes, I know I said I wasn't going to care about that, but even so—'

'Of course I want to tell people,' he said, laughing. 'I'm punching so far above my weight here I'll be a celebrity!'

'I don't think that's true at all, but as you put it so sweetly…'

She leaned back into him to give him a kiss. Beneath her, muscles tensed and twitched – nobody was leaving this bed just yet.

He broke off with a grin. 'Come to our gig next Thursday.'

Lara ran a lazy hand down his chest. 'You're sure you'd want me there?'

'Of course I do!'

'You say that but don't forget that I hate jazz with a passion.'

'Yeah, well, we're not actually proper jazz, you know. We're more sort of… pop jazz.'

'Pop jazz? Still sounds a bit jazzy to me.'

'Come,' he said, kissing her.

'Maybe,' she said, kissing him back.

Chapter Fourteen

The weekend had been taken up by work and visits to her mum and there hadn't been time to see Theo. In the evenings he'd had bookings with his band that were private functions and so Lara couldn't attend. In some ways this was something of a relief. It was still early days and she didn't mind waiting a little longer to embark on their first public outing together. There hadn't even been cause for her to collect Fluffy from his house, because unusually the contrary cat had camped out at her house for most of Saturday and Sunday, when, for once, she might have been glad of a reason to make the journey to Theo's to find him.

Betsy had called in sick on the following Friday. Lara had been concerned for her welfare, feeling that she hadn't quite been herself for a little while now – at least not since her teary breakdown on the morning she'd arrived to find Theo at Lara's house. Betsy had insisted everything was fine and she was just a little under the weather, but Lara could tell that she wasn't being completely honest about that. Still, she could only hope that whatever was bothering Betsy would pass soon.

On that same Friday, with things a little quiet in the office despite Betsy's absence, Lara had taken a few hours for herself in the afternoon to accompany her mum to the town hall for a new birth certificate. Then they'd gone down to the river to have ice cream and a walk, and then, later, Lara had treated her mum to supper at her favourite restaurant. All in all, it had been a pleasant enough day. Lara and Fay had chatted about everything, catching up on what they'd both missed since they'd last spoken, but one huge development in Lara's life was left unaddressed.

For some reason, Lara found herself unable to break the news that she had a new boyfriend, and she wasn't really sure why that was. Perhaps because, in spite of how compatible they were physically (there was no doubt in her mind there), she still wasn't sure of any long-term future with Theo. For a start, they were so different – their lifestyles, their friends, their habits and priorities. That wasn't to say that she didn't think it was possible to overcome those differences. She really liked him, couldn't keep her hands off him, found him funny and sweet, but even so, often she'd try to visualise a future with him in it and just couldn't see how they fitted together as a couple. Could it work? And there was the spectre of Lucien, too, always there, always waiting, in one way or another, to wreck things, just like he always did. She wanted to believe that curse was over, that his power over her was finally broken, but she couldn't quite.

When Theo had last seen her they'd said they were going to play it cool and they'd been forced to during their busy weekend, but on the following Monday evening he'd been on her doorstep, unable to stay away. And then again on Tuesday and on Wednesday, and by the time the Thursday of Theo's gig rolled around and Lara had turned off her computer for the day, she was so exhausted she was afraid she might fall asleep as soon as they came on stage.

She took plenty of time to get ready, carefully choosing her outfit of wide-legged black trousers teamed with a black halter-neck that showed her toned arms at their best, wondering all the while what Theo would like to see her in and hoping she'd got it right, her stomach churning and gurgling. By the time she was waiting for the taxi to pick her up she was feeling faintly sick from the nerves that had been building. Theo had gone to the venue early to help set up and carry out the soundcheck, and so Lara had been forced to follow later. Not only did that mean going into the club alone, but that particular club (as she'd only discovered once she'd agreed to go) was the Emerald Lounge, Lucien's favourite jazz haunt, the one they'd been in the night he'd dumped her.

Lara knew there was a strong possibility he'd be in there tonight, especially if the news had reached him that Lara was dating one of the performers. She tried to console herself with the thought that maybe he wouldn't. He couldn't possibly get to every gig and maybe, if he'd caught wind of the fact that Lara would be there, he might have the sense and decency to stay away for once. Admittedly, that didn't sound very much like the Lucien she had known, but maybe Siobhan had managed to exert some kind of good influence on him during the past year.

One thing she did acknowledge was that, however difficult, however scary it was, if she was going to stop letting Lucien influence her life once and for all then she had to do this. She owed it to Theo too, who was putting so much faith in her, who was sticking his neck out by making their relationship public when they both knew Lucien had seen to it that Lara had – at best – a questionable reputation and at worst sounded like someone who made the nutter from Fatal Attraction look like Mother Teresa.

A bit of her – the fighting bit – also wondered if it might not be such a bad thing to run into Lucien there, if only to confront him about the lies he'd been spreading. She wanted to know why, who he had told, what the extent of them was, but she had a feeling that, though it might provide some closure to find out, she probably wouldn't hear it from his lips. He'd deny he'd said anything, or he'd play games, show her that knowing smirk of his and clam up, and in the end she might come away from the encounter worse off than when she entered it. Honesty was not his style, and nor was motive when it came to toying with people. He did it because he could, on some kind of perverse power trip – if Lara had learned anything about him during their time together (even though she might not have recognised it fully at the time) it was that.

The taxi dropped her off and Lara walked into the Emerald Lounge for the first time in over a year. Nothing much had changed. The décor still looked the same – muted, stained and, she supposed, kind of cool in its scruffiness. It wasn't very emerald, that was for sure – more a sort of cigarette brown. There was always a musty smell early in the evening too, as if the building had an underlying damp problem, but later in the night it would warm up and give way to the smells of beer and spirits and sweat as the club filled up. She even recognised some of the same punters, sitting in the same corners in the same clothes. It was depressingly static, and suddenly Lara felt peculiarly like the same girl she'd been a year ago, as if she hadn't moved on either despite all the efforts she'd made to change her life.

She shook the thought as she turned her gaze to the stage and saw Theo looking back at her smiling. He looked good in the white shirt, black pencil tie and black jeans that was the uniform of the band. Though they were all wearing the same, only Theo wore it well. The sight of him lighting up at her entrance lifted her spirits and her stomach gave a little flip – not with nerves now, but with excitement. She didn't have to be that girl – she could be this one now, the one who had a gorgeous boyfriend.

It was still early enough that the crowd in the club was small and service at the bar was still quite straightforward. Lara ordered herself a double vodka and Coke and found a seat at an empty table as the band launched into their first number, Theo still looking at her, still smiling. His bandmates were looking at her now too, though with rather less affection. She could just imagine the conversations they'd had when Theo had broken the news that he was seeing her. She could understand them too, really; when she considered their last encounter at Chloe and Gez's wedding, she was only glad that she hadn't been able to hear any of it. If those conversations had taken place, as Lara suspected they had, at least Theo hadn't told her about them. Perhaps he thought it would have put her off coming tonight, and he'd probably have been right.

No one else in the club gave her a second glance. It wasn't unusual for a music venue like this to attract solo patrons – jazz enthusiasts that weren't necessarily interested in socialising but were there purely to see some live performances of their favourite pieces or to discover new bands with new songs. It was one of the few music venues in town where people felt comfortable enough attending alone. Lara sipped her drink as the band started up, and halfway through the first number she decided that she still hated jazz, but maybe she hated the stuff that Jazzy Chas and the Anglo-Sax-ons played just a little less than the rest of it.

The only person paying her any real attention was Theo, whose eyes never left her as he played, until he missed a cue and an irritated Chas jabbed him, raising warning eyebrows before turning to Lara and doing the same. It should have had the effect of making her feel uncomfortable, but for some reason she found it hilarious. She laughed, instantly relaxing, and when Theo looked her way she pulled a silly face to try and make him laugh too. He gave a slight nod Chas's way and raised his own eyebrows and now Lara laughed again. They were like naughty kids together, trying to wind up the teacher.

By the time they'd got halfway through the set, Lara's eyes were glazing over. All the songs sounded the same to her, and even Theo's presence wasn't helping to keep her focused. But at least it meant that she was feeling relaxed enough to be in that state of boredom, which had to be something positive.

The club filled up around her, though she remained at her table by the stage alone, many of the newcomers choosing to hover near the bar chatting to each other or the bar staff, or line the walls opposite the stage, tapping their feet or nodding in time to the music. There was no sign of Lucien either. Lara had scanned the crowd regularly, dreading to see him in it, but she hadn't. It looked as if she might just get her wish and could enjoy a night out for once without worrying that he'd ruin it.

'We're going to play some old favourites now,' Chas announced to rapturous applause and whistling. Lara steeled herself for some horrible, discordant, hardly-a-tune trumpet squealing when suddenly she was distracted by the sight of a figure walking towards her table. It took her a moment to realise who she was looking at but, when she did, every inch of her turned cold. It looked as if her luck had run out.

'Well, this is an unexpected surprise,' Lucien said smoothly. 'Enjoying the band?'

'Yes,' Lara said automatically.

'You remember Shane, don't you?' he asked, indicating another man who'd followed him across the room, and who now nodded at Lara.

'Yes,' Lara said again, recalling that Shane – Lucien's old friend – was as vain and self-absorbed as Lucien was.

'I'll get some beers in,' Shane said to Lucien. He didn't offer to get Lara anything – not that she cared and not that she would have accepted if he did. But it said a lot about the man she was dealing with. 'Where are you sitting, Luc?'

Lucien looked at Lara and gestured at the empty chairs at her table. 'Are these seats taken?'

It was tempting to say yes, but Lucien would know full well that they weren't. He'd probably been watching from a dark corner for a while before he'd come over, gauging her situation, and it wouldn't have taken him long to figure out that she was there alone.

'I didn't think so,' he said without waiting for her answer. He looked at Shane. 'These look as good as any, don't they?'

Lara wanted to say that he couldn't sit there, and even Shane looked faintly surprised by the suggestion, but Lucien just sat down anyway, leaving his friend to go off to what was by now a busy bar. On stage, Theo had just launched into some free-form riff and it was all disconcertingly reminiscent of the night when she'd last been here with Lucien, when he'd tipped her life upside down and she'd repaid the favour by tipping her drink over him.

'Where's Siobhan?' Lara asked.

'We're not joined at the hip,' he said.

'I never said you were; I was just asking.'

'Are you afraid you won't be able to trust yourself around me if she's not here?'

'That's not funny,' Lara said.

'I'm not trying to be.' He looked at the stage. 'The saxophonist isn't half bad. Is it him I hear you're banging?'

'Your manners haven't improved then,' Lara said. 'Still crass. Why are you here?'

'I've come to see the band, like you.'

'Then please go and see them from another table.'

'I like this one. I like the view.'

When he said this he looked directly at Lara and she knew he wasn't talking about the view of the stage. What was he getting out of this? Was it some kind of power trip? What was there to enjoy in this confrontation? She shook her head slowly.

'There's something seriously wrong with you.'

'Do you think so?'

She turned back to the stage and tried to focus on what was happening there. Theo was looking their way now, a deep frown creasing his forehead.

'Go away, Lucien.'

'OK, I think you're right,' he said.

Lara turned back to him. 'What does that mean?'

'There's something wrong with me. Well, not with me, but I did something wrong.'

'What the hell are you talking about?'

'I wonder... I wonder if I chose the wrong friend after all...'

Lara stared at him. 'Are you serious?'

'Deadly. Have you ever known me joke?'

'You *are* a joke,' Lara said with a scathing laugh.

He grinned. 'You always did look sexy when you lost your temper. Why do you think we had so many arguments?' He leaned forward, so close that she felt sick. 'The make-up sex was amazing, wasn't it? The things you did with that pent-up aggression. Remember the time we—'

'Stop it!' Lara shouted. 'I don't know how I ever let you touch me!'

Lucien leaned back in his seat. 'I don't know why I wanted to.'

'Well then, let's just call it a draw, shall we? You can leave me alone now.'

Lucien didn't make a move. He just folded his arms and looked at Lara as if scrutinising every inch of her.

'Does Siobhan know where you are tonight?'

'Of course she does.'

'But she's not here.'

'She didn't want to come.'

'Strange that. You knew I was going to be here, didn't you? Did Chas tell you? I suppose so,' she added, replying to her own question as she worked it out. 'I suppose Theo would have told him and of course he'd have told you. While we're at it, why don't you tell me why you're spreading so much shit about me? Why did you feed Chas all those lies?'

'Of course I didn't know you were going to be here. And did you really think you were so important that I'd rush to be here if I had? And lies? Tut tut, Lara... And you accuse *me* of being vain.'

'Don't bullshit me. I know what you've been saying. You can deny it all you like but it won't wash, because I know you too. You knew I was going to be here tonight as well, and that's why Siobhan isn't here. Don't think I've forgotten about those texts. Do you think Siobhan would be happy if she knew about those? Do you think she'd be happy if she got to hear about the things you've said to me tonight?'

'She's such a wet weekend I doubt she'd do much about it even if you told her.'

Lara's eyes widened. 'I knew you could be vile, but... that's my friend you're talking about!'

'*Was* your friend.'

'It still matters to me what happens to her. Why are you doing this? If she's what you say she is then why are you with her?'

'I never said I didn't want to be with her.'

'Do you love her?'

'So you're still as naive as ever...'

'Then what do you get out of it?'

Lucien paused for a moment, scrutinising Lara in that unnerving way again. 'You used to be ever so compliant, ever so agreeable. I'd clap and you'd jump. I used to think I liked that about you, but now I see the new you I'm not so sure I don't like this one better. It's more of a challenge and much more rewarding when I win.'

Lara bolted up out of her seat. 'I don't know what I ever saw in you!'

'Oh, I think you do.'

'Just leave me alone, Lucien. Stay out of my life!'

She didn't look back as she marched out of the club. Theo would need an explanation later, of course, and she felt bad that she couldn't stay for the whole show. Even as she walked, not daring to look back in case she caught the smug grin she knew Lucien would be wearing, she could feel Theo's eyes on her, watching her leave. Maybe he'd even be hurt and angry that she'd gone and maybe she'd have to talk him down, and she was sorry for that too, but what else was she meant to do? Lucien would have prodded and prodded and he wouldn't have left her alone until she'd snapped.

Even in the few minutes they'd spent talking she could feel him getting the upper hand. She'd never go back to him, of course, but even knowing that he was exerting any kind of influence over her, affecting her in any way, was enough to make her feel desperate and helpless. His behaviour tonight was no shock, but what she couldn't understand was why now, after he'd left her alone for so long. Was it because their paths had crossed and he'd been reminded of her existence? Was it because he was bored with Siobhan? Was it because Lara was dating Theo? Maybe there didn't even need to be a reason; maybe he just did it because he could.

The sounds of the club faded as the doors closed behind her, heat giving way to cooler air as she stepped onto the street. She began to

walk to the nearest taxi rank. A quick glance behind her told her that
Lucien hadn't followed her out, though, the mood he was in, she'd
half-expected him to. He was just lucky she didn't have Siobhan's
phone number anymore, because she would have been sorely tempted
to phone and tell her exactly what Lucien had been up to.

She stopped dead on the pavement. She didn't have Siobhan's
phone number, having deleted it when their friendship had ended on
such bitter terms, but she did know where she lived. As far as she was
aware, Siobhan and Lucien had yet to move in together and Siobhan
was still in her old place. Lucien shouldn't be allowed to get away with
this. Someone needed to tell Siobhan, and why shouldn't it be Lara?
It wasn't like they had a friendship to wreck – though Lara still valued
what they'd had before, despite what she'd often told herself. She still
cared that this man was obviously using her ex-best friend for reasons
clear to nobody, maybe not even himself.

She'd go, tell Siobhan, and what Siobhan chose to do with that
information afterwards was down to her; at least Lara would have done
the decent thing. She would have wanted to know if it had been the
other way around and she was certain that Siobhan would too.

Chapter Fifteen

Siobhan opened her front door, and the look of astonishment on her face might have been comical under different circumstances.

'I know,' Lara said, 'you weren't expecting anyone and certainly not me. Can I come in? It'll only be for a minute and I don't think you'd want to hear what I've come to tell you on the street.'

Siobhan hesitated, rocking back and forth slightly on the balls of her feet as if subconsciously trying out the two different options of out or in the door. Then she gave a short nod.

'I suppose you'd better.'

Lara stepped into the hallway. It was still painted pastel pink, as it had been the last time Lara had been to visit, but the harsh yellow of the lightbulb that hung from the ceiling washed it into a strange, yolky colour, and it wasn't doing much for Siobhan's complexion either. In fact, now that Lara looked properly, Siobhan seemed exhausted. But then, it was late and perhaps she was on her way to bed.

'Do you know where Lucien is tonight?' Lara asked.

'Of course I do,' Siobhan said tetchily, in a voice that sounded offended, as if Lara was questioning their relationship and Siobhan's trust of Lucien. But then, that was exactly what Lara was about to do.

'So you know he's at the Emerald Lounge.'

'Yes, you already know he goes there a lot. I don't always fancy it – Lara, what's this about? What's going on?'

'Do you know he texted me after Chloe Rowley's wedding?'

'Why would he do that?'

'Come on, Siob; I don't want to have to spell it out.'

'I think you do.'

'You must believe that it gives me no pleasure to come here and say this…'

'Say what? Stop beating around the bush. You seem to have something very important to tell me so why don't you just get on and say it?'

Lara paused, almost wincing. Now that she was here she didn't want to have this conversation, and yet, she felt certain it was the right thing to do. Siobhan wasn't going to make it easy though. She must have known to what Lara was alluding, and yet she was determined to make her spell it out.

'Really, Siob? You're going to make me say it? Why do you think he texted me?' she asked slowly.

'I don't know. Why don't you tell me?'

'I can do better than that – I can show you…' Lara reached for her phone.

'I don't want to see,' Siobhan said. 'I know what you're going to show me, but he wouldn't have meant anything by it; it's just what he does – you know that.'

'So that's it? You have to accept it? You're just OK with it?'

'Whatever you think it meant, it didn't. He's a natural flirt; he can't help it. He'd never go off with you even if he said it.'

'Funny – that's what I used to think. And then look what happened.'

Siobhan shook her head. 'We're different. He's different with me than he was with you.'

'What makes you so sure of that?'

'He's still with me, isn't he?'

'How long have you been together? About a year? And how long was he with me? Oh, I think about a year... Are you seeing a pattern yet?'

'We're not splitting up.'

'You'd be the last to know if he wanted to. Like I was when he went off with you.'

'We fell in love.'

'I thought we were in love too. I thought the same as you.'

Siobhan shoved her hand out to show Lara a diamond ring. It was big and ostentatious and everything that Lucien was – all show. It was probably as fake as him too, Lara thought privately, but it jolted her. She had to admit that in all the time she'd been with Lucien she'd never received any commitment of that sort, no physical symbol of an intended future, no matter what he might have said about their relationship.

'We're getting married.'

'So I heard. Have you set a date? Booked the church? Told his parents?'

'I have a ring. Isn't that enough?'

Yes, Lara thought, *but does that really mean anything where Lucien is concerned?*

'He's never going to marry you. And even if he did, is that really the life you want? You know what he's like – you've just told me as much. You can't be OK with that.'

'When you're in love you take the rough with the smooth, don't you?'

'Siobhan, I'm saying this because of the friendship we once had. You can't trust him and you don't deserve that life.'

'You're saying it because you're jealous that I mean more to him than you did. You wanted to be the one, you wanted the ring on your finger—'

'You know that's not true. I told you everything when we were together and I never once mentioned marriage. And I still think this engagement will fall through.'

'Well, I suppose when we're celebrating on our wedding day you'll be proved wrong, won't you?'

'Open your eyes, Siobhan, please! OK, maybe he will marry you but life with him will be horrible! You know how he can be; you must do!'

'Just because it was horrible for you, doesn't mean it will be the same for me.'

Lara fixed her with a frank gaze. 'Do you want to know what he was doing in the Emerald Lounge. What he said to me?'

'Stop it!' Siobhan cried. 'You're just trying to break us up!'

'After a whole year? If I'd wanted to do that I would have done it before now.'

'You can't move on! You never forgave us for falling in love and you can't stand that we're getting married now!'

'I'm sorry, Siob,' Lara said quietly. 'We may not be friends now but I have to say these things because I don't want to see you get hurt and – believe me – he will hurt you.'

'Just because it didn't end well for you doesn't mean it will end the same way for me.'

'It would end the same way for anyone because the only person Lucien loves is Lucien. Nobody else is perfect enough for him.'

'You don't know that – he's changed.'

'He looks like the same old Lucien to me.'

'You're wrong,' Siobhan cried, red blotches climbing her neck now. 'You're wrong! You're jealous and mean and spiteful and you'll do anything to wreck our happiness! I never imagined you could be this evil. Why are you doing this to me?'

'I take no pleasure in it, but my hand has been forced. I'm doing this because Lucien chose now to start trying to unravel my life again, to undo the progress I'd made. I'd come to terms with you two being together – I mean that. I'd come to terms with it because I had no choice, and I'd kept my mouth shut about so much, but I can't keep my mouth shut about this. He was coming on to me, Siob. I have no idea why, but I'm not mistaken or wrong about this. I know when someone is coming on to me. Maybe he thought it would be funny to play us both… I don't know. But he'll never be faithful to you because it just isn't in his make-up and tonight has proved that—'

'You never came to terms with us. You're here now because you heard we were getting married – that's it, isn't it? He told me about all the things you'd said, all the lies you'd told about us, and I didn't want to believe it because you were supposed to be my friend. You didn't think we'd last, you thought he'd come back to you, but he's not and you can't stand it!'

'You're wrong. I wouldn't have him now if he was the last man on earth. I'm with someone now and I'm happy. I just don't want to see you go through what I went through.'

Siobhan barked out a spiteful laugh. 'Oh, I've heard all about your new man.'

The hairs on the back of Lara's neck prickled and she suddenly felt cold. 'What does that mean?'

'He doesn't care about you – he's using you.'

'No—'

'The bike, they call you. He only wants you for sex.'

Lara felt the blood drain from her, the roots of her hair to the tips of her toes going numb.

'No,' she whispered. 'Who said that? Not Theo?'

'Everyone.'

'You mean Lucien?'

'Chas told him. It's what everyone in the band says about you.'

'Lucien's lying.'

'You come here painting me as the victim, holier than thou, telling me how sorry you are for me. Save your pity for yourself because you're the victim here; you're the one being played.'

'That's not why I came—'

'The bike,' Siobhan repeated. 'She's a bit rusty but climb aboard and she'll go like the clappers—'

Lara lashed out and, when she realised what she'd done, Siobhan was holding a hand to her cheek.

'Very mature,' she spat. 'Thank you for proving to me once and for all that Lucien was telling the truth when he said you were as mad as a box of frogs.'

Lara's eyes filled with tears. The palm of her hand tingled and burned from the blow she'd just landed, a wretched reminder of an instinctive step too far she'd instantly regretted, but one that had caused damage she'd never be able to undo.

'Siobhan, I'm so sorry. You know me, you know I wouldn't—'

'I don't though. I thought I did but all these years I was wrong about you; I couldn't see what you were really like. It's easy to be friends when everything is going well, but this was the test and we failed. *You* failed.'

'Siobhan…'

'Go. We have nothing more to say.'

Lara hesitated. But there was nothing else to say and nothing more to be done. She shouldn't have come here – she knew that now – but the girl who'd picked her scabs and unravelled sweaters had got her way and now the girl she'd become had paid the price. Right before her eyes, Lara's life was unravelling again, just like one of those sweaters.

She shot one last pleading look at Siobhan, but to no avail. Her old friend was not to be swayed on this, was not to be persuaded. They'd said too many harsh words and had both heard things that would cause untold damage for many years to come.

Without another word, she turned and stepped out onto the street, the slam of Siobhan's front door echoing around her.

Chapter Sixteen

She walked home. It was late and it was dark, and it would have been safer to call a cab. But Lara didn't care. She needed time to think.

Cars passed her, most of them cabs, headlights throwing long shadows along the pavement. Some of them beeped horns and she heard cat-calling from one through an open window. It bounced off her like rain from a tin roof. Perhaps she deserved it. Perhaps she really was the slut Siobhan had said she was. Was that what she looked like to people? Was that what everyone thought of her? Even Theo?

It started to rain, light and warm, drops tiny enough to be buffeted by the weakest breeze into chaotic squalls. It was how Lara felt right now: helpless, chaotic, blown where she didn't want to be, not strong enough to fight back.

Buttoning up her thin jacket, she walked on, head down against the weather.

Before she hit her own road, Lara had reached Theo's and by this time the rain had eased. She'd tried to phone him but there had been no answer. She thought about knocking to see if he was home yet, but she didn't know what she'd say if he was. Siobhan's comments bounced around in her head. They had to be lies, didn't they? And even if they weren't, even if that was what the band said, Theo wouldn't say that, surely? Theo would have defended her, wouldn't he? Theo would have told them to stop. The thought that he might not, that he might join in the scornful laughter, made her feel hollow.

She looked up at the house. It was in darkness. The gig should have been over by now and he ought to have been home. Maybe he'd stayed on for drinks. Maybe he'd seen that she'd left early and was angry, and had stayed out to spite her. Maybe he was laughing and joking and calling her names even now as he sat with his bandmates. Would Lucien have joined them, fanning the flames, adding his own fuel to the fire, making things worse just because he could?

Lara swallowed back the tears of self-pity. Perhaps none of that was happening. The set might have run over. He might be catching up with an old friend, talking to appreciative music fans, helping to pack the van. Perhaps there was a simple explanation. She took her phone out and checked it again. There was no message from him, but that didn't have to mean the worst, did it?

There was a faint mew from the darkness and Lara looked closer to see Fluffy sitting on Theo's doorstep, looking up at her.

'So much for staying with me,' she said, going over to pick him up. He wriggled to break free from her arms. 'Oh, taking his side now, are you? It's good to know I've got zero people I can rely on and now zero cats as well.'

He broke free and dropped to the ground with a grace that only a cat could possess. His tail went up in the air and he walked off down the road.

'Well, you meowed at me first,' Lara said as she watched him go. 'Stupid cat. Bite the hand that feeds you, would you? Wait until you come for your tuna tomorrow morning because you're in for a rude awakening!'

She started to walk again, following the road Fluffy had just taken. It led to her house anyway, and maybe he was heading there after all. She checked her phone yet again, not sure what she was hoping for. If there was a message from Theo it would probably only be something telling her how pissed off he was. But there were no messages – not from anyone. She'd expected one from Theo at least, even half-expected one from a furious Lucien after her visit to Siobhan, but perhaps he would play it cooler than that. He wouldn't have had to work all that hard on Siobhan anyway to smooth things out, so maybe Lara's visit had been nothing more than a minor inconvenience for him. Maybe the biggest regrets would be hers, as she now feared. Maybe the biggest casualty of this war would be her too. She didn't want to believe any of what she'd heard from Siobhan, about what Theo and his band had said about her, but they were lodged in her mind and she kept hearing them over and over, kept seeing Siobhan saying them to her. Had she placed her trust in the wrong man again?

As she turned the corner into her own street she spotted a man sitting on her garden wall. He was smoking, staring into space. As she got closer she recognised Theo.

'You smoke?' she said, frowning slightly as he pulled in another lungful, the cigarette glowing brighter momentarily.

'I gave up five years ago. It's not really a wise choice when you play sax for a living.'

Looking up at her, he flicked the remainder of the cigarette into the road and stood up. 'Where have you been?'

The question was so direct, so confrontational, it threw her. She'd arrived with questions of her own, answers she needed from him, but now he was quizzing her instead, demanding answers from her.

'I could ask the same of you,' she said. 'You haven't been home yet?'

'Neither have you.'

'You've been here?'

'For at least an hour.'

'Why didn't you text me? I'd have come straight here.'

'Instead of where?'

Lara pulled out her house keys. She needed to have this conversation but it wasn't one she wanted to have on the street. As she passed him to open up she caught the unmistakable whiff of spirits on his breath. 'Good night, was it?'

'It was alright. Where did you go when you left the club? I looked for you—'

'I'm sorry about leaving early,' she said, and on that point at least she understood the need to step back and admit she was in the wrong. 'It was Lucien… You saw he was there? I mean, we'd expected that he might be.'

'We did. But I didn't expect you to go off with him. Is that where you've been all this time? With him?'

Lara paused, her key halfway to the lock, and stared at Theo.

'What?'

'Have you been with Lucien?'

'Of course I haven't!'

'What else am I supposed to think when you left the club with him?'

'I didn't.'

'So, I look up and you're gone. Then he's gone.'

'That means we left around the same time, not that we left together. If he followed me out I have no idea about it.'

'So you haven't been with him? I mean, you looked pretty cosy when I saw you two sitting together.'

'He came to sit at my table – I couldn't do anything about it. He was trying to stir up trouble just like he always does.'

'You could have asked him to move.'

'I did but he refused.'

'You could have moved.'

'He'd have followed me. What the hell is going on here, Theo?'

'You leave together and then you're missing for hours. You never really got over him, did you?'

Across the road a light went on in an upstairs window. Lara saw the curtain move. Lovely old Mrs Shields who sometimes took in parcels for her. Lara would have to have a word to apologise about the noise tomorrow morning. She lowered her voice.

'Because that's what you say about me, isn't it? The bike. She's a bit rusty but climb on and she'll go like the clappers.'

'Who told you that?' Theo asked, and if it wasn't genuine shock on his face he was a brilliant actor.

'It doesn't matter,' Lara cried, her eyes filling with tears. 'You're saying it! You and Chas and those other pointless blokes who are so irrelevant I can't even remember their names! You're all saying that! Did you have a good laugh about it at band practice? Did you go to them after the first night for pats on the back?'

'Stop it!' Theo said, his voice low and urgent, all traces of his own outrage gone. 'I'd never speak about you like that and I can't believe you'd think I would!'

'Well, that's not what I heard.'

Theo stared at her. He shook his head. 'Tell me who said this.'

'Why should I? What does it matter? Is it true?'

'I can't believe you're asking me that.'

'Neither can I but I want an answer. Answer me, Theo – is it true?'

'I refuse,' he said quietly. 'I'm insulted and hurt that you're asking me. I thought we had something; I didn't want to listen to what the others said about you because I thought they were wrong, that they didn't know you like I did. I guess that makes me an idiot.'

'I'm the idiot for thinking you could be better than the other lowlifes I've been with.'

'Is that what you think? You think I'm a lowlife?'

'Just tell me it's not true. Tell me you didn't say those things.'

'If you have to keep asking me then we have nothing. We never had anything.'

'So you said it?'

Theo looked at her, as if to memorise the details of her face, and then he shook his head again.

'Bye, Lara.'

'That's it? You've got nothing else to say?'

'What else is there?'

'Fine. If that's how you feel, don't come back!'

He stepped away, onto her tiny path, out to the street. 'I wasn't planning on it.'

Lara stood at her front door, defiant, furious, desperately wounded, wanting him out of her sight but terrified that she'd never see him again. She wanted to say something; she wanted to make this right, but nothing was going to make this right, not now, not when so much had been said that was wrong.

He began to walk away. He didn't look back. When he'd turned the corner of the street and had disappeared, Lara went inside and shut the front door, falling onto it, heaving, wracking sobs ripping through her, as if she would cry her entire being out. Through her tears she made out the blurred shape of grey fluff at her feet and felt the soft fur of Fluffy against her legs. He'd do his best to love her, as he always did, but even Fluffy couldn't put this right.

Chapter Seventeen

Lara had struggled to get up the following morning. She was exhausted, of course, but part of her wondered what the point was. If she hadn't had a full working day to get through, and if not getting up hadn't meant letting Betsy down, she would have stayed in bed, staring at the walls.

Just before eight thirty she fed Fluffy and went to unlock the garden gate ready for Betsy. Her apprentice would want to know why Lara looked so awful this morning and Lara would probably have to tell her. She wasn't looking forward to that, but at least Lara's example might be a valuable lesson that would save Betsy some heartache sometime in her own future. If nothing else good came from this whole mess, perhaps there would be that.

As she was pocketing her key, Betsy arrived. Lara did an almost comical double take. As she'd looked in the mirror that morning, trying to do something with her make-up that might hide the bags under her eyes, she hadn't imagined that anyone could look worse – but Betsy had managed it.

'Good morning,' Betsy said, her voice so dull that Lara could barely recognise her as the girl who usually bounced in, full of beans and ready for the day ahead. At least, that was the girl who had first started to work for Lara – some mornings over the last few weeks Lara hardly knew who to expect. This one looked like it was going to set a new record for gloom.

'You look terrible,' Lara said.

'Sorry,' Betsy replied.

'I don't mean that. Are you OK?'

'Oh, I'm fine.' Betsy came in through the gate and walked past Lara, straight to the summer house. Lara swung the gate shut and hurried after her. In the office, Betsy was silent as she unpacked from her bag the things she'd need to start work.

'Are you feeling alright?' Lara asked.

Betsy looked up and gave Lara a smile that was clearly forced. 'Of course.'

'Hmm.' Lara didn't believe it for a minute, but if Betsy didn't want to tell her what was wrong she could hardly make her. 'Do you want a coffee?'

'Yes, please,' Betsy said. That was all. No mention of cakes, no banter, no 'Yes, boss'…

Lara's frown deepened as she watched her assistant log onto her computer. Betsy had been off for a couple of weeks now – one minute up, the next down. You could put only so much down to hormones or late nights. It was affecting the atmosphere in the office, but Lara had been patient about that, hoping that whatever was happening in Betsy's private life would resolve soon enough. It hadn't affected her work – yet. But if things continued to deteriorate, there was a chance it would.

'I've had some thoughts about your pay rise,' Lara said. 'I've been speaking to Terry and I think, between us, we've managed to come up with a figure. Shall we have a chat about it when I've made the drinks?'

'Thank you,' Betsy said.

Lara left the office, deep in thought, eyes on the ground as she went. It promised to be another dry day, though thankfully a little cooler than of late, with a sweet breeze rustling the olive tree that sat in a pot on her patio. If Betsy wasn't going to tell Lara voluntarily what was wrong, perhaps Lara could draw her into it without her realising she was giving anything away. Subtle, slow… that was the way to do it. Engage her in an unconnected conversation and gradually bring it round. It had to be worth a try.

She returned to the office a few minutes later with two mugs and a plan. She gave one of the mugs to Betsy.

'OK,' she said, perching on the corner of her desk and regarding Betsy over the top of her mug as she took a sip. 'Terry and I were thinking I could probably afford—'

Betsy's lip began to tremble and her eyes filled with tears. The time for subtle plans had already passed.

'OK, seriously,' Lara said in her best boss voice. It wasn't because she was annoyed with Betsy, but because she thought it might just be scary enough to get something out of her. Something wasn't right and Lara couldn't allow it to go unaddressed any longer. 'I know there's something you're not telling me and I need to know what it is. This isn't the first time I've seen you close to tears for reasons I just can't work out.'

Betsy shook her head miserably.

'No, not good enough,' Lara said sternly.

'I'm sorry, Lara, I can't…'

'Then I'll have to put you on a verbal warning.'

'No!' Betsy cried. 'Please don't do that!'

'So tell me what's wrong,' Lara said, her tone softening.

'You'll fire me.'

'I won't fire you,' Lara replied, faintly alarmed by the notion that Betsy might tell her something so bad that she'd have to fire her.

'Promise?'

'I can't do that. I don't know what it is. Is it something at home? Something you've done here that you daren't tell me about? If it's that I'm sure we can put it—'

'Oh, Lara,' Betsy said. 'I'm pregnant.'

Lara shuffled slightly on her perch, hands clasped round her mug. She had to be careful not to look shocked, because Betsy was clearly distressed and she didn't want to make it worse. But she was a little shocked. Betsy had never mentioned any kind of long-term boyfriend. She hadn't even mentioned a casual boyfriend, though Lara realised there must have been dalliances she probably wouldn't have heard about.

'You're going to fire me, aren't you?' Betsy sniffed.

'Of course not,' Lara said gently. 'How long have you known?'

'I did the test this morning.'

'That would explain the shell-shocked look you had when you got here. You must have suspected before now though? Why on earth didn't you say something?'

'I didn't know... I didn't want to say...'

'I suppose I might not want to either unless I was sure; I can hardly blame you for that. I take it this wasn't on your to-do list?'

'I only slept with him twice and then we broke up. I thought... it was only twice – I thought we'd be alright.'

'Oh,' Lara said, carefully. 'How long ago was this?'

'About three months ago.'

'And you've only just realised you might be pregnant?'

'No. I sort of guessed, but I didn't want to think about it. I was scared to check and I thought I might be wrong. And I'd only just started to work for you and my friend Shona got pregnant when she'd only just started her job at the kebab shop and her boss fired her because he said she must have known when she got the job and she was trying to fiddle maternity pay out of him; she hadn't, but she couldn't get her job back because he didn't believe her—'

'Betsy,' Lara cut in, 'I'm not going to fire you no matter when it happened.'

Betsy began to cry again. 'I've ruined everything, haven't I?'

'No, you haven't. We can work around it, I'm sure.'

'I was so scared to tell you,' Betsy said. 'I love working here; it's the best job I've ever had and all my mates are so jealous. I don't want to leave.'

'You won't have to. Unless you want to once the baby comes, of course…' Lara paused. 'This is a bit delicate, but I take it you are planning on having the baby?'

'You mean abortion? Oh, I couldn't do that.'

'And you're keeping it once he or she is born?'

'I think so.'

'What have your parents said?'

'Nothing yet – I haven't told them. There wasn't time this morning. Mum will kill me.'

'She might but they need to know. Besides, you're an adult; I don't think it's the big deal it might have been if you'd been a lot younger.'

'You say that but I know she'll be so disappointed.'

'She might be, but at the end of the day you're old enough to live your life as you see fit. What about the father?'

'I've texted him to say we need to meet up. I don't think he's seen it yet but I think he has a college lecture first thing.'

God help us, Lara thought, feeling sorrier for Betsy's predicament by the minute. The father of her child wasn't even out of education yet, which didn't bode well for financial support. She had to hope that Betsy's parents would come through for her when it really mattered.

'Right,' she said. 'Well, at least you didn't send him that kind of news in a Snapchat message. Have you made an appointment to see the doctor yet?'

'I need to do that?'

'I'm pretty sure you do so that you can be referred for pregnancy services.'

'Right. Will you come with me?'

'Don't you think your mum will want to do that?'

'She might. I just think you'd be less scary to go with. She'll keep telling the doctor what she thinks I should do.'

'But there must be someone else you'd rather go with? For that matter, wouldn't you rather go by yourself and keep it confidential?'

'I'd feel better if someone else was with me. The doctor will be talking all over the place and I won't remember all the things he says I've got to do.'

'Well, I can't imagine why you'd think I'm the best person, but if you want me to then of course I'll come along.'

'When do you think I should go?'

'As soon as possible. Call them now and make an appointment – you need to get all your help in place, especially considering you're so far gone.'

Betsy nodded. She looked better already and the sight of it cheered Lara.

'How are you so good at staying calm?' Betsy asked, sniffing as she sipped her drink.

That's a good question, Lara thought. Apparently she could be calm for anyone but herself. 'It's all an illusion. If you'd seen me last night you wouldn't have thought I was good at being calm.'

'What happened last night?'

'Phone the surgery. We've got more important things than that to worry about.'

'Did you have a row with Theo?'

Lara nodded.

'That's a shame,' Betsy said. 'I'm sure it will be alright.'

Lara knew there was no way it was going to be alright, but she wasn't going to bring that up now. She needed Betsy to focus on putting everything she needed in place.

'How do you feel in yourself?' she asked. 'Are you getting sick?'

'I'm feeling fine – just a bit weepy, you know.'

'I had noticed,' Lara said wryly. 'So you're OK to work right now? Not getting tired yet?'

'No.'

'Because we have that double booking next week and if you're not going to be up to it I need to know.'

'Oh, I will be,' Betsy said, looking almost like her old self again. Bulletproof, Lara thought, reflecting on how lovely it would be if she could be that resilient. 'I would never let you down.'

At least that's one person I can rely on then, Lara thought. *Please don't completely destroy my faith in the human race by buggering up that promise now.*

Lara was sitting across from her mum. They were in Fay's favourite tea shop overlooking the river. Lara had often commented that she thought it was overpriced for what it was – probably paying for the view – and Fay had often agreed. But whenever Lara suggested they meet up for a chat somewhere other than her mother's cramped and cluttered house, that was where Fay wanted to go.

Lara couldn't blame her really, as she looked out on it today. They had their favourite seats by the window. The skies were a little grey, but the scene was still pretty – the river, moving sedately along, flanked by lush greenery, pleasure boats going up and down, a rowing team just getting into the water for their evening practice, families wandering along the promenade with children or dogs, often both. In the distance they could see the ornate and sturdy iron structure of the River Dee suspension bridge, gleaming as it spanned the waterway.

Lara had work waiting back at the office, but it was gone six thirty and well past the end of her official working day, and she was just too tired and tetchy to do it tonight. Whether an hour listening to her mum's gossip would cheer her up or make her feel worse remained to be seen. At least she'd never told her mum about Theo, which meant she didn't need to now explain why she and Theo weren't together any longer. It was one less person to gossip about.

Lara had ordered an Americano while Fay had ordered a coffee so full of syrup, whipped cream and marshmallows it practically counted as a meal. When the drinks arrived at their table, Lara saw that her mum had also ordered chocolate cake when Lara hadn't been looking.

'How your blood sugar isn't through the roof I'll never know,' Lara said, pouring milk into her coffee.

'I won't have any other treats this week,' Fay replied a little defensively as she dug a fork into her cake. 'I can have one every now and again, can't I?'

'I suppose so. I just worry about you, that's all.'

'I know. I can't complain about that. I do wonder when that all switched around though.'

'When what switched around?'

'When I started to worry about you less than you worry about me.'

'Are you saying you don't worry about me now?'

'Oh, I'll never stop worrying about you because that's what mothers do. But you never worried about me like you do now. I expect it's because I'm getting old.'

'Don't say that – I don't want to think about it.'

'Well, we'll have to think about it one day because it's coming. Unless I die soon.'

'Great. Now I feel cheerful.'

'Well, that's going to happen too so there's no point in shying away from it.'

'Can we stop talking about you dying please?'

Fay rammed another forkful of chocolate cake into her mouth and chewed solemnly.

'I bet you never have this conversation with Sean,' Lara said.

'I never have any conversations with your brother these days,' Fay said. 'He never calls, never comes round. It's all about Michaela these days.'

'At least he's settled.'

'Well, there is that,' Fay said, taking a sip of her coffee that left her with a cream moustache. 'So what's young Betsy going to do? I'd have liked to have been a fly on the wall when she told her mum.'

'I don't think she's actually told her yet. Yesterday, when she told me, she said she was going to, but this morning when I asked her she said it hadn't been the right time.'

'There's never a right time for that sort of news. Best to just get it out.'

Lara gave a slight shrug. 'She's hardly a slip of a girl anyway. She's eighteen – I can't see how her mum can really make a fuss about it. It's not all that shocking.'

'But it's not about her age; it's about the resources she has to bring up a child. She doesn't have her own home and she doesn't have a man by her side. That's going to make life difficult for everyone, isn't it?'

'I suppose so. I never really thought of it like that.'

'Well, you wouldn't, because you don't have children. Don't forget that I did it alone so I know what I'm talking about. It's harder than you can imagine.'

'Hmm. I suppose I didn't really think about it that way.' Lara stirred her coffee, her gaze going to the window. She could see a couple on the bridge. Suddenly, they stopped in the centre and the man got down on one knee. She watched as the woman threw her arms around him. Another love story with a happy ending. Lara smiled slowly. It was hard not to be cheered by that, no matter what was happening in her own life. 'Someone's just proposed on the bridge.'

'Oh!' Fay squealed, leaning into the window to get a closer look. 'Oh! I didn't see it! I wish I'd seen it! I wonder if they'll come to you for their wedding? It's a good business to be in,' she added sagely. 'Plenty of money in weddings. People are getting married all the time.'

'I'm doing something wrong then because I'm not seeing all that money.'

'You don't charge enough.' Fay sat down on her seat again.

'I can't yet; I'm not established.'

'No, but you're good. I tell everyone about you. I'm so proud of you.'

'I know, Mum,' Lara said, her smile returning. She'd been feeling low and lost again all day, still missing Theo. She was reeling from the way it had ended, driven half-mad by his lack of contact and desperate to make the first move and contact him, no matter how angry she felt and no matter how convinced she was that it was better left alone.

She was also worried about Betsy and how she was going to support her through the pregnancy – both as an employer and a friend. Though when she really thought about it, she was blessed, more than she often appreciated. She only had to sit here and look at her mother to know that. She was loved, she had a thriving business, a beautiful house and the cutest cat in the world. To want anything else was just plain greedy. She decided, there and then, that she was going to start counting those blessings instead of dwelling on what she felt was missing. She had it a lot better than many others.

'You know what,' she said. 'I might get a slice of that cake.'

Fay raised her eyebrows. 'You never eat the cake here.'

'I know. But there's a first time for everything, isn't there?'

'Let me get it,' Fay said, taking out her purse and sliding a five-pound note across the table.

'No, Mum, you can't—'

'You never let me treat you and I want to. Do what your mother says and take the money.'

'OK,' Lara said, laughing. She got up and went to the counter, returning a few minutes later with a slice identical to Fay's.

'I think yours is bigger,' Fay said, eyeing it. 'I'll bet it's because it's nearly the end of the day and they want to get rid of it.'

'Well they do say good things come to those who wait.' Lara grinned and started to eat. It was gooey and rich and just the sort of comforting thing she needed right now.

'You'll never guess who I saw yesterday,' Fay said.

'President Nixon? Madonna? Ronald McDonald?'

'No,' Fay said, and Lara had to stop and wonder why she wasn't laughing. 'I saw Siobhan.'

'Oh,' Lara said, all her good humour and promises to herself evaporating in that one instant. Suddenly, the gooey, indulgent chocolate cake had lost its appeal. She put the fork down on the plate and pushed it away.

'Oh, she looks bad,' Fay said. 'Terrible. She looks ill.'

'Does she?'

'Dreadful. Getting big around the jowls too. And I could see her roots.'

Siobhan had looked tired when Lara had seen her last and on that point she had to agree with her mum, but she certainly hadn't noticed any of the other things.

'I'm sure she's fine,' Lara said. 'Everyone has an off day. You probably just happened to catch her on one of hers.'

'She said hello to me,' Fay said. 'Crossed over the street to ask how I was. She hasn't done that since… well, you know.'

'Did she?' Lara leaned forward now. It seemed surprising that she'd do that, especially given what had happened between them at Siobhan's house the night Lara had split from Theo. 'That's nice of her. She always did like you. She used to say she wished you were her mum.'

'She shouldn't have said things like that,' Fay said, though clearly she was flattered and pleased to hear it. 'Her own poor mum wouldn't have liked to hear her say that.'

'I don't think her mum was all that interested. Siobhan always said she was the accident her mum and dad hadn't wanted to happen and by the time she was born they were fed up with raising kids.'

'It was a very big gap between Siobhan and her sister,' Fay agreed. 'I'm surprised her mum and dad were still doing… *things*… at that age.'

'I don't think they were *that* old,' Lara said with a faint smile.

Her mind went back to the first time she and Siobhan had got chatting. They were thirteen years old. Lara had seen Siobhan at school but they'd never spoken. But then, one day as she walked home, she saw her shivering outside her house in the rain because she'd lost her front-door key. Lara went to see if she could help. They could see her mum through the window, watching TV, but it was so loud that no matter how much they knocked she didn't hear them.

Lara often thought in the years that followed that Siobhan's mum simply hadn't wanted to hear them. Siobhan's dad had died the year before, and Lara sometimes wondered if Siobhan's mum been the victim of some mental illness that nobody had known about. Siobhan was often neglected as she grew up. That first day, Lara had invited her back to her house to dry out, and Fay had made them hot chocolate and toast. Lara had been a bit embarrassed that her home was so chaotic, but Siobhan had told her she loved it and, after that, she was there almost every afternoon once school had finished. When Lara thought back to the friendship they'd had and lost, she hated Lucien more than ever.

'What did she say?' Lara asked.

'She just said it was nice to see me looking well. I didn't ask about... you know who. She didn't ask about you, I'm afraid, but I expect she's too ashamed to. Oh, but she looked terrible. I almost asked her if she wanted to come to my house for hot chocolate like she used to in the old days. I think she needs someone to take care of her.'

'I don't think that would have been a good idea,' Lara said, vaguely alarmed by the prospect. What if any of her last conversation with Siobhan had been relayed to Fay? Lara didn't think that even Siobhan would want to drag Lara's mum into their spat, because she knew Siobhan thought a lot of Fay, and she didn't think for a minute that

Fay would have taken any of it on board anyway, but she couldn't be certain and the idea unsettled her.

'Oh no, I wouldn't have done. I wouldn't have her in the house,' Fay said. 'Not after all that business. It wouldn't be right.'

'I know you wouldn't,' Lara said, despite the brief doubtful thoughts that had flitted through her mind.

'It's such a shame about you two, though.'

'It is,' Lara said quietly, her gaze back on the river beyond the windows. 'Nobody knows that better than me.'

Chapter Eighteen

It was almost nine by the time Lara arrived back at home. She'd driven her mum home and had left there feeling lighter than she had in days. It had done her good to be out and thinking about something other than her altercations with Theo, Siobhan and Lucien, although what her mum had told her about Siobhan troubled her. It was nothing more than the usual gossip, of course, and Fay always saw illness and drama when it wasn't necessarily there, but, in this case, Lara thought she might be right. But what could Lara do about it, even if she was inclined to? And she wasn't really inclined to do anything. She could feel sorry for Siobhan but the fact remained that Siobhan had hurt her badly and continued to hurt her. If Siobhan was unhappy, if Lucien was wearing her down, then she only had herself to blame and why should Lara care?

She killed the engine outside her own house and got out of the car. It was then that she saw the flowers on the doorstep. They were gorgeous – pink carnations, white roses and lilies, eucalyptus stems adding a touch of lush greenery. There was a note attached. Lara picked it up. She'd expected them to be from Theo but was shocked to see that the note was from Siobhan.

I'm sorry for what I said to you on Thursday night. I know you don't owe me any forgiveness, but please know that I didn't mean to hurt you.

Always your friend,
Siobhan

Lara took the flowers inside. Fluffy padded down the hallway to greet her and she was gladder to see him than she'd ever been. As she searched for a vase he wound around her legs, his soft fur and contented purrs a comfort, and as she arranged Siobhan's flowers, tears splashed onto the kitchen worktop. There was no bitterness in them now, only a profound sadness. What had happened to the two girls who had grown up together? Hadn't they been like sisters once? All this warring was over a man who wasn't worth either of their tears.

She wanted to call Siobhan and thank her but she didn't have her phone number anymore. She guessed that was perhaps why Siobhan hadn't called her either. But then, even if they could speak to each other, what would they say that hadn't already been said? This peace offering didn't change any of the material facts. Siobhan was set to marry Lucien and, once that happened, they could never be friends again. They might see each other in the street, say a brief hello, a nod of acknowledgement maybe… but that was all it could ever be now.

She gazed at the flowers, now in a pristine white vase. They warmed her and saddened her in equal measure, but they represented a line: before the grown-up Lara and Siobhan had understood each other and afterwards. Because now, Lara thought that perhaps they did have an understanding. There was no animosity, no hatred, only an acceptance that they had once had a friendship to cherish. If nothing else, at least they could treasure the memories of that and not let what had gone on since taint them. This was Siobhan's way of asking Lara not to forget, and Lara wasn't about to.

*

Betsy had managed to get a last-minute appointment for an ultrasound on the Thursday after she'd told Lara her news. She still hadn't broken it to her parents yet, though the father of her baby had been stoic about it all and had promised to do the best he could by her. At least that was something, Lara had said as Betsy repeated her request for Lara to accompany her to the clinic for the scan. So they'd shut the office for a couple of hours on Thursday afternoon and driven to the hospital together. Betsy had been chatty on the way and, if Lara hadn't known better, she'd have said that her apprentice was almost excited at the prospect of seeing the evidence of what she knew was growing inside her.

Finding a parking space had been a challenge, but eventually they got one. It was outside the elderly care building and was a good twenty-minute walk to the maternity block, but they'd allowed themselves plenty of time to get to Betsy's appointment. It was a fine, breezy day and the grounds were planted with beds of vibrant begonias, antirrhinum and fragrant lavender, so the walk was no hardship.

As they passed the entrance of the building they'd parked in front of, Lara heard her name being called. She turned to see Selina coming out of the main doors, waving at her.

'Oh, hi!' Lara said, trailing back to meet her.

'Fancy seeing you in these parts,' Selina said, digging her hands into the pockets of her nurse's tunic. 'Not poorly, are you?'

'Oh, no, I'm fine,' Lara said.

'Visiting then?'

'No, we have an appointment at the maternity block. In fact…' Lara glanced at the time on her phone. 'We kind of have to go or we'll be late.'

'Oh, yes,' Selina said keenly. 'It's a bit of a walk, especially when you're carrying an extra passenger.' She smiled at Betsy and then turned back to Lara. 'You take care, eh? I'll pop round and see you. What number is your house again?'

'Twenty,' Lara said.

'Ah, I'll remember that – it's just my age.'

Selina grinned and suddenly pulled Lara into a hug. It was completely unexpected, filled with surprising affection and had never happened before. When she let go, Lara smiled uncertainly. 'We'd better go. Pop in any time; you'll always be welcome.'

Lara and Betsy hurried away.

'Who was that?' Betsy asked.

'Remember the nurse I told you about who lives a few streets away? She often tells me when she's seen Fluffy roaming around so I can find him. That's how we got chatting the first time actually. It's funny how that cat brings all sorts of people into my life.'

'Yes,' Betsy said quietly. 'Thank you for not telling her it was me who's having the baby.'

'It's not my place to tell anyone,' Lara said. 'It's for you to do when you're ready. I would never just say it in front of anyone, even if they don't know you.'

'I know that, but it's still good to hear. She seems nice,' Betsy added. 'Very friendly.'

'Yes,' Lara replied. 'More friendly than usual if I'm honest.'

Her brain chugged, turning it over and over. And then she realised... Selina must have heard about her and Theo. Perhaps she felt sorry for Lara. Had she been talking to Theo? What had he said? As far as Lara was concerned, she wasn't even aware that Selina knew they'd been dating, though she realised Selina had guessed there was an attraction way before Lara even realised it. That had to be the reason for this sudden show of affection. She wanted to go back and ask her what Theo had been saying about her. Had he said he was sorry? Was he missing her? Had he been too scared, too proud, too anxious to come and talk to her about it? Or had he told Selina all the wrong things that he believed to be true about Lara? Had he told her about his suspicions around Lucien?

'Maternity's that way,' Betsy said, pointing to a signpost. Lara shook away her thoughts. There was a time to worry about all that, but right now Betsy needed her.

The waiting room was cheerful enough, painted a warm apricot with posters of cute babies all over the place bearing various bits of new parent advice and messages. In the corner there was a box of toys, currently being assaulted by a couple of toddlers who were playing happily, blissfully unaware of the baby siblings soon to turn their little worlds upside down. There were women with partners and some with older women, perhaps mothers or grandmothers.

Lara couldn't help but feel that Betsy ought to have been here with her own mother, or even with the baby's father. She and Betsy were good friends, but this wasn't a responsibility that sat well with Lara. However, Betsy had insisted that she come. Perhaps it was because she wanted to be with someone who wouldn't judge or lecture – Betsy had said that her own mother would do that, though Lara suspected that, even if she did, it wouldn't last long.

After this visit, once everything was confirmed and care in place, Lara would talk to Betsy and persuade her that the best people to see her through things like this were her family. And besides, if Betsy's dates were correct and she was twelve weeks gone, even Betsy wasn't naive enough to think that her family weren't going to notice the changes in her sooner rather than later. The boy's parents would surely want to be involved too, and all that meant getting everything out into the open.

Lara held in a sigh as she looked at Betsy, who was poring over an Instagram page full of baby clothes. Betsy swung from being totally terrified to resembling a little girl getting a new doll. It was hard to know how she would handle motherhood once it smacked her right between the eyes. Even more worrying was how Lara was going to handle having a pregnant apprentice. She barely knew anything about it herself, without having to worry about guiding Betsy through it. Then there were her obligations as an employer, which were about as clear to her as mud right now, even though she'd spent two hours that morning reading through a document about it. And there was the work too. How was Betsy going to keep up when she started to get tired towards the end of her pregnancy? What if she wanted to finish early? What if something happened to her or the baby while she was working?

One thing was clear to Lara: once they got the double-booked weddings out of the way the following Saturday, she couldn't send her assistant on any more jobs alone. It wasn't fair to her or the clients, and Lara would worry constantly that Betsy was going to be taken ill. Betsy wouldn't like it and she would argue that she was capable, but that had to be the final word. It was too late to do anything about the two they had booked for the weekend, of course, and so that would have to stay as it was. At least the wedding Betsy was covering was a day occasion only and would be finished by mid-afternoon. Although, Lara couldn't help but wish that they could swap, because the wedding she was working at just happened to be the one Theo was playing at, and how many levels of awkward was that going to be?

A lady sitting next to Lara nudged her.

'Excuse me, I don't want to pry and I don't know if the receptionist told you, but you're supposed to be drinking water.'

'What?'

'It helps the sonographer to see the baby better. You have to drink until you want to go to the toilet. Didn't they tell you?'

Lara, of course, hadn't spoken to the receptionist when they'd arrived. She'd left Betsy to register, choosing to look around the room and try not to seem as if she was listening in.

'There's a water fountain and cups over there,' the woman added, pointing to a little water station.

'Right, thanks.'

Lara was about to nudge Betsy to tell her when the door to a side room opened.

'Betsy Blake!'

A woman in a grey tunic called and Lara leapt up. 'That's us,' she said briskly, nudging Betsy, who jumped up too. She glanced at Lara.

'Oh shit,' she said under her breath.

'Oh shit indeed,' Lara replied. It was too late for water – too late for anything. Betsy was about to come face to face with her future.

They'd been sent away the first time because Betsy hadn't drunk enough water, but at least when they went back out to the waiting room, the woman who'd been quizzing Lara had gone. They went back in ten minutes later, Betsy now complaining that she was desperate for the toilet, to try again.

'I can't see anything,' Betsy said from the bed as the sonographer rolled the scanner over her tummy. 'It's just grey. Does that mean I'm not pregnant after all?'

Lara couldn't help but remark that she looked almost disappointed by the idea. She was standing to one side, unable to see the screen properly but perfectly placed to see the back of the sonographer's head and Betsy's face. But then they heard a faint noise, like someone was bashing a steady rhythm on a tiny sheet of metal.

'There's the heartbeat,' the sonographer said. 'You're definitely pregnant.'

'Oh!' Betsy said faintly as the sonographer moved to get some different angles. 'Oh…' she said again, looking as if she was about to cry.

'It's hard to tell right now but you can just make out baby's head there. Looks happy enough.'

'Is it a boy or a girl?' Betsy sniffed, wiping a hand across her eyes.

'You can find that out at twenty weeks if you want to know,' the sonographer said.

She moved again and, suddenly, Lara could see the screen too. It looked grainy and unclear, and she could understand why Betsy might think there was nothing there. But then she spotted a faint fluttering at the centre of the picture, which seemed to be in time with the sound they were hearing, and she realised with a shock that it was the baby's heart. She stared at it, the strangest, most profound mood sweeping over her. She was there, witness to the start of a new life, and she felt privileged and awed and somehow unworthy. It was the most beautiful thing she'd ever seen, and if she lived to be a hundred years old this moment would always stay crystal clear in her memories.

Before she could comprehend it, she realised that she was crying too.

'That's your baby,' she said, beaming at Betsy.

'I know,' Betsy said, looking back at the screen, tears streaming down her own face. 'It's in there right now.'

'Are you OK?' Lara asked, drying her eyes and doing her best not to look like an emotional mess. 'It's a lot to take in.'

'I'm OK,' Betsy said. She turned to the sonographer, her mood instantly buoyant again. Lara didn't know if it was hormones or just the shock of the situation, but her mood swings were disconcerting and hard to keep up with. 'Can I have a photo?'

'You can pick up a copy of the scan at reception,' she said. 'You have to pay a small fee but—'

'No, I mean a photo of me here having this done?'

The woman stared at her. 'I don't know if that's appropriate.'

Betsy shrugged. 'I just thought I could put it on Insta once everyone knows.'

'Maybe you could just put your scan on there,' Lara said, trying not to laugh. Betsy was Betsy, and it was nice to see that motherhood probably wouldn't change her all that much.

Lara was still laughing as they left the ultrasound room, Betsy looking happier and more content than Lara had seen her in some time. Perhaps the first and biggest hurdle had not been Betsy telling people but believing and accepting the pregnancy herself. Now that she had, she seemed at peace with the idea, ready to get on with it, excited for what lay ahead.

They went to get a copy of her scan, and then they made their way out of the department. Betsy said she was starving and, as most of the afternoon was now gone, Lara wondered if there was any point in making her go back to work. She could just as easily let her go home and pick up anything she needed to do tomorrow. For that matter, Lara could probably do it herself later. And perhaps it would give Betsy the opportunity to speak to her parents too.

She was just about to suggest this when the doors to the department opened and Lara looked up vaguely, only to stop dead.

Siobhan had just walked in.

It was hard to know who looked more shocked out of the two of them as they both stopped and stared at each other.

'Hi,' Lara said.

'Hi.'

Siobhan looked awkwardly from Lara to Betsy and back to Lara.

'I'm sorry, but I'm late for my appointment…' she said finally.

'Of course,' Lara said. 'I hope…'

What did she say? Did she acknowledge the likely reason Siobhan was here? Did she congratulate her, wish her well? Did she say she was happy for her and Lucien?

'Thanks for the flowers,' she said. 'They meant a lot.'

Siobhan gave a short nod and a pained smile. 'I just wanted to say… well, you know.'

'I know. Bye, Siobhan. I hope everything goes well.'

'You too,' Siobhan said, before hurrying away.

'Is there anyone you don't know?' Betsy said as they left the department, Lara deep in thought.

'Hmm?'

'Everywhere we go you bump into someone you know.'

'It doesn't usually happen like this. It's been a bit of a weird day.'

'You can say that again.'

'I can, can't I?'

Chapter Nineteen

Later that evening, Lara was boiling pasta when the text came through.

Can we talk?

She gazed at the phone for a moment. She wanted to talk to him, more than anything, but after the way they'd left things she was afraid.

What about?

Us.

Not sure.

I know you didn't go with Lucien. Please let me explain my stupidity.

Please let me come and see you.

OK. When?

Now

?

I'm outside.

Lara took the pasta from the heat before rushing to the living-room window. Theo was standing on the street, a spray of carnations clutched in his hand. She threw open the front door and beckoned him in.

'Thanks,' he said as she closed the door and he stood awkwardly in her hallway. 'I didn't honestly think you'd see me.'

'You were outside. It would have been really mean of me to turn you away if you were already here.'

'I've missed you,' he said.

'I've missed you too,' she said, her heart beating at a rate that couldn't have been healthy.

'I'm sorry. How have you been?'

'I've been better, to be honest. Not that it matters.'

'It does matter. I was an idiot. I know now you didn't go with Lucien that night. I know now he went with Shane to another club. Not enough action in the Emerald Lounge, so Chas said.'

At least he could be honest about some things, Lara thought to herself, but as Theo was clearly finding this apology hard enough, she didn't see the point in making it worse by saying so.

'I'm sorry for what I said to you,' Theo continued, 'but I saw you with him and I just saw red; I assumed the worst, which was ridiculous and so unfair. This is all new to me and I don't know how to deal with it. I've never felt like this about anyone before and knowing your past with Lucien, I just thought…'

'Hmm,' Lara said. It was an apology of sorts, but he was still, in a roundabout way, turning the blame back onto her here. She wasn't sure she was happy with it. He was digging a hole when a simple 'Sorry, please forgive me' would have sufficed. 'So I'm supposed to fall into your arms now? Happy to be proven innocent after all and grateful that you've never felt like this and so it means you don't know how to act?'

'No, of course not.' He thrust the flowers towards her.

'I don't want them.'

'But they're for you.'

'Taking them means I've forgiven you and I haven't.'

'You said you missed me too.'

'I have. But that doesn't mean I can forgive what you did.'

'But it was an honest mistake…'

'You didn't trust me. You let things you'd heard from other people colour your decisions.'

He looked devastated and, if she was perfectly honest, he looked exactly the way she felt. Rejecting his peace offering was ultimately a rejection of him, but how could she take his flowers? That would mean everything was alright again and it wasn't. She'd been excited to see him when she'd opened the door to him, but it was quickly becoming obvious that she should have tried to temper that excitement with the voice of reason. Was there really a future for them, no matter what either of them wanted, no matter how much they might miss each other? It was only a matter of time before the suspicion and accusations started again. All it would take was one well-placed word from a so-called friend, one incident in a club, one late night home…

'What do you want me to do?' he asked helplessly.

'Nothing. I need time.'

'What for? What is there to think about?'

'You being here doesn't change the fact I'm still hurting about the things you said.'

'I told you I know about Lucien—'

'The other things,' Lara said. 'When I asked you to deny what I'd heard you'd said, you refused.'

'I was angry.'

'So was I, but you could see how much I needed to hear it from you. What you did was cruel. You could have set it all right, there and then, with just a word, but you chose not to. That's the bit I can't forgive. Tell me now – did you say those things?'

'No! I would never say them! I thought we had... I was crazy about you!'

Lara paused to let his words sink in before she allowed herself a small smile. He was crazy about her. She'd been pretty crazy about him too. Maybe she'd been too hasty after all...

She held out her hands for the flowers.

'They're pretty,' she said, putting her nose to them.

'So we're good?'

'Maybe.'

'We can talk?'

'We are talking, aren't we?'

'Yes,' he said. He drew a deep breath. 'So, time to lay the cards on the table.'

'I thought we were doing that too.'

'Lara,' he said. 'I know about the baby – I just need to know... is it mine?'

It took less than a second to work out exactly what had happened here. Siobhan had told Lucien about seeing her at the hospital, who'd told Chas, who'd told Theo. A perfectly efficient grapevine delivering perfectly flawed information. Was that the real reason he'd come? Not to try again because he wanted to, but because he had a duty to?

'There is no baby,' she said.

'But…'

'I'm not pregnant. Is that why you've come?'

'Well, yes, but—'

'You wanted to know if it was yours?'

'Yes. I wanted to do the right thing.'

She handed the flowers back to him. 'Give these to your mum or something. She'll appreciate them.'

'I don't understand.'

'And that's exactly the reason why we can't be together. After all you've said, after you made me believe that you had faith in me, that I could trust you to trust me and show me some respect, you come to me and ask me if the baby is yours?'

'I'm sorry, I thought you were pregnant; it's just that I was told—'

'It's not that you came to me because you thought I was pregnant. Actually, that's a decent thing to do. It's that you had to ask if the baby was yours. Who else's was it going to be? I'd told you I hadn't slept with anyone else since Lucien and yet you come here asking me who the father is? Doesn't that say everything about what you really think of me?'

'It wasn't meant to sound like that; I just wanted to check before I said something—'

'Well, it did.'

Lara walked to the front door and opened it.

'That's it?' he asked.

'Yes.'

'You can't just tell me to go.'

'I can. This is me, telling you to go.'

'Let me explain—'

'I could, but I have a feeling you'd make it worse. You're good at that.'

'Lara, I'm sorry…'

'Please go now.'

Theo threw her one last pleading glance, but Lara turned her face away, afraid that if she looked she'd crumble.

Chapter Twenty

Betsy had been missing the following afternoon at an appointment with her midwife. Lara had told her not to worry about coming back, but she'd insisted on seeing out the rest of the working day and, though Lara appreciated the commitment, for once she wished her assistant would go home. It had been difficult to keep her mind on anything they had to do in the office when there was so much else to think about. Her sleep had been crappy and that hadn't helped. Betsy had been the same, often bending her head to a file only for it to snap up again and for her to start talking about something that had happened at her scan, or some new thought about motherhood that had occurred to her:

'I wonder if I'll eat weird food.'

'I wonder if I can have it in a swimming pool.'

'When do they start walking?'

'Does it hurt a lot giving birth?'

She'd messaged a copy of the scan photo to the baby's father, Reece, and he'd messaged a smiley face back. That had sent Betsy into contemplating whether the baby might bring them together as a proper couple and how she felt about that. Lara was content to let her talk and to offer the odd word where she felt it necessary but, in the end, this was Betsy's life and only she could decide it. Besides, Lara hardly felt qualified to offer anyone advice on life choices.

At five, Betsy left for the day. Lara hurriedly locked up the office, rushed to put down fresh food for an absent Fluffy in the expectation he'd be back soon enough, pulled on a cardigan and headed out.

Outside the house, Lara scanned the street for a sign of Lucien's car. She couldn't see it, and she hoped that meant he wasn't there. As far as Lara knew, he ought to be still at work and, once he got home, he'd take his time preening and grooming before he headed out again. Siobhan would have finished her working day and be in by now, but again, this assumption was based on what Lara knew of her friend's schedule before the split. She had to acknowledge that this might have changed, though she hoped it hadn't. If Lara was right about all this, it gave her perhaps an hour or so to do what she needed to do. She knocked a shaking hand at Siobhan's door and waited.

After perhaps thirty seconds, the door opened. Siobhan didn't look surprised to see Lara standing there, but she did look wary. Lara couldn't blame her for that when she thought back to what had transpired the last time she'd stood on this doorstep.

'I haven't come to start anything,' Lara said quickly. 'I just wanted to say... well, I just wanted to say congratulations.'

Siobhan gave a tight smile. 'I suppose I ought to say the same to you.'

'I'm not pregnant,' Lara said. Siobhan looked confused now, and Lara wondered whether the flawed information that had been fed to Theo had indeed come from her. 'We were at the hospital for my colleague, not for me.'

'Oh,' Siobhan said again. 'I didn't realise—'

'It's an easy mistake to make,' Lara said. 'Look…' she glanced up and down the street. 'Can I come in? It's kind of weird having this conversation on the street.'

'What conversation is that going to be?' Siobhan asked, and Lara could see her guard go up.

'Please. I'm sorry I lost it with you – it won't happen again. I just feel that we have a past we really should show a bit more respect for. And I don't think that's down to you,' she added quickly. 'I realise I need to take some blame for that too.'

Siobhan moved aside and let Lara step into the hallway before closing the door.

'Will Lucien be coming over tonight?' Lara asked.

'Not for a while yet,' Siobhan said, 'so you needn't worry about running into him as long as you're not planning to stay long.'

'I'd rather not,' Lara said. 'It would be a bit awkward.'

Siobhan folded her arms tight across her chest and nodded. She looked tired again; she had shadows around her eyes and was paler than usual. Lara wondered whether the pregnancy was draining her.

'How far along are you?' Lara asked, glancing at Siobhan's tummy. She wasn't showing yet – at least, Lara couldn't see that she was, though the sweatshirt she'd probably just chucked on over her work clothes was baggy enough to hide quite a lot.

Siobhan didn't reply; she simply folded her arms tighter across her chest. Lara took that to mean that she didn't want to discuss it with her and, if she was honest, Lara could see why she'd be reluctant. Perhaps Lara had been very unreasonable the last time she'd been at her house and perhaps Siobhan didn't want to give her any more personal information than she needed to. She might have been worried that Lara would use it as ammunition somewhere down the line should she find herself in a less forgiving mood than the one she was currently in. Lara wouldn't do that, but again, she could see why Siobhan might be wary.

'I honestly don't know where to start,' Lara continued, taking the cue to leave that particular line of conversation. 'While I was driving over here I kept thinking about what to say and I couldn't figure it out. I still don't know. I don't even know why I've come, except that something just told me I needed to.'

'I'm sorry about what I said the other night,' Siobhan said. 'I know it was all rubbish and it was mean to repeat it to you.'

'I know you are. I'm sorry for what I said and did too.'

'You still think you were right, though.'

'I should have butted out, right or wrong. It's not my place to come here and tell you the things I told you.'

'No,' Siobhan sighed. 'I would have done the same if it had been the other way round. At least, I would have done once upon a time.'

When we were friends and the telling me wouldn't have involved you being with my boyfriend, Lara thought – though that much was obvious and didn't really need saying.

Siobhan scratched the length of her arm, still hugging herself. Lara recognised her all-too-familiar troubled look – she'd seen it enough over the years they'd been friends. 'What did Lucien say to you that night at the Emerald Lounge?'

'Siob, I was angry that night and I steamed over here without thinking it through. I don't think it's something we want to start again now… is it?'

'I want to know.'

Lara paused as she took in Siobhan's tired features. 'He was coming on to me – that's all. Just like I said the other night. But then, like you said, he does that. It's in his nature; it probably didn't mean anything.'

'I'd just told him I was pregnant. Before he went out I told him.'

Lara stared at her.

'I think he was a bit freaked out,' Siobhan continued. 'I think that's why he did what he did.'

Lara didn't believe that for a second; after all, it wasn't the first time Lucien had played that game. But she could see how desperately Siobhan wanted to believe it. What kind of person would that make Lara if she let her? But if she tried to persuade Siobhan otherwise, would this conversation end in exactly the same way it had the night she'd flown here from the Emerald Lounge?

'I confronted him about it,' Siobhan said. 'I asked him and he said you'd come on to him.'

'But that's—'

'A lie, I know – I'm not that green,' Siobhan cut in. 'Even I can see that much. I told him so too. And do you know what?'

Lara shook her head.

'He said he was sorry, and I actually think he meant it. We talked about the baby and I've never seen him so serious before. I think it actually did us good to acknowledge the way he is and tackle it for once instead of me always turning a blind eye. I told him that if he wanted to be a part of this baby's life then he had to clean up his act. And he promised me he'd change, Lara. He promised me he'd change for the baby. I want to believe him, and I think I do but… You know him; do you think he can? Do you think that's even possible?'

'I don't think I really knew him at all,' Lara said. 'I thought I did. I can't answer that question – only you can. And if you can't then you have no choice but to go with your gut.'

'My gut says he wants to, but that's not the same as being able to, is it?'

'Well,' Lara said slowly, 'maybe he'll surprise us both.'

Siobhan gave a small smile. 'You never know.'

'I don't think he would have even tried for me, so you're winning there.'

'I never wanted to win,' Siobhan said. 'You have to believe that I never wanted things to be like this.'

'I do,' Lara said and, as she said it, she realised it was the first time she'd actually believed it. Talking to Siobhan now, like this, almost like they used to be, she realised the truth of what her friend was telling her. They'd shared too much history for Siobhan to have wanted them to end up like this. 'I hate us being enemies.'

'We can't be friends – not now. Even if we tried really hard.'

'I know that too. We don't have to be at war though.'

'You were the one waging war; I was just here—'

'In my place—'

'And that's why we can't be friends,' Siobhan cut in. 'You're never really going to forgive me for what happened, even if you say you can. It will always be there, in the back of your mind.'

'I'm sorry – that came out wrong.' Lara sighed. 'You're probably right. It's going to take some effort but I think we could move past it eventually. As long as I don't have to see him.'

'You're suggesting we start socialising again?'

'No… of course not. But perhaps we could make it so things aren't so horrible and awkward every time we bump into each other somewhere. I'd like that and I hope you would too.'

'I never wanted that.'

'But you can understand why it happened, surely?'

Siobhan nodded. 'I've always regretted the way all this panned out. Not the being pregnant with Lucien's baby – I'm thrilled about that. But the things that it did to you – to us. You've always meant a lot to me.'

'I know. I feel the same way – you know I do.' Lara gave her a brief smile. 'In a way, I suppose I ought to thank you. I did complain quite a lot about him.'

'You did,' Siobhan said. 'If I'm honest, I find him quite high-maintenance too.'

'I think anyone would. But you're happy?'

'Yes.'

'I don't know, looking back now, that I could have honestly said that and meant it when I was with him. I thought I did but now I realise that I wasn't seeing it clearly. We were never really suited.'

'But you loved him?'

Lara paused. Had she ever loved Lucien? It had felt that way at the time, but now that she thought about it, she couldn't tell. Had she been swept along by the dream of the handsome, well-connected boyfriend? Had she mistaken those feelings of validation for love? Now that she really thought about it, perhaps she'd never been in love at all.

Her mind wandered to Theo, even though she hadn't asked it to. Had that been love? It had been complicated, messy, confusing, but at times utterly joyous… perhaps that meant it had been love, or at least the beginnings of it. As a woman of twenty-nine, it was frustrating to think that she was still so clueless in these things, but it seemed that she was.

She looked to see that Siobhan was waiting for an answer, an answer that Lara couldn't give because she didn't know it herself anymore.

'I certainly didn't love his parents,' she said instead, not knowing what else to offer.

'Nobody loves his parents,' Siobhan said with a sudden wry smile. 'Apart from Lucien, and even he has his moments of doubt.'

'They don't exactly make themselves loveable, do they?'

Siobhan gave an uncertain nod. Perhaps she was wondering whether this conversation was wise, but at the same time, perhaps she was finding it cathartic to share her feelings with the one other person who would understand. 'Did his mum used to do that thing to you when she'd look over your hair with a sort of sneering face?'

'And then in the next breath mention the salon she goes to and how amazing the stylists are there; as if to say that you need urgent help from her crack team.'

'Yes,' Siobhan said with more eagerness now, 'or tell you that such-and-such-a-body has had their hair done and it takes years off them – also to make out that your hair looks like shit?'

'Oh, and when you'd take your shoes off in the hallway she'd peer inside to see what the label was, and if they weren't Jimmy Choo or something ridiculously expensive she'd pull a face?'

'Oh God, yes!' Siobhan said.

'Always talking about other people's sons or daughters who are the same age as you but own half of Hong Kong or something because of their meteoric rise to the top?'

'She has so many ways to make you feel crap she ought to put them in a how-to guide,' Siobhan said with a genuine smile now that made Lara's heart soar. They might never be friends again like they once were, but she was glad to see that once they put all the bad feelings to one side, they could still communicate and they still had all the things in common that had once made them so close.

'His dad's no better.'

'He's almost worse!' Siobhan agreed fervently. She looked at Lara, her smile fading, replaced once more by that tired, slightly wary look. 'So this is closure, of sorts, isn't it? This isn't making up; it's only making peace?'

'I suppose, realistically, it is.'

'And what about you? Are you OK?' Siobhan hesitated. 'This thing you have going on with Chas's bandmate…'

'Theo?' Lara shook her head. 'It was never meant to be.'

'It's over?'

'Yes. And before you add "already", yes, that too. I'm proving to be quite careless when it comes to men – I keep losing them.'

Siobhan looked awkward. 'It wasn't because… well, because of what I said the other night? I mean, did you split over that? Because if you did then I feel just—'

'No,' Lara said. They had, but what was the point in making Siobhan suffer for it? And besides, perhaps once Lara had been given time to dissect just what her relationship with Theo had meant, she might find that even if Siobhan's comments hadn't finished it, something else would have done sooner rather than later. 'It wasn't. Tell me, though: do you know whether Theo said any of this stuff, or was it just Chas and Lucien?'

'I don't know. I only heard it from Lucien and he said it was the band, but I don't know if that means all of them or only some of them.'

Or even if Lucien was telling the truth, Lara added internally, aware that he got a peculiar kick out of causing mischief.

'I feel just terrible about that—' Siobhan began, but Lara stopped her.

'I had you backed into a corner – it would have taken a saint not to retaliate. It doesn't matter now. If people had been saying that stuff behind my back, especially if it had been my boyfriend, then better that I know, and better that I get rid of the boyfriend.'

Siobhan nodded slowly. Lara drew in a breath.

'I should go.'

'OK.'

Lara turned to the door.

'I'm glad you came,' Siobhan said. Lara turned to face her again.

'Me too. Take care of yourself, won't you?' She gave a last, brief smile before stepping out onto the street. She had a feeling that this might be the last time she set foot in Siobhan's house, but that was OK. If she never got the chance to speak to her again, that was OK too – not because she didn't want to or because she hated Siobhan that much, but because she felt as if, finally, she'd been able to close that chapter of her life in a way that would let her look back on it and remember the good times they'd shared instead of just seeing betrayal. She'd never forget it, of course, and she still found it hard to forgive, but at least she felt she could understand it, come to terms with it, not let it cast a cloud over her own life. That was, unless Lucien chose to cause more trouble. She could only hope that Siobhan was right, and that he would change. As for whether he was even capable of a change that monumental, only time would tell.

Chapter Twenty-One

It was lucky that the wedding Betsy was meant to be covering that day was a low-key affair. Well, as low-key as it was possible for a Roman-themed wedding to be. The couple were remarkably undemanding in all respects – apart from the fact that the groom had dressed as a centurion and the bride was robed in a diaphanous white toga complete with gold diadem. The service was to be conducted in the quite recently excavated amphitheatre paying homage to various Roman gods, where the guests were dressed as various members of Roman society, and where food such as fermented fish sauce and fire-baked apples was to be served to guests lying down on blankets. (This was how, Lara discovered from a very enthusiastic groom, the Romans would have eaten it.). They were more concerned with having fun than anything else, and Lara was as sure as she could be that if the odd mishap occurred, they'd probably just shrug it off and store it in their anecdotes of the day.

At least that was what she hoped, because Betsy had chosen this day to get her first bout of morning sickness.

'All the books say it's supposed to stop by now, not start,' her apprentice complained as Lara went with her to set up at the amphitheatre and run through once more everything she had to do before going. Lara didn't want to leave her to it, but she really didn't have a choice.

'Perhaps it's a one-off,' she said hopefully. 'Maybe it's just nerves about today. After all, it's your first solo run. Perhaps once it gets underway you'll relax a bit and feel better.'

'I hope so,' Betsy said, 'because, right now, if I see one of those fermented fish things I'll be chucking up all over the place.'

'Well, if you happen to be near the feasting then please avert your eyes.'

'My mum wanted to come with me to make sure I was OK.'

Lara smiled. 'Well, that would have been OK with me.'

'I didn't want her to. She'd be sticking her nose in all the time.'

'I'm sure she's just got your best interests at heart. I'm glad that the talk with them went OK and that they took it so well. It just goes to show, doesn't it?'

'What?'

'That sometimes when we're scared of doing something, there's really no need to be. It's usually not as bad as we fear.'

'Do you think that about your wedding later?' Betsy asked with a sly look. 'You'll have to see Theo, won't you?'

'Only on stage – probably not to talk to.'

'What if he wants to talk to you?'

'I'll be working so I won't have time,' Lara said briskly. She hadn't told her assistant about Theo's visit two nights ago and she wasn't about to. As far as Betsy was concerned, Lara hadn't seen Theo since they'd split up.

'What if he comes to you afterwards?'

'He's not going to come to me afterwards. I'll be busy then, anyway. Listen, have you got that list?'

Betsy held up her phone. 'It's on my notes.'

'And your phone's charged?'

She nodded.

Lara was thoughtful as she looked at her. 'I might get my mum to come down and see if you're alright once the service is over. You shouldn't need to get too involved in that, apart from making sure the board is up with the order of the day before it's over. You need to make sure the caterers know where to set up to hand out the champagne – or whatever that weird wine is they've chosen – for the toast and that they don't start uncorking the bottles until the registrar has pronounced Dave and Patricia man and wife. But make sure there's enough being poured so that everyone gets a drink as soon as they arrive at the table. That OK?'

'Yes, boss.'

'Then you need to make sure the speeches run on time. You've got the schedule for that?'

'Yes, boss.'

'There's going to be some Roman music or something while they eat and then that's it. Dave's taken care of that but you need to make sure it doesn't run over or they'll get charged extra for the use of the amphitheatre. So if you need to get a bit bossy and boot people out, Dave says you can.'

'OK,' Betsy said.

'You need to make sure the caterers take everything away with them afterwards,' Lara added. 'And check round for rubbish or damage once everyone is gone.'

'Yes, boss.'

'If there is anything, call me and tell me what it is and we'll figure out what to do.'

'I will.'

'You're sure you're going to be alright?'

'Yes,' Betsy said, though she didn't look all that sure.

'I'll call my mum. Would it make you feel better to have her around?'

'Yes…' Betsy began, 'as long as…'

'What?'

'Well, sometimes she makes things worse, doesn't she?'

Lara paused. She had to concede that Betsy had a point there. 'It'll just be moral support more than anything – I'll make sure she knows that you're in charge.'

'Oh, OK,' Betsy said, looking far happier at the prospect of being in charge. The fact was, she wasn't in charge of very much if it was just Fay, but Lara didn't say so. A little confidence boost never hurt anyone. 'Just don't let her carry any vases. Or talk to the wedding party. Or get on any ladders… It'll be just fine… On second thoughts, perhaps you'll be alright on your own after all.'

Betsy nodded, but then she clamped a hand to her mouth. 'I think I might be sick again…'

Lara watched as she rushed off for the nearest public toilets. With a sigh, she called her mum.

'Hello,' Fay said. 'I thought you were working today.'

'I am. Today's the day that we have that double booking. Betsy's supposed to be doing one and I'm doing the other. But today's the day that Betsy has also decided to be sick.'

'Oh, does that mean you don't have her?'

'She's here but I've seen her in better shape.'

'Poor thing.'

'I know. Listen, Mum, what are the chances of you coming down for a few hours to help her out? It wouldn't be much – just a bit of moral support and to keep an eye on her in case she really gets sick.'

'Well, I said I'd take some jumble down to St Dominic's…'

'Oh, well if you're busy it doesn't matter.'

'I suppose I could do it another day.'

'This wouldn't be all day here – I reckon you'd be done by around five. We have to be out of the venue by then anyway. I'd be ever so grateful; I am a bit nervous about leaving Betsy alone considering it's her first one and she's not at her best.'

'It might take me a while to get to the town centre – buses are terrible on Saturdays.'

'Don't worry,' Lara said, 'I'll come and pick you up now. We can be back before the service starts.'

When Lara arrived at her mother's house, she was amazed to discover that miracles did happen. Fay was ready and waiting outside on the pavement. Perhaps Lara could see it as a good omen – she'd have to consult one of the Roman gods at the amphitheatre before she went off to Fiona Wilson's wedding just to be sure.

'Thanks so much, Mum,' she said as Fay got into the car at the passenger side.

'That's alright,' Fay said. 'I can sort out my jumble another day.'

'What are you sending?'

'A few of my books and magazines.'

'Bloody hell!' Lara said as she pulled away from the kerb. 'Don't tell me you're actually letting some of those go!'

'I decided they were getting in the way. Sometimes you have to clear away a bit of clutter, don't you, even if you'd quite like to keep it.'

'If you need some help, let me know.'

'You're so busy I don't like to ask.'

'I know, but I'd make time for you.'

'You're a good daughter.'

'I try to be.'

'You know, I've been thinking about young Betsy all morning.'

'Have you?' Lara turned a corner and joined the main road. She slowed to a halt as a set of lights turned red and looked at her mum.

'Yes,' Fay said. 'And then do you know what happened?'

'What?'

'Mandy told me that she'd seen Siobhan. Did you know she's pregnant?'

Lara turned to face the road again as the lights went green. 'Yes,' she said quietly. 'Actually, I did.'

'I said she would be. Why else would that man marry her?'

Lara shrugged. She'd had a lot of time to think about all this and the last conversation she'd had with Siobhan, and she'd come to the most unlikely conclusion. For all his faults, for all his vanity, for all the games he liked to play, maybe Lucien did actually love Siobhan. Maybe they did have a future, and maybe their marriage would be a success, and maybe they'd be brilliant parents. Siobhan would make a fantastic mother – of that Lara was certain, even if she couldn't be certain of anything else. Siobhan's child would want for nothing and would be loved like no child was ever loved – at least by its mother. And maybe fatherhood would be the making of Lucien too. So far, there'd been no more mischievous texts from him trying to stir things up. That was either because he felt he'd done all the damage he'd set out to, or because he was genuinely trying to keep the promise he'd made to Siobhan to change his ways.

Lara allowed herself a rueful smile. Stranger things had happened. It meant one thing – in an odd way, Siobhan's pregnancy had also drawn an unexpected line under that episode of Lara's life. Siobhan and Lucien were about to be parents, and that changed everything. Perhaps it was why Siobhan had been so keen to make peace in the end. Now that they'd resolved things, Lara wished Siobhan well. It didn't change the circumstances of the betrayal, but it did mean that Lara was finally ready to put it behind her. She hoped for Siobhan's sake, for the sake of their baby, who was innocent of any wrongdoing, that Lucien would be the husband and dad they deserved.

Fiona arrived at the register office in a classic Rolls-Royce, while a large number of her guests were ferried in aboard vintage open-topped buses. She stepped out from her car looking regal and a little bit enormous. Not because she was in any way big, but because the skirt of her dress was full enough to take up a good four feet around her. It consisted of layer upon layer of white tulle, overlaid by a final layer that was embroidered by vibrant scarlet roses. It was finished with a boned scarlet and black bodice with a dramatic sweetheart neckline. Her dark hair was scraped into a huge bun and studded with red roses that matched those on her dress, and her make-up was equally striking.

In comparison, her husband-to-be, Connor, looked like a forlorn bank manager who'd found himself in the wrong place at the wrong time and now seemed to be getting unexpectedly married. His suit was charcoal grey and exceptionally ordinary, as were the suits of his ushers and best man. In contrast, Fiona's bridesmaids all wore dresses of white tulle that, for some, could be wedding dresses in their own right. It was only when they stood against Fiona that the difference was obvious.

Once the short service was done, Fiona wanted photos on the main street of Chester before they went on to the reception venue for the wedding breakfast. They began with her standing on the Rows in front of shoppers like some minor celebrity, then photos under the old clock that stood over the gates and greeted visitors to the city. And then she wanted photos in front of the many Tudor buildings that lined the main streets, and so everyone had to trail behind her as she went from place to place. And then she insisted that she needed some in front of the weathered old stone cross that marked where the market used to be. And then some in the Roman Gardens, and atop the city walls, and on the Victorian bandstand and by the river.

When Fiona suggested driving out to the zoo, the photographer had to draw the line, which was just as well because if she hadn't, Lara might have had to. A trip out to the zoo just to get photos – lovely as the old manor house that provided the zoo its grounds was – would have seriously upset the finely tuned schedule of the day. In fact, they were already running late for the sit-down meal. In the end, Fiona seemed content that she'd drawn quite a crowd everywhere she went.

So they'd gone on to one of the poshest hotels in the city centre for their reception. Lara went ahead in her own car, leaving everyone else to follow in the transportation that had been provided for them by the wedding couple. Many of the guests had already taken full advantage of the fact that they didn't need to drive and were well on their way to inebriation, helped by the fact that Fiona had taken so long having photos that some had been forced into the many bars and pubs that lined Chester's streets just to stave off the boredom while they waited for her.

Jazzy Chas and the Anglo-Sax-ons were already in the tiny car park at the back of the venue, unloading equipment from their van.

'Alright?' Chas called.

'Fine,' Lara said coldly. 'Everything alright here?'

'Yep. Don't worry; we'll all be on our best behaviour for you.'

Lara nodded. Chas showed no signs of knowing what the situation was between her and Theo, but she assumed that he did. She didn't know where the conflict that had split them had originated from – had Chas said the horrible things about her that Siobhan had repeated, or had they come from Lucien? She wanted to ask Chas, but if it had come from him she didn't want to give him the satisfaction of knowing they'd had such a devastating effect on her.

The next moment, Theo himself emerged from the back of the van. He looked at her silently, and she wondered whether he'd try to strike up some kind of conversation. But then he simply looked away again.

'Is there any chance the soundcheck can be done before the speeches begin?' Lara turned back to Chas. 'It wouldn't do to interrupt them with a load of noise.'

'We'll do our best,' Chas said. He looked as if he might say something else but then seemed to catch a warning look from Theo and immediately clamped his mouth shut again. Lara held back a frown. Had something gone on between them? Was it to do with her? Theo said nothing and continued inside with an amp he was carrying.

'If you could I'd appreciate it.' She had to keep reminding herself that she was here to work and she needed to focus. Getting into that kind of conversation right now wasn't professional and wasn't particularly helpful either.

Pushing the idea from her mind, she began to walk towards the hotel. Her gaze trailed over the exterior of the building. It was like so many – a relic of Chester's long history. It had been built around the sixteenth century, beautifully clad in hefty timber, but unlike the Tudor buildings that had been restored during the reign of Queen Victoria – painted the black and white that most people associated with Tudor architecture – this one had been restored to what would have been its

original browns and beiges. It had window boxes at every frame filled
with trailing lobelia and ivy, and heaving flowerbeds ran along the
outside walls, the smell of lavender, sage and rosemary filling the air,
busy with bees and butterflies.

Her attention was caught by a movement at one of the darkened
windows, and she turned to look. She found herself staring right at Theo.
He held her gaze for a second, before he moved away from the window and
was swallowed up by the interior of the building. Her heart was hammering,
as it had when she'd seen him at the van a few minutes before. She looked
cool and collected, but it was a pretence, and a moment's real inspection
by anyone would undo her. She'd thought, as she started to work that day,
that she'd be able to deal with this. She'd thought she could be professional about it and put her emotions to one side while she went about
her duties. She was beginning to think she'd been very much mistaken.

Lara stood in a dark corner of the room and watched the stage. Jazzy
Chas were into their third number and a lull in Lara's duties meant
that she found herself distracted by them. Actually, distracted by one
member in particular.

He looked good, she noted with some regret. The hands that had
travelled her body on so many nights now travelled up and down the
keys of his saxophone. The lips that had been pressed to hers were
now moulded around the mouthpiece. The eyes that had gazed into
hers now looked blankly out at the room. He was doing a good job of
looking like he cared about his performance, but then, wasn't he first
and foremost a showman? Lara could see the truth, and it made her
ache to go to him and tell him he was forgiven, that everything would
be alright. She saw that he was sorry for what had happened between

them, that he wished things could be different, because she recognised the look she'd seen in the mirror, of someone strangely incomplete where once they had been whole. She wondered…

Maybe she'd been too hasty in sending him away the night he'd come to make peace. Perhaps she'd reacted too quickly and too hotly. He'd got it wrong and he'd said it all wrong, but she thought now that perhaps his intentions had been sincere, even if he'd messed it up. He'd asked if the baby he'd thought she was carrying was his but perhaps that was a perfectly reasonable question given how long they'd actually been together. And perhaps it was an automatic first question that might come from the lips of any man. When he'd heard that Lara was pregnant, he could have run from that knowledge, he could have put his fingers in his ears and hummed to drown it out, he could have avoided coming to her and tried to evade his responsibility, but he hadn't. He'd come to talk to her about it and he'd wanted to be involved – though she was sure the news would have been a shock had it been true. He would have stuck by her, and that said a lot about the man he was.

The song was winding down, and Lara caught another strange look pass between Chas and Theo as they played the final notes. She'd always known them to be on amiable terms, but she couldn't see any of that now. What she saw now was distrust. She watched as Chas gave a curt nod at Theo and then pointed to something on a sheet of paper that Lara had to presume was the running order of the numbers they'd planned to play. Theo returned the nod with one just as short and began to play the opening bars of the next song.

'There you are!'

Lara turned, shaken from her musings, to see Mrs Wilson, Fiona's mum, glaring at her.

'Have you tasted these blinis?' she asked. 'They're foul; we can't have these out.'

'No, I haven't,' Lara said, tempted to add that it wasn't her usual habit to go around stuffing handfuls of food from her clients' buffets into her mouth and, if she did, she was certain that Mrs Wilson, for one, wouldn't be happy about it. 'What's wrong with them?'

'They're soggy. The salmon is too wet – any fool can see that.'

'Nobody seems to be complaining. In fact, I've heard people saying the food is lovely.' Lara was doing her best with her customer-service face, but the way she was feeling she feared it was going to fail her today for the first time.

'Well, I don't think it's lovely,' Mrs Wilson said. 'I want a refund.'

'For the whole thing?' Lara asked. 'I don't think—'

'The whole thing is below par. If M&S had sent this out in an order I would have sent it straight back to the store.'

'If you're unhappy with it, don't you think the caterers need to be told before anything else is done?'

'Yes, I do.' Mrs Wilson looked expectantly at Lara.

'Ah, I see,' Lara said. 'You want me to talk to them.'

'That's what I'm paying you for.'

'Right. Well, I'll have a word.'

But I'm not asking for a refund, she added internally. Tightwad.

'While you're at it, get someone to open the windows; it's like an oven in here. Don't they know it's summer? Someone will faint.'

'Right.'

'And the dance floor is slippery. I don't know if it's sweat from everyone being so hot, or polish. I've a good mind to sue the venue either way because I nearly lost my footing a moment ago.'

'I'm not sure what can be done at this stage considering the dance floor is full of people right now.'

'Well, if a guest breaks their ankle, it's you I'll be sending them to.'

Lara said nothing, but for the first time since she'd set up Songbird Wedding Services she was beginning to wish she'd chosen something else to offer services for, something that didn't turn people into raging psychotic blini haters.

'I'll leave it with you,' Mrs Wilson concluded, puffing out her chest and marching off, the fuchsia feather fascinator on her head trembling madly like a psychedelic twig in a storm.

Lara sighed. With a last glance at the stage, where her gaze once again found the empty stare of Theo and made her feel more wretched than ever, she went to find the catering manager.

She'd barely reached the kitchens when she was stopped by Fiona.

'Has my mum seen you?'

'Yes. I'm just trying to find someone to sort it all.'

'Have you tried the blinis?'

'No,' Lara said again, tempted once again to verbalise the sarcastic comments she'd held back from Mrs Wilson.

'Honestly I was nearly sick. I've never tasted anything so disgusting – they're like eating slime. And the chicken wings aren't much better. We're not going to pay for this food, you know. We want a refund – you can tell the catering people that.'

'Your mum said that but I don't know what—'

'And my mum nearly broke her neck on the floor over there. I'm sure they polished it with chip fat this morning. And the hand dryer isn't working in the ladies' toilet. Honestly, this venue is shocking and

I've got a good mind to tell them so. We could get some money back for all this, couldn't we?'

'Oh, I really don't think—'

'Oh, I need to go and warn my cousin before he eats the salmon!' Fiona cried, cutting Lara off and rushing back towards the buffet, almost taking out a small child with her enormous skirts as she passed him.

I need a pair of ruby slippers, Lara thought bleakly. *Three clicks and I could be home, curled up on the sofa with my little Fluffy.*

Having set her phone on vibrate so, while the room was noisy, she'd know if someone was calling, she felt it go in her blazer pocket now. Taking it out she saw Betsy's name flash up and rushed out of the function room to find a quiet spot to talk to her.

'I knew you'd be worrying,' Betsy said. 'So I thought I'd call and let you know that everything was OK at our wedding today.'

With all that was going on here, Lara had almost forgotten that Songbird Wedding Services had other clients today.

'That's good,' she said. 'So they were happy?'

'Very happy. They said they'd tell everyone how good we are.'

'That's one less thing to worry about then.'

'How's it there?'

'Awful.'

'Oh, no! Do you want me to come down?'

'No, I can manage,' Lara said. 'I'll tell you all about it on Monday. You need to take it easy. You were alright today – not too ill?'

'No,' Betsy said. 'I mean, I was a little this morning but it passed. Your mum was worse than me.'

'Mum? She hasn't called me to say she's been ill! Is she OK? What was it?'

'Oh, I think she's OK now.' Betsy laughed. 'She tried the fish sauce and it made her sick. She was alright after it had come up.'

'She tried the fish sauce?' Lara asked. 'That fermented stuff?'

'We both did. I was asking someone whether the food was nice and Patricia heard me and got us both a plate. Your mum thought it was so cool lying down and pretending to be Roman and she looked so funny. Do you know, Patricia is so lovely – I wish she'd get married every week.'

Lara wasn't entirely comfortable with how familiar Betsy and Fay had apparently got with the guests at the wedding they were meant to be working at and, if it had been anyone else, she might have felt very uncomfortable. But she had a feeling that Dave and Patricia would have loved introducing Betsy and Fay to their Roman cuisine and might even have been a little offended had their offer of food been refused. She certainly couldn't imagine them complaining.

'So, how was it?' she asked.

'I actually thought most of it was quite nice. It was just shrimps and octopus and stuff. Patricia gave us some dormouse, and your mum looked like she'd faint, but then Patricia said they hadn't actually used real dormice; they'd just cooked some chicken or pork or something and were pretending it was dormouse because apparently it's quite hard to get hold of. So that was OK. It was nice.'

Lara had to laugh at this. Her own evening might be one she'd want to forget very quickly, but at least Betsy and Fay had enjoyed their day. Apart from the bits when they were being sick, at least.

'And Mum managed not to break anything?'

'Yes. Honestly, I was really glad to have her there in the end. I felt better – not so nervous. Is yours really horrible then? Is it because you have to see Theo there?'

'I wouldn't mind so much if it was just that, but I've had nothing but complaints. And they do whatever they like – hang the schedule. It's a complete nightmare.'

'I bet you wish you'd done my one now.'

'God no! Imagine you being here alone with this lot for your first wedding! I'm sorry I missed Dave and Patricia's – it sounds like it was lovely – but it's far better that you worked that one and I did this. Don't worry about me – it's nothing I can't handle here; I'm probably just being a grump about it all really.'

'I suppose you might not be feeling quite so stressed if you didn't have Theo's band playing there.'

'Probably,' Lara agreed. There was no point in denying that. 'But I have to put work before my feelings on the matter. Hopefully it will be some time before I have to deal with them again – if ever – and I might be a bit stronger by then.'

'Oh, Lara,' Betsy said. 'Oh, it's such a shame about you two.'

Lara gave a wry smile, her eyes on a spot on the opposite wall. 'There's no need to feel sorry for me – you've got enough of your own going on.'

'Oh, that's alright,' Betsy replied. 'Mum's been lovely since I got home today. She's running me a bath now. And she went out to buy folic-acid tablets for me this afternoon.'

'And you were so worried about telling her!'

'I know, though she did say she's not happy about being a granny because she doesn't even have any grey hair yet. She said she's not going to give up her gin club just to babysit for me.'

'She's not too upset that I went to the scan with you instead of her?'

'I think maybe a little bit, but she hasn't said. I've told her there's always the next one, and then we'll get to find out the baby's sex together.'

'That's probably a better one. You'll be able to see things more clearly at that one too.' From the corner of her eye, Lara saw Mrs Wilson making a beeline for her. 'Have to go… Speak to you Monday!'

If Betsy replied, Lara didn't get to hear it. She ended the call and stuffed the phone back into her blazer pocket.

'My mother-in-law has just found a hair in her apple-roasted pork bap!' Mrs Wilson huffed. 'What do you think about that!'

'Did you keep hold of it?'

'Keep hold of it?' Mrs Wilson cried, eyes bulging. 'What on earth for?'

'So we can show the caterers.'

'We most certainly did not! Surely our word is good enough – we're not liars! What did the catering manager say about all the other things?'

'I haven't spoken to him yet.'

'Not spoken to him yet? What have you been doing?'

'Looking for him,' Lara said, which was half-true, although she'd spent the last few minutes talking to Betsy. She was feeling belligerent about the whole thing, though, because Mrs Wilson and her picky daughter were really beginning to wind her up. 'As soon as I find him I'll add the hair to the list of complaints.'

Along with a request to add some arsenic to your bloody salmon blinis, you cantankerous old bag!

The catering manager had been sympathetic to the complaints Lara had relayed to him and perhaps understood that she was repeating gripes that she didn't necessarily think were all that big a deal. They went to the buffet to fetch some of the offending articles to inspect, and both thought that they tasted fine. Lara had a suspicion that the Wilsons were just trying to save some money on their bill, and she thought that perhaps the catering manager felt that too, but both were too professional to say so out loud. Instead, he offered to remove the blinis that the bride had been unhappy with and put some new ones out because that wouldn't take him too long to do. The chicken was a bit more of a problem because he didn't have enough left over to replace it. As for the hair, he couldn't do anything about that because he hadn't seen it and so couldn't comment on where it might have come from. All his staff wore hair nets, he said, and left it at that.

Lara thanked him and turned her attention to the other issues Fiona and her mother had flagged up. But what she was supposed to do about most of them she had no clue. She found someone who would open the windows for her, but that was the easiest bit. Then she went into the function room again and weaved in and out of the crowds on the dance floor, trying to get an idea of where the floor was slippery, but if there was a dangerous patch, she couldn't find it. All the while she was conscious of Theo's eyes on her; she didn't even have to look up at the stage to know, because she felt it, as if there was a psychic link between them.

She'd given up on the greasy floor as Chas announced their last song to a disappointed groan from the audience. The evening would continue through to midnight with a disco, he said, but it didn't seem to make anyone happier. Once again, it seemed that they'd proved very popular and had got many of the wedding guests on their feet. The audience might not have been happy but Lara was, because it meant that Jazzy Chas and the Anglo-Sax-ons would pack up and leave and she could get on with her work without feeling Theo's eyes on her wherever she went.

Without meaning it to be, she felt her gaze drawn up to the stage again where it settled on Theo. Maybe she'd been staring at him as much as she felt he'd been staring at her. Perhaps neither of them could help it.

As she watched, she saw Chas walk across the stage to him and say something in his ear, and then Theo whirled around looking furious, before one of the other band members came up behind both of them and settled a hand on each man's shoulder, as if to cool heated tempers down. Lara knew she was staring as she watched the subtle drama unfold but she couldn't help it. What was going on with those two? It was likely that nobody else in the room would have noticed anything untoward because they didn't know the men – or at least one of them – like she did, but Lara could see otherwise.

Suddenly, she was grabbed by the arm and whirled round, finding herself face to face with a tiny old man.

'Care for a dance, young lady?' he asked.

'Oh, I'm sorry, I can't…'

'Oh, come on! It's the last song! Don't be a stick in the mud!'

'You don't understand; I'm not actually a guest—'

'What are you doing here then?' he asked. Then he laughed and tapped his nose. 'Gatecrashing, eh? Heard the party and thought you'd come and have a look? Don't blame you! Have a dance with me and I won't tell anyone!'

'No, I'm…'

Lara tried to shake her arm free, but his drunken grip was tighter than he looked capable of. As she gave it another, rather fiercer shake, sorely tempted to give him a piece of her mind, she saw a couple close by turn to look in the direction of the entrance to the function room. Then one of them tapped the person next to them and pointed, and they tapped someone else who turned to look too. Lara felt the grip of the old man slacken and, when she glanced at him, she saw that he'd noticed something at the doors as well. She followed his gaze and saw that there was some kind of altercation going on. She looked closer, trying to work out what was happening and who was involved, suddenly going cold at the thought that it might be Mrs Wilson shouting down some poor staff member.

Fiona's mother was at the centre of it alright, and that was no huge surprise given how the day had gone so far. What was far more surprising was the person arguing with her. Lara stared, straining to confirm the improbable scenario that her eyes were telling her she was seeing, because it just seemed so unlikely.

Pulling her arm free, she made her way over, pushing through oblivious guests. As she drew closer she could hear their argument, even over the music.

'You don't understand – this is an emergency!'

'You're not coming in!' Mrs Wilson shouted.

'But I need to see her!'

'Absolutely not!' an outraged Mrs Wilson retorted.

'Could you get her for me if you won't let me in?'

Lara hesitated and hung back for a moment. She was already unpopular with the Wilson women and getting involved here might make it worse. But Lara was mad with curiosity and actually quite concerned.

'I don't pay her to stand around chatting! Contact her in her time, not mine!'

Lara suddenly realised that she might be the person they were talking about. She stepped forward.

'Selina?' she said, frowning. She couldn't imagine what business Selina had at this wedding. Did she have some connection to the bride or groom? Clearly not to Mrs Wilson, who looked as if she wanted to have her arrested. But what other reason could she have for being there?

'Oh, Lara!' Selina cried, looking almost faint with relief to see her. 'I've been looking all over for you!'

'Me?'

'And then I remembered that Theo had said he was playing here for you tonight, and I hoped you'd still be here because I just didn't know what I was going to do if you weren't—'

'Selina, what's wrong?'

Mrs Wilson's voice boomed over the exchange. 'I simply won't allow this business to be conducted here!' She glared between the two of them, daring an argument.

'But if you could just let Selina tell me what it is she's—'

'No! No, no, no!'

Selina glared at Mrs Wilson now. But then she turned to Lara and her defiant expression became one of sudden misery.

'I'm so sorry, but I've hit your cat!'

Lara's eyes widened. Surely she hadn't just heard that right?

'He ran out into the road and I couldn't stop. I've been all over looking for you!'

'Where is he?' Lara asked, her legs feeling suddenly weak.

'I took him straight to the emergency vets; I didn't know what else to do. I'll pay the fees, of course. I feel just terrible – I'm so sorry.'

'When was this?'

'About two hours ago – I'd just finished my shift. They're going to do emergency surgery. I had to give them consent – I hope that's OK. I said I'd come to find you.'

'Which vets?'

'The one near the leisure centre.' Selina looked close to tears. 'I'm really sorry, Lara.'

Lara turned to Mrs Wilson. 'I've got to go.'

'Absolutely not!' Mrs Wilson barked. 'What about the wedding?'

'I'm not asking your permission,' Lara said. 'I'm telling you I'm going.'

'But…'

'The night's almost over – surely you can spare me now?'

'The gifts!' she boomed. 'The clearing up! The settling of bills!'

'Could you have a word with the hotel manager?'

'I could not!' Mrs Wilson cried, her chest heaving and staring at Lara as if Lara had just offered to sign her death warrant. 'What am I paying you to do?'

'I'm sorry but this is an emergency. I wouldn't be going if it wasn't important.'

'It's only a cat!'

When Lara spoke again there was steel in her voice.

'Not to me.'

'If you go I won't pay you!'

'Fine. Don't pay me.' Lara turned to go.

'I'll ruin your business!'

'So be it,' Lara called back as she hurried away, leaving both Selina and Mrs Wilson to watch her go. 'If I have to choose, I'll choose my cat every time!'

Lara raced to her car. She'd always used a different vet for Fluffy, but she knew where the one Selina had taken him to was. She was tense but she tried to stay calm. There was no point in panicking until she got there and heard for herself what she was dealing with. But still, in the back of her mind was a treasonous little voice full of fear.

What if the news was the very worst? She couldn't bear to lose her beloved Fluffy, not on top of everything else.

Chapter Twenty-Two

The waiting room had pastel-coloured sofas and bright cushions with cartoon pictures of cats and dogs on them, and it looked as if the owners had at least tried to make it welcoming. But no matter how cheerful it was, no amount of cute, colourful décor was going to make Lara feel anything other than miserable. They might have tried to pretend that it was a warm, happy place, but the floor was a heavy-duty vinyl and the walls were covered in a shiny, washable paint and the smell of disinfectant hung in the air. To Lara it said sick animals.

She sat on one of the pastel sofas now, leaning forward, tense, the only person waiting. She'd arrived during the out-of-hours surgery time and so she'd had to buzz for access. There had been no receptionist on duty, and a nurse had shown her in and then disappeared into a side room. All around was profound silence, apart from the faint buzzing of the strip lights and the occasional slam of a distant door. She'd wanted to call her mum, but it was late and Fay would probably be in bed by now. Despite this, it was tempting, if only so she didn't have to sit here alone and stew over all the worst outcomes.

She hadn't been able to speak to the vet on duty, who was still with Fluffy. The nurse had said he was trying to stabilise him and get a full picture of his injuries. They knew for certain that one of his back legs was broken. There were also rib fractures and one of the broken ribs had damaged his lung. They suspected additional internal bleeding but were assessing that now. It didn't sound good, especially when the nurse asked if, rather than trying to save him and bearing in mind that if he recovered he might never be the same cat again, did she want him put to sleep? The bill was going to be big, the nurse said, possibly in the thousands. Selina had apparently told the nurse she'd pay it, but even if Lara had been forced to find the money herself then she would have.

Still, she'd been torn between her selfish desire to save him because she loved him so much and guilt that by doing so she was subjecting him to a life of pain from his injuries. She asked the nurse if it would be kinder to let him go rather than save him, but the nurse wouldn't give an opinion either way. In the end, Lara had decided to go with the treatment, heartened slightly by the suggestion that what she was being told about his prognosis could well be the worst-case scenario. Things might not actually turn out to be anywhere near as bad.

It hadn't been all that hot over the past couple of days, but someone had switched on the air conditioning, perhaps thinking to make Lara comfortable. She shivered under the vents now and wished she had something thicker to wear than her blazer.

She wondered what was happening at Fiona's wedding, but she couldn't let it worry her. She'd made the decision to be here and she'd just have to try and smooth it out with the Wilsons if she could on Monday, though she didn't see that going well. More likely she'd have to forfeit her fee, but it was what it was, and if it made their appraisal of her services a little kinder for having them for free, then it was a small price to pay. Perhaps it might even salvage the damage she'd done by walking out on them tonight, though truthfully, if it had been a choice between possibly losing her business or not coming here tonight, she would always have chosen to come. Songbird Wedding Services was a hugely important part of her life, but nobody could know what Fluffy meant to her, and nobody could hope to understand. It didn't matter. Let people say she was foolish, let people say he was only a cat – she didn't care what they thought.

She'd spent perhaps twenty minutes with these thoughts when the intercom behind the reception desk buzzed. The nurse who'd seen Lara in appeared from the side door again and spoke into it.

'Hello? Can I help?'

'It's Selina Marquez,' came the reply. 'I brought a cat in earlier and I wondered if I could come and see how things are.'

Lara had never been so glad to hear a friendly voice.

'Just a minute,' the nurse said, and then she pushed a button. There was a loud click and then Selina came in. Lara looked up with a tense smile, ready to thank her for coming and to reassure her that she placed no blame upon her, when her attention was drawn to a second figure, hands deep in his pockets, coming in behind her.

'Theo?'

'Selina told me what happened and she said she could give me a lift down here. I know he's not my cat anymore but…'

'He's always been every bit as much your cat as mine,' Lara said. 'We were kidding nobody but ourselves there.'

He nodded. 'I guess you're right.'

'What about the gig?'

'We were just about finished anyway.'

'Yes, but what about… well, didn't you need to pack up and stuff?'

He gave an evasive shrug and Lara wondered if there was something he wasn't telling her, something to do with what she'd seen pass between him and Chas earlier, but he didn't volunteer any information.

'So you're OK with me coming?' he asked instead.

'I'm glad you care enough to come,' Lara said. She meant it too, because she realised just what it would have taken for him to be here now after all that had happened between them. It meant a lot to her.

Selina dropped into a seat next to Lara. She looked as if she'd been crying. Theo kept his distance, taking a seat on a nearby sofa.

'Is he going to be alright?' Selina asked.

'I don't know yet,' Lara said. 'It's still too early to tell. They told me he has a lot of complex injuries.'

'Oh, God,' Selina said. 'I can't tell you how bad I feel about this—'

'Don't,' Lara said. 'You'd warned me about this before – if it's anyone's fault it's mine.'

'I don't see how it's either of your fault,' Theo said. 'You can't tell a cat where to walk, and you can't stop him from running in front of a car when you're not there. For that matter, you wouldn't be able to stop him from running in front of a car even if you were.'

'I was probably driving too fast,' Selina said. 'It was dark and I didn't see him until it was too late.'

'I doubt that either,' Theo said. 'If you'd been driving too fast, there'd be no surgery that could save him. Don't keep beating yourself up over this – there was nothing you could have done. He ran out in front of you and you did your best to stop. You brought him here straight away. You did everything you could.'

'He's right,' Lara said, forcing an encouraging smile for Selina. 'You can't blame yourself.'

Selina sniffed, and though she was still clearly upset, she seemed to relax a little.

'You should go home,' Theo said to her. 'You've done a long shift at work and then you've been driving all over the place because of this.

You must be worn out, and if you're not sensible about it you'll end up having an accident that hurts you as well.'

'I'm alright,' Selina said.

'There's no point in all three of us sitting here all night,' Lara said. 'Theo's right about that too. Why don't you go? I'll phone you as soon as I have news, I promise.'

Selina looked as if she might argue, but then she seemed to make a decision.

'You're probably right,' she said. 'I'll be a danger on the roads if I stay awake much longer. I'll go.'

She got up, and Lara rose too and pulled her into a hug.

'Don't feel bad,' she said. 'It's going to be fine.'

'Give me your mobile number,' Selina said. 'I'll phone first thing to see if you know any more.'

Lara pulled out her phone and they exchanged numbers. 'It's probably about time,' Lara said. 'We've been chatting for months and never done this.'

'Now I'll always know where to find you,' Selina said. 'That's if you're still speaking to me after this.'

'Of course I will be. Go home; get some sleep. I'll talk to you tomorrow.'

With a last hug, Selina left. Lara sat down again with a heavy sigh. She looked up at Theo.

'Can I ask what was going on with you and Chas tonight?'

'What?'

'Come on, I need something to distract me. I could drive myself mad worrying about Fluffy but there's nothing I can do except wait. You can tell me while I do.'

'You don't want to know.'

'I do.'

'Right…' he said slowly. 'I'm leaving the band.'

Lara blinked. 'But you love that band!'

'I did. Not anymore.'

'What's changed?'

He shrugged. 'I just realised that it wasn't a healthy place for me to be. Chas… well, he can be an arse at times. We had a falling-out, earlier this evening, and it all just came to a head. I was thinking I might start a band of my own. One with a less stupid name.'

Lara had to smile, despite everything else that was going on around her. But it faded as quickly as it had come.

'At the risk of sounding arrogant, I hope this decision wasn't anything to do with me.'

'Maybe. I'm not expecting you to do anything about it though.'

'What did he do?'

'It wasn't so much what he did, but what he didn't do. He couldn't keep his mouth shut.'

'About what? Us?'

Theo nodded. 'I'll admit that I told him about us spending the night together that first time. Not details, of course, but that it had happened. It was just mate to mate; I didn't think it would go any further. But then Lucien had told him things about you, and he told Lucien what I'd told him about us spending the night together, and somehow it all blew up from there. He didn't say any of it to me, though – the first time I heard of it was when you told me.'

'Why didn't you say then that it hadn't come from you?'

'Would you have believed me?'

'Of course I would. I just wanted to hear it.'

Theo shook his head. 'I'm not so sure. I was angry with you anyway because I thought you'd gone with Lucien and that just made things worse. I guess both of us could have handled things better.'

'I suppose so,' Lara said. 'We can't change it now.'

They were silent for a moment, and the slam of a door somewhere in the building brought Lara back. She looked at him, eyes misting as she thought of Fluffy, even now under the vet's knife.

'Are you really OK?' Theo asked. 'You put on a good show for Selina there but I know you better.'

She shook her head, sniffing away her tears. 'Honestly? I could do with a cuddle.'

Pointing a finger at himself, he raised a questioning eyebrow and she gave him a watery smile.

'Why not? There's nobody else here to do the job.'

He moved to sit next to her and wrapped an arm around her, pulling her close. She closed her eyes, silent in his embrace, and let herself drift. Selina wasn't the only one who was tired – it had been a long day for her too. In fact, it had been a long week. A very long and lonely week.

As she sat, wrapped in Theo's arms, she realised just how right it felt. Did she really care about all that other stuff? Did she care about the petty things that would keep them apart? Was it all worth giving this up for?

They stayed like that, the strip light buzzing and a door slamming occasionally in a distant corridor, and Lara was content to feel him against her, to smell him, to feel comforted by his presence. In their brief time together, their relationship had always been so physical and his body had meant something different to her than it did now. Right now, it felt like an anchor, something to hold on to that would steady her. Right now, it felt like home.

He stroked a hand along the length of her hair and she lost herself a little further in him. His gentle breaths sounded like everything there was and his touch felt like the only sensations she'd ever want to feel again.

'You'll stay with me?' she asked.

'Of course.'

'Thank you.'

'He's going to be OK, you know.'

'How can you sound so certain?'

'One of us has to be.'

'You didn't talk to the nurse earlier. I want to be positive but it all sounded so hopeless. She asked if I wanted him put to sleep.'

Lara felt Theo's breath catch briefly before he spoke again. 'I take it you said no to that,' he asked in an even tone, suggesting a calmness that Lara didn't buy for a moment.

'I did,' she said, but she had to wonder whether, if she'd given the nurse a different answer, he would have been angry. He'd once told Lara that she could keep Fluffy as her cat alone, but did he really feel that way?

'I'm sorry,' she said. 'I should have asked you first.'

'I don't suppose there was time. If it had been the other way around I hope you would have supported the decision I made for him. I'm glad you didn't have him put down, though.'

'We might still have to if things don't go well tonight. We have to consider that.'

'We will. But I hope it will be OK if we consider it together. I know what I said about him not being my cat but—'

'Absolutely,' Lara said. 'If I'm honest I think I'd appreciate the support. I'm terrified that I won't do the right thing by him, but at least if there are two of us making the decisions we might stand a chance of getting it right.'

He pulled her closer, and that was all she needed to know that he felt the same way.

The side door opened, and Lara looked up at the clock to see that an hour had passed since Selina had left. She and Theo had spent it silently together. There were things they needed to talk about but Lara had been content that they didn't need to do that yet. She'd simply been grateful and comforted by the fact that he was there. As the nurse came into the waiting room, Lara sat up and stretched, suddenly taut and expectant. The nurse gave them a brisk smile.

'We've done as much as we can do for the moment.'

'And?' Lara asked.

'Time will tell. He's stable and we think he'll pull through, but there are no certainties at this stage.'

Lara allowed herself a deep sigh of relief, her shoulders slumping from sheer exhaustion.

'Perhaps you want to go home,' the nurse said. 'There's nothing more happening here tonight. We'll be open at eight in the morning – you can call then for an update.'

'You might as well,' Theo said. 'This is not a place you want to sit all night and you must be tired.'

'You too,' Lara said, looking at him.

'A bit. I've survived worse.'

'Alright,' Lara said. She got up, feeling stiff and cold, but less tense now.

'We'll be in touch if anything changes overnight,' the nurse said. 'Otherwise phone us in the morning.'

*

'Thanks for the lift home,' Theo said as they stood outside his house. The sky was heavy with rapidly moving clouds, though the night was mild and dry.

'I wasn't going to leave you standing there in the vet's car park when you'd gone to the trouble to come and sit with us.'

'I know, but still... I wouldn't have blamed you if you had.'

'Even I can't stay that angry at anyone.'

He looked at her, his face illuminated at one side by the glow of a street lamp, his eyes dark and warm. 'I'm sorry you were angry. I deserved it but I didn't mean to upset you. I said and did stupid things and I realise that now.'

'I know.'

'I was... well, I thought a lot of you.'

'I thought a lot of you too.'

'I guess this isn't the time to talk about that, eh? Are you worried?'

'About Fluffy?' Lara asked. 'Yes. I'm trying to be encouraged by what the nurse said to us, though. I don't think she really would have sent us away if she thought he wasn't going to make it.'

'That's a good way to look at it.'

'Perhaps luck will be on our side. We can only hope.'

'He's a tough cookie. I have a good feeling that he'll be OK.'

'You do? I wish I could be as optimistic. But everything else seems to be turning to shit these days so I can't help but feel there's a trend emerging here.'

He gave a rueful smile. 'I can't help feeling that might be my fault too.'

'It's not all about you, you know.'

'Maybe some of it's about me?'

Lara couldn't help a tired smile of her own. 'Maybe some of it. Don't let it go to your head, though.'

He turned towards his house, but then turned back to her. 'You'll be alright? On your own tonight?'

'Do you have an alternative?'

He shrugged. 'You could come in and stay with me. We wouldn't have to do… As friends, that's all I mean. As one friend supporting another. You don't have to spend the night worrying alone. You could spend the night worrying with me.'

'It wouldn't be us getting back together.'

'Perish the thought.'

'This is only because Fluffy is our cat.'

'Obviously.'

Lara looked towards the house. She sighed. This was a terrible idea. This was possibly the worst idea she'd ever had. They could make as many promises as they wanted to the contrary, but if she went inside with him now it would all start up again and where would that lead them?

But then she looked back up at him, dark eyes full of promises, of memories of better times, and she knew that she didn't want to be alone.

'I'd like that,' she said. His hand closed around hers. She should have slipped hers free, shaken him off, but she didn't. It felt too good, too right for that. It felt like comfort and friendship and, if there was nothing else on offer, God knew she needed some of that right now.

'Come on,' he said, leading her to the door. 'I'll fix us a drink.'

Chapter Twenty-Three

Lara turned up the dial on the oil-fired radiator and sat back at her desk. The office of Songbird Wedding Services was well equipped to deal with cold weather but a particularly bitter late-winter snap had tested her facilities to the limits. She looked up as the door opened, bringing a blast of icy air into the room.

'Ugh! Shut the door!'

'Sorry, boss.'

The door slammed shut. Lara grinned and took the mug that was being offered.

'Maybe you should start making your drinks in here rather than trekking to the kitchen in the main house every time you want to brew up.'

'Maybe you should know your place and stop having opinions on how I run my office,' Lara said with a fake scowl. 'You can be replaced, you know.'

'I thought I *was* being replaced. Just as soon as Betsy comes back. That's no threat at all, is it?'

Lara's grin spread. She rolled up the case from a fairy cake and threw it at the occupant of the other desk.

'Oi! What was that for?'

'I felt like it.'

'Seems a bit harsh!'

'You'll have to clean it up now.'

'What?'

'Well, you forced me to throw it so technically it's your mess.'

'My God, you're an absolute nightmare to work for; so unreasonable! Thank God Betsy is due back this week! I don't know how she puts up with you but she must be some kind of saint!'

'I'm not *that* bad, surely?' Lara teased. 'I mean, there must be some perks to working with me…'

'Well, I suppose the lunch breaks are pretty good.'

'Pretty? Is that the best you can do? Surely the lunch breaks are like little pockets of heaven on earth?'

'Well…'

Lara put her coffee down and walked slowly to the other desk. She leaned over it. 'Is it lunchtime yet?' she whispered.

'It's ten thirty.'

'Close enough,' she said, leaning in closer. 'Do you want your lunchtime treat now?'

Theo grinned. 'Well, I do think I deserve a medal for helping you out over the past few months. But as there are no medals on offer, I guess I could settle for that.'

She pulled him into a fiery kiss.

'We're not getting much work done,' he said as she let go.

'So tell the boss,' Lara said.

'I am telling the boss. She's not taking much notice.'

'Hmm. The boss has decided she doesn't care.'

She kissed him again. And then the office phone rang.

Theo gazed dreamily at her as she left his desk and went to answer it.

'Betsy!' she said, grinning at Theo. 'We've just been talking about you!'

'No we weren't,' Theo mouthed, but Lara just threw another ball of paper at him.

'Seriously?' Lara squeaked. 'That's so exciting! Hang on, I'm coming to open the gate now!'

Lara leapt up, grabbing her keys from the desk drawer. 'Betsy's here with the baby!'

Without waiting for Theo's reply, she rushed out. The garden was icy, the shrubs dusted in sugary frost, and if she'd been less excited she'd have taken more care on the path. As it was, her footing went suddenly and, with a squeal, she landed on her back, looking up at the sky. As she pushed herself up to sit, Theo appeared in front of her.

'Are you OK?'

'I'm fine,' Lara said with a sheepish grin. 'Just clumsy.'

'I can't leave you for a minute. Have I got to start carrying you everywhere now?'

'It couldn't hurt,' Lara said with a coquettish look that made him chuckle as he helped her to her feet.

'Give me the keys,' he said. 'I'll get the gate while you go back to the office. It's safer all round that way.'

Lara almost began an argument. Old habits die hard and she was used to doing everything herself, unable to let even the smallest task go. But then she remembered the progress she'd been making in that regard, and the promise she'd made to let Betsy have a lot more responsibility once she was back at work, and she relented. She held up the keys for him.

'Thanks.'

A minute later, she was rubbing her backside, trying to dry her wet trousers in front of the heater when Theo came back with Betsy and her baby. She raised an eyebrow when they were followed in by a young man, though her surprise didn't stop her from running to Betsy to get a look at the bundle she carried in a papoose.

'Oh, he's growing so fast!' she cooed. 'And getting more gorgeous every day!'

'He smiles all the time,' Betsy said. 'Even in his sleep. And he's rolling now – I have to watch all the time because the minute you turn your back he's off rolling across the room and out the door.'

Lara ticked a finger beneath the baby's chin and he offered a beautiful smile in return. Lara broke into one of her own.

'How are you so handsome?' she said softly. 'How is that even possible?'

'I remember when you used to say that to me,' Theo cut in with a grin.

'Oh, but you can't compete with this little man, can you?' Lara replied.

'Oh, Lara…' Betsy said. 'This is Reece.'

'Corey's dad?' Lara said, extending her hand in greeting. The slight young man who had been standing silently behind Betsy since they came in looked awkward. He blinked hard and ran an uncertain hand through mousey hair before he responded. Lara supposed he knew that she knew all about them and perhaps was wondering what Lara thought of him. She gave him her brightest, most friendly smile in a bid to reassure him that she wasn't about to judge, although she couldn't help but muse on the fact that he was here at all.

'Yes,' he said, shaking Lara's hand before slinking back into the shadows again.

'Reece has been coming over this week to learn how to look after Corey,' Betsy said. 'To help out when I come back to work. I mean, you'll be starting your engineering apprenticeship soon, won't you?'

Betsy asked, turning to Reece, who nodded. 'But you have Fridays off so you'll be having Corey to give my mum and dad a break.'

'My mum will be there too,' Reece said, as if to reassure himself of the support more than anyone else. Lara supposed it was only natural to feel nervous at the prospect, but she couldn't be anything other than pleased that he was taking an active role in bringing up their baby, especially as Betsy had stated categorically that she didn't want a romantic relationship with him now and that he didn't want one either. If they could work well together as a parental team, that was the best anyone could ask for and a lot more than some children got. And they both seemed to get along quite well in spite of the new responsibilities that must have seemed truly daunting at times.

'So I thought he ought to come here to see what I do and to meet you, so you'd know him in case he has to come and get me for anything ever,' Betsy continued.

'I'm glad you did,' Lara said. 'It's lovely to finally meet you, Reece.'

'So,' Betsy said, turning to Lara again. 'Are you excited to have me back?'

'Of course I'm excited to have you back,' Lara said with a laugh. 'Your replacement has been absolutely useless.'

'She bullies me!' Theo said with a mock whine. 'Come back and save me, Betsy!'

'See what I mean?' Lara said. 'Can't take orders at all.'

'Again with the bullying!' Theo said. 'I don't have to work here, you know; I'm a world-renowned musician!'

'You don't work here,' Lara said. 'You just hang around and look pitiful until I give you a biscuit.'

'What, like Cupid?'

'Where is Cupid?' Lara asked, looking around the office. 'Don't tell me he ran out when you opened the doors just now.'

'He's got to go out sometime,' Theo said. 'Probably feels like he's joined a cult being stuck in all the time.'

'Cupid?' Betsy frowned. 'Who's Cupid?'

Lara looked sheepish. 'The cat. We sort of renamed him.'

Betsy looked confused, but the new question hanging from her lips was cut short by Lara giving the office another sweep.

'We'd better have a look for him,' she said.

'I'm sure he's fine,' Theo replied, going over to have a closer look at baby Corey himself.

'He can't get around well with his dodgy leg; you know that,' Lara said, her tone more serious now. She might well be in a committed relationship with Theo but they both knew that her cat would always be her number-one guy and, since the accident that had nearly taken him from them, she worried about him more than ever. 'I'd feel happier if I could…'

There was a purring sound, and a blue-grey tabby cat appeared from behind the radiator.

'There you are,' she said, scooping him up. 'Naughty boy. You got me all worried.'

Theo turned to her. 'I think he's having an identity crisis?'

Lara pursed her lips. 'You keep saying that – it's ridiculous.'

'Well, he keeps hiding – perhaps he's trying to tell you something.'

'I expect he was just cold.'

'But he is on his fiftieth name now. Probably having a breakdown trying to remember them all.'

'Fluffy, Satchmo, Cupid… I don't think he cares what his name is. He wouldn't answer to any of them whatever they are.'

'I'm sorry…' Betsy interrupted, stroking a hand over Corey's little head as he fussed and grizzled. 'What's his name now?'

'Cupid.'

'What was wrong with Fluffy?'

'Nothing,' Lara said as Cupid leapt down from her arms again and curled up in front of the radiator. 'I just thought Cupid because romance is my business, and it's Cupid because that's what he does.'

Theo smiled. 'Because he brought us together.'

'Exactly. Like our very own little Cupid.'

'Oh,' Betsy said, throwing a quick grin at Reece, who didn't grin back, instead looking deeply mortified to be caught up in a conversation that he didn't have a clue how to respond to.

'A cat called Cupid,' Theo said, putting an arm around Lara. 'All the other cats are laughing at him, you know. Only slightly less than they did when he was called Fluffy, but you're not exactly giving him any more street cred here.'

'The other cats can laugh, but I bet they don't get yellowfin tuna for breakfast.'

'True. He has got it pretty good here.'

'I think so. There are worse places to live.'

Corey reminded everyone of his presence with sudden force in the form of a loud wail.

'Oh, I knew he wouldn't last until after lunch,' Betsy said. 'He's so hungry lately.'

'You need to feed him?' Lara asked.

'Yes.'

'You can use the house if you want some privacy. You know where everything is.'

Betsy nodded. 'Can Reece come in too?'

'Of course,' Lara replied. She couldn't help but feel that even if Reece felt a little uncomfortable watching Betsy breastfeed, it would still be preferable to making awkward conversation with her and Theo, and he hardly seemed like the gregarious type anyway.

'Come on.' Betsy beckoned him to follow as she left the office and made her way to the main house. Lara watched them go with a fond smile.

'I think maybe that's going to work out.'

'You think they might get together?' Theo said doubtfully. 'Do you think that's a good way to start a relationship?'

'I don't know about a relationship, but they seem keen to make a go of parenthood as a team, and that's not a bad result, is it? A lot of lads wouldn't want anything to do with the baby, but he seems willing.'

Theo came up behind her and circled his arms around her waist, leaning into her. 'You know you sound about sixty when you say that.'

Lara nudged him with her elbow and laughed. 'Thanks so much. I just mean that it's good to see them taking it seriously. I had my doubts at first.' She turned and looked up at him. 'Which reminds me; I wanted to ask you something.'

'You don't have enough sugar in your coffee? I'll get right on it.'

'Never serious for a minute, are you? We've been together for almost a year now and I think it's going well, right?'

'I think so,' he said, kissing her nose. 'I suppose you're not too taxing to be around.'

'And we've got a good balance here – you can be a bit choosier about what gigs you play now that you've ditched Jazzy Chas, and we've got on well while you've been helping me out here. You've been here quite a lot so it's a good indicator of how well we might get on should you choose to be here a whole lot more… Like… permanently…'

'You're asking me to…?'

'Move in.'

'Seriously?'

'Why not? I wouldn't ask you to keep working with me because I'd have Betsy back but... Unless you'd rather not let your house go?'

'That leaky old hovel with rent that would be too expensive for a shoe box? I think I could tear myself away.'

Lara smiled. 'So you think it's a good idea?'

'Well, yes, but I didn't think...'

'It's OK,' Lara said with a vague frown. 'You can say if you don't want to and I won't get offended.'

'God, of course I do! I just never imagined you'd want me to!'

Lara smiled up at him. 'Why on earth would you think that?'

'Because...' he sighed. 'Because you're so far above me. Because you're this go-getting, independent, smart, beautiful, savvy woman and I'm just... well I'm just me. A sometimes musician with no discernible prospects.'

She tapped his chest and smiled. 'A very sexy sometimes musician with no discernible prospects.'

'I'm being serious now. You really want to be saddled with me?'

'Of course I do. And that reply sounded more generous in my head than it does saying it out loud.'

'I know what you meant,' he said with a laugh. 'I still can't believe how lucky I am to have you.'

'I can't believe how lucky we are that we met at all. If I hadn't been looking for Cupid that night and you hadn't been out looking for him at that same time...'

'We never would have bumped into each other. Well, what I mean to say is you never would have beaten the crap out of me.'

Lara narrowed her eyes. 'You're never going to forgive me for that, are you?'

'One day. I think you have a lot of making up to do first.'

'We could start right now.'

'Betsy's in the house…'

'She'll be a while yet…'

He dipped his head to hers and kissed her, hands travelling down her torso and settling on her waist to pull her in close.

'Yes,' he said.

She giggled. 'We haven't done anything yet.'

He pulled away and grinned. 'Yes to moving in,' he said. 'But once I'm here you're never getting rid of me.'

'Maybe I don't want to. At the very least we owe it to Cupid.'

'I don't think us being here together will stop him roaming.'

'Probably not, but perhaps he'll have more of a reason to roam a little less often and a little less far away.'

'True. I mean, we must be his two favourites, surely.'

'*I'm* obviously his favourite,' Lara said with another giggle.

'You're my favourite too. Have I told you today that I love you?'

'No and it's almost midday. I was beginning to think you'd gone off me.'

'Never. I love you.'

'In that case, I love you too.'

Theo gently tilted her head up and pressed his lips to hers once more.

In the corner of the room, warming himself by the heater, Cupid the blue-grey tabby cat with a wonky back leg and more names than he'd had tuna dinners let out a little mew of approval.

A Letter from Tilly

I want to say a huge thank you for choosing to read *The Break Up*. If you did enjoy it, and want to keep up-to-date with all my latest releases, just sign up at the following link. Your email address will never be shared and you can unsubscribe at any time.

www.bookouture.com/tilly-tennant

I'm so excited to share *The Break Up* with you. It's a book I've wanted to write for some time now, and once I got the go-ahead from my editor I loved every minute of working on it. I truly have the best job in the world and I've been so proud to share every new book with my lovely readers.

I hope you loved *The Break Up*, and if you did I would be very grateful if you could write a review. I'd love to hear what you think, and it makes such a difference helping new readers to discover one of my books for the first time.

I love hearing from my readers – you can get in touch on my Facebook page, through Twitter, Goodreads or my website.

Thanks,
Tilly

 tillytennant

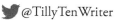 @TillyTenWriter

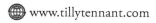 www.tillytennant.com

Acknowledgements

I say this every time I come to write the acknowledgements for a new book, but it's true: the list of people who have offered help and encouragement on my writing journey so far really is endless and it would take a novel in itself to mention them all. I'd try to list everyone here, regardless, but I know that I'd fail miserably and miss out someone who is really very important. I just want to say that my heartfelt gratitude goes out to each and every one of you, whose involvement, whether small or large, has been invaluable and appreciated more than I can express.

It goes without saying that my family bear the brunt of my authorly mood swings but, when the dust has settled, I'll always appreciate their love, patience and support. I also want to mention the many good friends I have made and since kept at Staffordshire University. It's been ten years since I graduated with a degree in English and creative writing, but hardly a day goes by when I don't think fondly of my time there.

I'd also like to shout out to Storm Constantine of Immanion Press, who gave me the opportunity to see my very first book in print. Nowadays, I have to thank the remarkable team at Bookouture for their continued support, patience, and amazing publishing flair, particularly Oliver Rhodes, Lydia Vassar-Smith – my incredible and long-suffering editor – Kim Nash, Noelle Holten, Peta Nightingale, Leodora Darlington and Jessie Botterill. I know I'll have forgotten someone else at Bookouture who I ought to be thanking, but I hope they'll forgive me. I'll be giving them all a big hug at the next summer bash whether they want it or not! Their belief, able assistance and encouragement mean the world to me. I truly believe I have the best team an author could ask for.

My friend, Kath Hickton, always gets an honourable mention for putting up with me since primary school, and Louise Coquio deserves a medal for getting me through university and suffering me ever since, likewise her lovely family. I also have to thank Mel Sherratt, who is as generous with her time and advice as she is talented, someone who is always there to cheer on her fellow authors. She did so much to help me in the early days of my career that I don't think I'll ever be able to thank her as much as she deserves.

I'd also like to shout out to Holly Martin, Tracy Bloom, Emma Davies, Jack Croxall, Jenny Hale, Clare Davidson, Angie Marsons, Sue Watson and Jaimie Admans: not only brilliant authors in their own right but hugely supportive of others.

My Bookouture colleagues are all incredible, of course, unfailing and generous in their support of fellow authors – life would be a lot duller without the gang! I have to thank all the brilliant and dedicated book bloggers (there are so many of you but you know who you are!) and readers, and anyone else who has championed my work, reviewed it, shared it, or simply told me that they liked it. Every one of those actions is priceless and you are all very special people. Some of you I am even proud to call friends now – and I'm looking at you in particular, Kerry Ann Parsons and Steph Lawrence!

Last but not least, I'd like to give a special mention to my lovely agent and champion, Madeleine Milburn, who always has my back.

Printed in Great Britain
by Amazon

39302615R00177